AS TIME GOES BY

Henry Ellis regarded Jalian d'Arsennette across his desk-top. His eyes did not waver from hers. "What is your question?"

She showed the first emotion he had seen in her; a deep, quivering breath. It seemed to him that he could almost *hear*, /after all these years, the answer . . ./ She was holding the edge of his desk.

"Is it possible to prevent Armageddon?"

Sweat was trickling down the back of Henry's neck. He was thinking, *this isn't happening*, while something deep inside him assured him, *yes, it is too happening.* "May God help you, whoever the hell you are. I can't. I just don't know. Even Nigao could not answer that question, given your assumed parameters. Our field is very young."

Jalian was sitting back in her chair, eyes closed. She wasn't sure what her reaction was, relief or despair; only that it was strong. He had not said yes, but he had not said no. She could still *hope*.

She stood to leave, and Henry said, "Miss d'Arsennette? Where are you going?"

Jalian pivoted slowly, and smiled at him. Henry felt his perception of everything in the world but those silver eyes fade away, and was thinking with a cool, rational detachment that silver was the most erotic color that he knew, when Jalian said, "I am going to save the world."

"An impressive debut. Moran is a writer worth watching, and *The Armageddon Blues* is a novel worth reading."
—Richard Bowker, author of *Replica*

THE ARMAGEDDON BLUES

A TALE OF
THE GREAT WHEEL
OF EXISTENCE

DANIEL
KEYS MORAN

SPECTRA

BANTAM BOOKS
TORONTO • NEW YORK • LONDON • SYDNEY • AUCKLAND

THE ARMAGEDDON BLUES
A Bantam Spectra Book / April 1988

Grateful acknowledgment is made for permission to reprint the following: "Rage, rage
against the dying light," Dylan Thomas, *The Poems of Dylan Thomas.* Copyright 1952 by
Dylan Thomas. Reprinted by permission of New Directions Publishing Corporation. "As
Time Goes By" copyright 1931 by WARNER BROS. INC. (Renewed). All rights reserved.
Used by permission. "My Father's House" used by permission from Bruce Springsteen.

ISBN 0-553-27115-6

Published simultaneously in the United States and Canada

Bantam Books are published by Bantam Books, a division of Bantam Doubleday Dell
Publishing Group, Inc. Its trademark, consisting of the words "Bantam Books" and the
portrayal of a rooster, is Registered in U.S. Patent and Trademark Office and in other
countries. Marca Registrada. Bantam Books, 666 Fifth Avenue, New York, New York
10103.

PRINTED IN THE UNITED STATES OF AMERICA

KR 0 9 8 7 6 5 4 3 2 1

DEDICATION

The Armageddon Blues should probably be dedicated to George Scithers, a very nice man whom I have never met, for reasons too numerous for me to list. But George has at least two books that I know of dedicated to him already, so he's going to have to settle for a mention here; mondo thanks, George.

The Armageddon Blues is dedicated, with love, to Kari Lynn Moran, my sister, for couch and hamburgers during hard times.

ACKNOWLEDGMENTS

For their various contributions:

The quotations of President John F. Kennedy, as they appear herein, are taken from *To Turn the Tide*, a collection of the speeches from the first year of his tragically short-lived Presidency; as edited by John W. Gardner.

A very useful research source was *Jane's Guide to Strategic Weapons Systems*. This is a fascinating work for its weapons ads alone. Other important reading can be found in G. Harry Stine's *Space Power*, and Ben Bova's *The High Road*.

I am monstrously indebted to Gregory McDonald, John Dos Passos, and Robert A. Heinlein, for teaching me how to build this; to Tom Robbins, for showing me how to paint it, and to Hunter Thompson, for explaining that sometimes it's okay to burn the bitch down—and for other reasons. Thanks, Uncle Hunter.

A NOTE FROM THE AUTHOR

The following is compiled from a number of sources, including humans. It may therefore be inaccurate in a number of details. In fact, considering the humans involved, I will go farther than that.

What follows is not accurate.
It is not truth.
It is . . . elegant.
I am a computer.

THE ARMAGEDDON BLUES

The story went around during the glum diplomatic dog days in the late '30s. The 13-year-old son asks his father, a retired senior diplomat: "Daddy, what was your role in the world war?" Lord Cecil looked up from his newspaper: "I tried to prevent the bloody thing."

—William F. Buckley
Editorial
February 19, 1985

ALL THE TIME
IN THE WORLD

Consider the explosion of a thermonuclear weapon.

From an insignificant collection of radioactives and supporting hardware, the bomb expands within seconds to a thundering mushroom cloud of stunning size and power.

(Psychedelic mushrooms, yeah, yeah, *yeah*.)

Hold this image most clearly in mind, please—small metal egg of the technological demons to the fires of a somewhat less sophisticated era's hell; *flash*. Do you see it, do you have the image, do you *understand?*

To comprehend the essence of the personality of Georges Mordreaux, take this image, this process, and reverse it.

(Add the sound of Japanese wind chimes. Georges Mordreaux is a happy man.

(Naturally.)

A brief aside: It is the opinion of the author that the sound of an atomic bomb exploding in reverse is *squilchgmp!*

The author is willing to concede that he could be wrong, but adds that until such time as he is proven incorrect, he will continue to hold this opinion.

DATELINE 2052 GREGORIAN.

Marchand the Hunter went into the deep Burns after her daughter.

The child was five Coldtimes, and she knew no better; the nighttime glow of the Burn beckoned, and she went.

The Clan of Hammel, migrating through the Big Desert by the Waters, pressed on. It was death to enter the Burns. They knew they would never see Marchand again.

Three days later Marchand d'Loria y ken Hammel staggered out of the darkness, past the Clan's sentries and into the ring of campfires. Dilann, her daughter, was clutched in her arms.

Marchand died the next morning.

To the awe of the entire Clan, Marchand's daughter survived. Before Dilann's sixth birthday, the Clan, or what was left of the Clan after the desert trek, had reached the forests by the Big Waters of the North Coast.

What was left of the Clan prospered. Dilann became known as Dilann d'Arsennette, the lady of the fires.

Only one of Dilann's three children survived to adulthood. All three of Dilann's children were mutant, as was to be expected of the offspring of one who had survived the banked fires of Armageddon.

The child who lived was a girl, Rhia, tall and fair and strong.

Her eyes were bright silver.

Dilann's grandchildren, every one, had silver eyes.

DATELINE 1917 GREGORIAN.

Verdun, France: the western front.

When Georges was a younger man—not a young man, no, but younger—the world had gotten together for a while and declared a social event called the Great War, the War to End All Wars, and later, World War One. (Rumors to the contrary, there was no American aviator named Snoopy, famed for his duels with the Red Baron. That all came later.)

Georges Mordreaux, through some bad timing on his part and the jealousy of the husband of a wife, found himself in the middle of this silly conflict, yes *sir*.

What should have been his last thought, as the German soldier came up out of the rain-soaked trench, bayonet in hand, was *That's a muddy bayonet,* as though it could possibly make any difference whether he was killed with a clean bayonet or a dirty one. (Georges was a perfectionist of sorts; even when it was in style, some years in his future, he refused to drink his milk out of a dirty glass.)

Georges came to some hours later—so the overhead sun, peeking cautiously through gray clouds, informed him. He was being dragged away from the front. All around he saw the rest of the French army, retreating methodically and with great haste. Georges's corporal, Henri, who was nineteen and who, Georges later heard, became a hero taking a hill that nobody gave a damn about anyway, saw that Georges's eyes were open, and motioned to the soldier holding Georges's right arm to drag him the rest of the way to his feet. Georges stumbled a few steps over the ragged, shell-torn ground, before gaining his balance.

Georges could not think clearly; there was a vast pain in his neck that was only beginning to abate. The terrain about them seemed vaguely familiar. After nearly a kilometer, the retreat slowed, then stopped; they began digging in, grimly determined that the Germans would go no further.

Night descended like a raven. Soldiers were still stringing barbed wire on grimy, rotting wood posts and the shattered fragments of shell-torn trees. They had to pull dead men off some of the trees before they could use them. Georges and the remains of his company—Henri—sat in the muddy trenches, trying to nurse a small fire raised a few inches over the mud. They were having some success, more than anyone else, but still the flame was weak.

Georges had not spoken since awakening. When Henri spoke to him, he found himself unable to answer, having, uh, no vocal cords to speak of. They knitted as the night wore on; the scar on his neck began to fade. Near midnight, he whispered, in a voice like ground glass, "Henri? What happened to me?"

Henri was hunched over the small fire, trying to light a damp cigarette that was already half smoked. He finally produced a dim glow in the tip of the cigarette, and sat back against the trench wall. "Don't know, Georges. German stuck you . . ." He hesitated. "It looked like your head came off. That's just what it looked like." He shrugged indifferently. "I shot the German. When I looked again your head was in place and there was a bleeding gash all around your neck."

Georges touched the skin above his collar. There was

a thin ridge he could barely feel. He nodded. "I used to wonder if I could die."

"Georges?"

"This area looks familiar," whispered Georges. "I think this is where General Dumouriez stopped the Prussians, when they were trying to help King Louis restore the monarchy. The day after the battle . . ." He shook his head, and winced at the faint ghost of pain. "That was September 20. In 1792. The next day the National Convention declared we were a Republic." Henri was staring at him, wide-eyed, across the fire. "In January," said Georges in a voice distant with memory, "we cut King Louis' head off."

Henri turned his face away from Georges, and drew his coat about himself. He clutched his rifle tightly. (In the morning he was gone, and that was the last time Georges saw him, because three days later, while taking a hill that nobody gave a damn about anyway, he became a hero of the French Republic, his last thoughts being of Georges Mordreaux. Ironically, it was a German boy with a bayonet who got him too, although the resemblance stops there. The German boy—he was actually younger than Henri, and his name is unimportant, since like Henri he did not survive the war—this German boy put his bayonet in from behind, and the corporal did not resurrect. Ah, well.)

Georges spent the rest of the night trying to whistle. He did quite creditably.

Georges thought, with some irritation at himself, that there ought to be some point to be learned from having one's head cut off, and surviving the experience. He could not think of one, however, aside from the obvious. He was very glad to be alive.

In some ways, thought Georges Mordreaux, *I am a very shallow fellow.*

Ah, well.

The author notes that in the year 1917, Georges Mordreaux was two hundred and five years old.

Perhaps he was a bit shallow, at that.

One of the definitions of the word "entropy" is: "The degradation of the matter and energy in the universe to an ultimate state of inert uniformity." Put more simply: "Things run down."

Georges never read dictionaries. He considered them, being as they were largely artificial attempts to impose order on the anarchistic languages of man, very much beneath him.

About order-imposers, as dictionary compilers: Georges was better at it.

Indeed, one might consider Georges Mordreaux "The Enemy of Entropy."

Georges liked to.

When the Big Crunch came, and the superpowers decided to sterilize the face of the planet, the freeways survived.

(Vista: A thousand and one mushroom clouds dotting the face of a small planet. Terminal acne. Winding lazily among the mushrooms, strips of concrete, overextended roads, observed the goings-on, and later, when the barbarians and the mutants came howling out of the radioactive Burns to trek the surface of the freeways among the dead shells of the automobiles, the freeways might have giggled to themselves. Eventually the cars were dragged from the freeways for use in making weapons, and the freeways were left alone to contemplate their freewayness.)

DATELINE 711 A.B.C. (AFTER THE BIG CRUNCH).

Ralesh caught her before she had even reached the hills beyond the forest. The little girl had fallen asleep beneath an old willow, at the edge of the grassy meadow that led up to the foothills. Ralesh, a woman of early years, awoke the five-year-old unceremoniously, and ran the child the kilometers back to the Clan House without comment.

She whipped the child publicly. Five lashes; she was not a severe mother. When the punishment was over, she took her daughter back to the Girls' House. She put her daughter to bed; kissed her on the forehead, and said gently,

"Child, the woods are dangerous for children. There are bears and Real Indians. There is nothing at the end of the Big Road; the stories are lies."

Her daughter stared up at the oak planks of the Girls' House. She did not speak.

Ralesh sighed. "Daughter, understand this: I will catch you. You cannot run so far nor so fast that I will not find you. Remember that." She left, and left the girl alone.

When she was gone, Jalian d'Arsennette, the straight-line female descendant of Dilann d'Arsennette, finally let the tears come. It was strange, though; the tears were external, they tracked down her cheeks and she could hear herself sobbing, but inside none of it mattered.

Inside she was as cold and calm as an elder Hunter. They would be watching her now; but now was not always. Summer would come again.

Ralesh's words stayed with her, though, like a curse that would not be shaken.

"You cannot run so far nor so fast . . . I will catch you."

Jalian's hands clenched into fists. Summer would come.

DATELINE 712 A.B.C.

They gave Jalian few duties on the day the Hunters came back; she finished them early, and slipped out of the Clan House when nobody was watching her. She wandered through the village aimlessly, stopping to play a game of strike with one of the boys. (She was only beginning to understand that boys were not fit company; she had not yet learned why that was so, except that in all the stories it was the boys who caused the Big Crunch and the Fire Times.)

By the time the watch was preparing to change, she had reached the clearing that separated Selvren village from the forest. She squirmed into what cover she could find at the south end of the clearing; brown-haired and brown-clothed, she would have been hard to see in any case. Against the brown summer meadow grass she was next to invisible.

The clearing was a ten-second run for Jalian, from one

end to the other, and it was in clear view of the Clan House. Out in front of the Clan House the men were tending the fires that would be used to smoke the catch the Hunters returned with.

Ten seconds.

The watch's replacements arrived. The women stood together, gossiping for a few moments before the new guards assumed their posts.

Jalian drew her legs up under her, checked her knife to make sure the sheath was securely tied down, peered toward the Clan House one last time . . .

She ran.

Ten seconds was a long time; long enough to think of exactly what Ralesh would do to her if she was seen, if she was caught. *Run,* and *run,* and *run.* . . . Jalian reached the trees at the north end of the clearing, running as fast as she had ever run before. Her foot caught in a tuft of the long brown grass at the last instant and sent her tumbling. She did her best to convert it into a roll as she had been taught, but still the wind was knocked from her lungs and she had trouble breathing when she regained her feet. Fighting silently to pull air into her emptied lungs, Jalian squirmed up to the edge of the decent cover and peered out. There was no unusual activity over at the long wooden Clan House, nothing out of the ordinary for early morning in the late thaw-time . . . she had not been seen.

Jalian grinned fiercely. It would be late afternoon now before she was missed, and by then she would be long gone. They would know where she had gone, when she failed to show up to help with the preparation of the Ceremony meal, but by then, with luck, it would be too late. If the Hunters started out after her the instant they became aware of her absence, Jalian would still have a third-day start.

With luck, before nightfall Jalian would be in the land of the gods and demons that was at the end of the Big Road. She did not think that anyone but Ralesh would try to follow her there—and perhaps not even Ralesh.

Jalian turned, her long brown hair swirling out behind her, and vanished into the trees. She left no trail.

None.

Consider a time traveler.

Her name is Jalian. Yes, Jalian d'Arsennette, except that there have been, well, changes.

She is no longer six years old, and her hair is no longer brown. It is white, ice-white, completely untinted. She is twenty-six years old. Her eyebrows and eyelashes are still brown, and it gives her features an artificial seeming. Her skin is extremely pale; she does not tan. Rather than melanin her skin holds pigmentation that whitens under the sun. She is lovely in a strange, erotic way.

None of the above is important.

She has eyes. Even in the twentieth century Gregorian, her eyes are exceptional. The irises are silver. They have always been silver, of course, but now they are something else and more: a maelstrom of swirling color, silver and blue and pink and purple and green and gold-red, but somehow still only silver when faced with the lens of a camera; the effect is not reproducible.

(Clan Silver-Eyes prospered where the Real Indians and the barbarians did not, at least partially because of the silver irises; they were quite lovely, true, but they also detected abnormal radiation levels quite capably, as a sort of staccato flashing in their peripheral vision. After the Big Crunch, this became a survival mechanism.)

Jalian's eyes can and do cause almost instant desire in any functioning male, and in not a few women besides. They are the eyes of someone who has seen too much and knows too much, and knows that there is nothing she can do about what she knows.

Because, of course, Armageddon is coming.

Jalian d'Arsennette is viewed, by the twentieth century, as a tall, rather elfin beauty; a woman whom destiny rides like a demon.

She has the strange habit of not meeting other people's eyes.

DATELINE 712 A.B.C.

Jalian pushed herself, moving through the light woods silently nonetheless. The sun, striking down through the trees, rarely touched her; she was a silvered shadow, mingling with the other shadows of morning. The light did not find her, she made no sound. It would have taken an Elder Hunter to track her; no lesser tracker would have discerned any trail.

It was late morning when Jalian reached the hills. There was no cover in the hills to compare with that in the forests; automatically she made the most of the sketchy scrub, and refrained from worrying about it. She would make it across the hills or she would not.

It was near noon when she reached the place.

Ruins of the old world lay all about them, wherever one looked. Old buildings, the frames of karz; even, in some places, where ancient builders had lined concrete with polymer bases, stretches of good roads. Still, for Jalian, none of these, not even the few good roads, matched the straight and clean and serene beauty of her place:

The Big Road.

Like the path of a thrown knife, the Big Road stretched away as far as the eye could see, west and north toward the far hills that ringed the other end of the valley, toward the mountains that legend said the Clan had walked down from in the days after the Big Crunch. For as far as Jalian could see, the Big Road ran true.

The Big Road, where Jalian came to it, was bordered by one of the largest and worst of the Burns. If one had known the Big Road before the bombs fell, that person might have been able to tell Jalian that the Big Road was not supposed to be partially melted; but there was nobody to tell Jalian that, and she supposed that the Big Road had always been that way.

(Even before the missiles came burning from the sky, this spot had held a laboratory in which there were radio-active materials stored for testing. When the bombs went down and then up again, strange things had happened there.)

That was more than seven centuries ago; to Jalian's eyes, the Burn still sparkled faintly.

Jalian stood at the spot where she usually ascended to the Big Road.

It was a desolate area at the edge of the concrete, where a plant that resembled ivy had survived the radiation long enough to breach the Big Road's protective guardrail. Dirt and dust, working their ways into the body of the dead ivy mutant, had formed a small, natural incline that Jalian was able to scramble up and make her way onto the concrete of the Big Road itself. She paused at the edge of the Big Road, her feet still on dirt but only a step away from the concrete.

This would be only the second time that Jalian had set foot on the Big Road.

The first time, one of the Hunters—Jalian could not remember who it had been, except that it was not an Elder Hunter because she did not wear the white tunic of an Elder Hunter—had taken a group of children from the Girls' House with her on routine patrol of Silver-Eyes borders. The patrol had made camp at the edge of the hills, while the four- and five- and six-year-olds scrambled over the Big Road. Later, one of the younger women in the patrol told the children about the land of gods and demons at its end.

Then she had tried to run away, and been caught by Ralesh.

This time, Jalian had a third-day start. They would not catch her.

They would not.

The twentieth century, as viewed by Jalian d'Arsennette, consists of freeways.

(The twentieth century saw the birth of the thermonuclear explosive and the freeway. Jalian could almost forgive one for the other.)

(Almost.)

DATELINE 712 A.B.C.

One step, and then two, and Jalian stood for a frozen timeless moment on the concrete of the Big Road itself.

Then the paralysis broke, and, shivering slightly, Jalian walked to the center of the road, where the melted ruin of a lane divider stood a lonely vigil.

The freeway ran away from her, straight and true and clean, protected as though by the gods. (The winds, here, were too sporadic to erode much. Plants, which in other places grew up through the asphalt and crumbled the man-made structures, here stood no chance against the radio-active Burn. The freeway itself, cambered from the center, was regularly cleaned of the dirt that built up on its surface by the summer rains.)

At the age of six, to Jalian d'Arsennette, it made sense that the Big Road was protected by the gods. (Or the demons, perhaps, although Jalian did not like to think about that.)

For how long Jalian simply stood on the Big Road, the sun burning down on her, her eyes seeking into the distance for the end of the Big Road, she never knew. She came back from infinity, slowly, with the thoughts in her mind:

Mountains beside me, desert behind me. Forest and hills and sun, and the Big Road far ahead. . . .

That moment, her thin body touched with the ecstasy of a dimly perceived greater reality, Jalian remembered for the rest of her life.

The moment ended and she ran.

Jalian had not made it to the end of the Big Road when she was five because she had squandered her lead time. This time she would not make that mistake.

Run and *run* and *run*. . . .

The freeway stretched before her; a road of possibilities.

Georges Mordreaux is an interesting man. Aside from the fact that entropy tends to decrease in his vicinity, there are eight of him.

Yes, eight. Not all on the same timeline, of course.

(It is a shame, but Georges will not admit to any of the eight having been present during the explosion of a thermonuclear weapon. He may be lying, of course; humans are notorious liars. Evidence suggests that he may be engaging in this common human pastime. For reasons too lengthy to go into here, asking any of the other seven directly would be . . . difficult.)

(Georges Mordreaux, of the base timeline that led to divergence 1962, did once meet Einstein. This is not the same as being present when a thermonuclear weapon is exploded, but it is the closest that Georges is willing to admit to. The author, commenting in a negative fashion on this subject, has been blessed with the response, "Ah, well."

There are times when the author agrees with Georges that he is in some ways a very shallow fellow.)

(All eight of him.)

DATELINE 712 A.B.C.

Jalian ran automatically. Her body pushed itself without conscious attention. She was thinking about the end of the Big Road, and what she would find there. It would, she thought, be a strange place indeed . . . something with bright, bright colors, and loud noises. Very loud.

Jalian liked loud noises.

With a shock more immense than anything she had every felt before in her young life, Jalian focused on an object some ways ahead of her. There was something *on the Big Road*. Her legs stumbled, then stopped. She stood there in the middle of the old freeway, her chest heaving, her short brown tunic splotchy with sweat, looking at the building that had grown up on her freeway.

She stood in the sun, quiet and motionless but for her breathing, for two minutes that stretched into three. Once she drew her knife from its sheath; then, looking back to the large building, she shook her head against the silliness and put it back with an impatient movement. Jalian, even at the age of six, knew the uses of a knife.

The action broke her paralysis, and Jalian found a strange, powerful fury growing in her. Here, in her holy place, on *her* Big Road, someone had grown a building.

The six-year-old Jalian d'Arsennette, even through the worst anger that she had ever experienced in her life, knew there was nothing she could do about the building on her Big Road. She backed away from the building a few steps, eyes still locked to it; then, reluctantly, turned and began the long run back to the Clan House. She would be home nearly a twelfth-day before she would be needed for the Ceremony meal, but that was of no account. When she told Ralesh what she had done, she would be badly punished, perhaps even ceremonially scarred; but Jalian's mother would do *something* about the tall, thin building that had grown up on Jalian's Big Road.

Jalian d'Arsennette had no way of knowing that the "building" was a starship.

DATELINE 1968 GREGORIAN.

Georges Mordreaux sat behind the wheel of a green '66 Camaro. He was traveling north on the Pacific Coast Highway. Georges Mordreaux was a tall, broad-shouldered man, with cheerful nondescript features, light blue eyes and light brown hair. He smiled a lot.

The Camaro ran smoothly, with the sort of leashed power that a jet pilot might have recognized, but which was utterly out of place in a green 1966 model Camaro. (Or any other color Camaro.) Both the passenger's and driver's windows were down, and wind was blasting through the car. The air conditioner was on. So was the heater.

The machine ran . . . well, *better than new* was the term that came immediately to Georges' mind. Georges did not think that the car would break the sound barrier, even if he pushed it. The car was too aerodynamically inefficient.

Georges had owned the car for two weeks now. He'd bought it from a used-car dealer in New Jersey who swore that it had been driven by a retired couple who simply liked Camaros. Georges had not put gasoline into the car once on the way west.

"Better than new" was probably the correct term.

Georges whistled as he drove. He was not very good at it, and besides, the car radio was competing; the Beatles were singing "I Want To Hold Your Hand." Georges was whistling "Marseillaise." It did not occur to him to turn the radio off. (To be fair, it is not likely that he *could* have turned the radio off.)

Georges whistled, driving north. The Pacific Ocean sparkled in the sunshine off to his left. He smiled quite a lot.

How likely is it that the world's only time traveler would encounter Georges Mordreaux?

Not very. But then, there are things that are more improbable. That an object should spontaneously gain more energy, assume a more orderly pattern, is vastly more unlikely—and yet, still *possible*. In a world ruled by quantum mechanics, there are no certainties; entropy is a function of probability theory.

One might best consider Georges Mordreaux as an improbability locus.

There.

DATELINE 1968 GREGORIAN.

Forty miles north of San Luis Obispo, Georges Mordreaux saw a hitchhiker walking briskly along the right shoulder of the highway. A second closer look altered his impression slightly. Walking along the roadside, yes; but she was not a hitchhiker. She paid no attention to the cars skimming by her on the freeway.

The drivers passing her certainly paid attention to her; they were almost unable to do otherwise. She stood out from her surroundings like a Corvichi fusion torch at night. She was dressed in a white jumpsuit, and carried a light blue satchel on one shoulder. Her hair hung to the small of her back, long and straight and undeniably white, reflecting the sunlight brilliantly. Her skin, where the rolled-up sleeves of the jumpsuit showed the flesh of the arms, was bleached-white, with little pink in its makeup. The jumpsuit legs were tucked into the tops of calf-high black boots.

Georges smiled to himself absently, and brought the Camaro to a halt next to the girl. He leaned over and called out through the right-hand window.

"Do you need a ride, miss?"

The girl continued to walk when he stopped the car; she did not turn when he spoke to her, in a voice that held faint traces of a French accent.

Georges called, "Miss?" a bit more loudly.

Jalian d'Arsennette y ken Selvren turned around, intending to inform this stranger that she was quite content walking. She would do so in the iciest tone of voice of which she was capable, which was considerably so

/light blue eyes smiling at me and there is power that shines on him and pours from him broad shoulders plain face and the power the power he is smiling at me. . . ./

/silver eyes. . . ./

when something strange happened.

"Freeways," said Jalian d'Arsennette, in an accent that Georges had never heard the like of before, with a voice so soft and clear that it sounded like running water, "were made to be walked upon."

Georges got out of the car, and Jalian watched him, waiting; not unsure or confused or wondering, simply waiting for what would happen next.

Georges Mordreaux stood at the side of the still-running green Camaro, looking at the girl who stood at the edge of the cement, on a small stretch of gravel, who was looking back at him with very silver eyes, and suddenly he was more in love than he had been since the age of nineteen.

You know, *that* was in 1731.

DATELINE 1969 GREGORIAN.

Ralesh d'Arsennette y ken Selvren, Eldest Hunter of Clan Silver-Eyes, lay comatose in the hospital that the ambulance had taken her to. The doctors who examined her fully expected her to die. Her entire system was in shock; she appeared to have suffered radiation burns of some sort.

Her personal effects the doctors found vastly strange: a white overtunic and white leggings, three knives, and two devices that they found themselves unable to understand in any regard. One of the gadgets looked like a meter of some sort, or a compass; the other looked like a hand grenade. The local police were still debating whether or not they ought to call in the FBI, two days after Ralesh had been admitted.

For two days, while the police argued among themselves, Ralesh lay in a coma, a glucose solution dripping slowly into her veins.

On the third day, the silver-eyed freak was gone from her room in intensive care, and her personal effects were missing from storage.

In place of the items that she took, the Eldest Hunter of Clan Silver-Eyes left two things: a male intern and a female nurse. The nurse had been tied and gagged and knocked unconscious. The intern, who had simply not been born the right sex, had his throat cut from ear to ear.

DATELINE 1968 GREGORIAN.

"Walk?" asked Georges blankly. "On the freeway?"

An eighteen-wheeler blasted by them. The wind sent Jalian's hair streaming backward. She nodded silently.

"Walk on the freeway," Georges repeated. He considered the idea. "Where are you headed?"

"Anywhere." Jalian shrugged. "Nowhere. One place seems as good as another, as long as it can be reached over a freeway. The freeways," she added, "the freeways are beautiful."

"What are you?" Georges was staring at her.

Jalian studied him, without meeting his eyes particularly. "I might ask you the same question. . . . I'm a wanderer. I walk the freeways, and I wait for the fires that you destroyed yourselves with. There are," she said with the gravest expression Georges had yet seen on her, "thirty-eight years until Armageddon."

"Thirty-eight—what do you mean?"

Jalian said abruptly, "I return your question. What are you? You are unlike any male I have ever known. You are much like a person," she said courteously.

"Well," said Georges. "Thank you. . . . Where are you from? I don't recognize your accent." Jalian's lips parted as though to reply, then closed. She made a gesture of helplessness, and turned to leave. She stopped in the act and said to Georges, "There is a bridge on my map. It is. . . ." She paused, converting time units in her head, ". . . fifteen minutes' walk from here. I will wait for you there, for a little while." She gestured to the car, somehow managing to convey supreme contempt. "Do not come in that, if you come." She began walking without waiting for a reply.

Georges watched the retreating figure for a long time, until she had passed from sight. He was horribly tempted to get back in the car and leave and never be faced with this white-haired woman again.

Georges Mordreaux tended to think of himself as something a cut above the ordinary mortal, almost semi-divine, and it was a fact that Georges tended to awe people. It was strange to find someone who had the ability to set herself up as his equal on their first meeting.

It was a long time before he started after her, on foot.

Behind him, the Camaro's engine began to falter.

Jalian d'Arsennette and Georges Mordreaux stood at the edge of the bridge. A small, nearly dry river passed underneath. Far overhead, a front of dark, rain-heavy cumulus clouds moved toward the bridge. Second by second, its shadow killed the sunlight on the moving water.

"I like bridges the best," said Jalian. Her hands were resting on the guardrail. "There were no bridges on the Big Road, not even any places where bridges used to be." Beneath them, the murmur of the river was barely audible. Georges reached out, and ran one finger along the profile of her jaw. "The first time I came to a bridge, I was almost afraid to cross it."

Georges sighed. "You know I don't have any idea at all what you're talking about?" Jalian did not reply. Georges whispered, "Look at me."

Jalian kept her eyes averted. She was looking at the guardrails of the bridge. The rails were made of iron, and were badly rusted. They reached to Jalian's waist. Jalian ran her hands over the rough metal, as though she were studying the texture and shape. After a long and stretching silence, she said, "What is your name?"

Georges said, "Georges," absently. The breeze was blowing her long, silky hair toward him. His hand dropped from her chin and tentatively, he ran his fingers along its surface. Jalian shivered, and brushed his hand away.

Georges said, so softly that his voice could not have

been heard more than a meter away, "*Je ne sais quoi.* What am I to do about you?"

"Georges what?"

"Eh?"

"Is Georges all there is?" Jalian persisted.

Georges leaned back against the railing, not looking at her. Where Jalian's hand had touched the rail, the rust was smeared faintly. Small patches of clean steel began to appear with creeping slowness. "Mordreaux," said Georges finally. "Georges Mordreaux."

Jalian straightened and brushed her hands off on her white jumpsuit. Her hands left faint orange splotches behind. "My name is Jalian. Jalian of the Fires of the People with Silver Eyes, in the long form." She moved closer to him, and lightly touched one of his hands with one of her own. "Does your name mean anything?"

Georges shook his head no. He was more aware of her touch than of any other physical contact with a woman that he could recall in all his long life. "Not that I know of." With the hand that hers was not covering, he touched her chin. He would have turned her to meet his eyes; before he could do so she looked up of her own accord

/self. life is calm power running through deepquiet channels worn smooth. control is necessary and uncertain./

/self. most alone. rivers of black concrete freeze in grief, melt in fire. there are thirty-eight years until Armageddon./

and Jalian's desolate grief and aloneness slashed through Georges as though it were his own.

Jalian's voice trembled. "How old are you?" Her eyes were averted again.

"Two . . ." Georges licked his lips and said, "Two hundred and fifty years old. About."

Jalian turned slightly away from him, so that even by accident she could not meet his eyes. "I think I had better leave." She took a step away from him, turned, and took another before Georges found words.

"Ni." Jalian froze. Georges Mordreaux said in silver-speech, "I am not Ralesh and I am not ghess'Rith. I am myself, and I will never hurt you."

Jalian started to speak, and her voice broke on the first word. She had to begin again. "All of the people I have ever loved, Georges, they have wanted me to be things other than what I was; things other than what I could be. I . . .'' She seemed at a loss for words.

Georges shrugged. "I know what you are. I know you as well as you know yourself. And I'm more objective about it."

"The ending of things, Georges. . . ."

"Is not your fault," he said mildly. "Jalian, when you left your own time you meant to change things for the better—"

She interrupted him. "I am not sure that it can be changed. Georges, it *happened*."

"Oh, to be sure," agreed Georges cheerfully. "It happened once. Need it happen twice?"

Jalian's voice was steady. "What do you mean?"

"The nature of time," said Georges solemnly, "is a mystery to the best of us." He paused. "Einstein said that to me, the one time we met."

"I do not understand."

"Second Precept of Semi-Divinity," said Georges, "is 'Don't Worry About It.' "

"I shall not worry about it, then," said Jalian hesitantly, "but . . . who is Ine-stine?"

"Well," said Georges comfortably, "that's rather a long story. You see . . ."

They walked away down the freeway together.

In the spot they had vacated, for five meters in either direction, the iron railings were completely free of rust.

And so it came to be that Jalian d'Arsennette and Georges Mordreaux walked the freeways of the world together, for a while.

Let us note, here, the two Precepts of Semi-Divinity:

(1) Mind Thine Own Business.
(2) Don't Worry About It.

The alien gods came to Earth in the early part of the twenty-eighth century, as measured from the death of a man who was nailed to a tree for telling people that it was all right to love each other.

Their landing craft dropped out of a clear blue summer sky, and set down on a strip of what appeared, to them, to be a sort of primitive road. They sought the civilization that would produce such a road, and found nothing.

They were not surprised, these alien gods. They had seen other deathworlds; they recognized the signs. If they were surprised in any degree, it was only by the obvious recency of the cataclysm; the previous owners of this world had destroyed themselves less than a cycled running cycle ago.

The alien gods—the Corvichi spacetime gypsies—set down to work. The Ship that was their world was in trouble. Biosphere degradation, resource depletion, failing machinery; they had traveled a long, long way around the Great Wheel of Existence, had braved the Chained One and Chaos itself, and much of their equipment was designed to operate on timelines whose physical law was vastly different from the one on which they now found themselves.

And so they set to work.

Three days after they set down, eighty of Clan Silver-Eyes' most blooded Hunters climbed onto the steelstone of the Big Road, and began the long, long run toward the ship.

Many of the women wore the white of Elder Hunter; they did not lag behind their younger comrades.

At their head was a woman named Ralesh, who would one day be Eldest Hunter.

DATELINE 712 A.B.C.

In the Clan House, well past sunset, lights glowed and flickered. The flicker came from the central fire pit, where lopers and bluewings were roasting on a spit. The glow came from several strange, floating balls, about two hands across, that emitted an eerie blue radiance.

Sitting on the faded green tatami mats nearest the fire pit, the eight Eldest Hunters, including Morine, the Eldest Hunter, conferred with the alien gods.

For reasons of their own, the gods had insisted that Jalian be allowed to attend the meeting. Morine d'Arsennette y ken Selvren was at first inclined to say no; the child was willful and headstrong, and was not to be rewarded for her asinine behavior.

The alien gods insisted.

Jalian sat in a dark corner of the Clan House's central hall, separated from the alien gods by fire and the eight white forms. The alien gods spoke to the Elder Hunters through a machine that spoke understandable silverspeech, in the voice of the first ken Selvren that had addressed it. It was strange for Jalian, listening when the alien gods talked; the machine's voice was her mother's.

That they talked in her mother's voice was not the strangest thing about them. The things they talked *about* were not even the most interesting things about them, although they were interesting enough:

Of the eight Elder Hunters present, five, including Morine and Morine's daughter Ralesh, knew how to read and write. Sylva de Kelvin and her daughter Jenna knew the basic rudiments of chemistry and mathematics. Other Hunters, not present because of low status, knew the arts of medicine and construction. Though the wastefulness of the Men's World forced a simple lifestyle upon them, the Silver-Eyes, ken Selvren that was ken Hammel, had the capability, as the Real Indians and mutants did not, of reconstructing a technical civilization, given power and metal.

It was this that the alien gods were offering them; but first they had to explain what an alternate timeline was, and that took a long, long while.

Like everything else about them, their explanation was strange; but it was not the strangest thing.

What was strangest was the way they looked.

If it is true, as said, that it is only the first time a human looks at a thing that she truly sees it, then it is probable that Jalian saw the gods more clearly than any of the others in the House's central Hall. Even Jalian's mother, the youngest of the Elder Hunters present, looking at the gods, was able to put aside her preconceptions of what a creature should look like only to the point where she perceived a sort of very large, squarish bear, with tentacles and something like strings of lace hanging about its upper regions.

To Jalian, at the age of six when most things are new and strange, the alien god was a four-limbed, nearly cubical hunk of furred flesh; there was a double-jointed leg, as thick around as both of a normal person's legs put together, at each corner of the body. Atop the cube there rose a lattice of interweaving bars that looked like exposed black bone.

Lace was strung about the lattice; in some spots tightly, in others more loosely. Their tentacles grew out of the base of the bone lattice; there were about twenty of them, and four of those twenty were thicker and longer than the rest. The tentacles were covered with a fine, purplish fur that faded to show purple-black skin at the tips of the tentacles. While Jalian watched, the lace stretched and loosened, as the bones beneath them shifted positions slightly. Watching the lace, she had the sudden strange, intense sensation that she could read expression in them.

/?/

Before the machine spoke to the Silver-Eyes, it was always preceded by a high-pitched whine that only a few of the Silver-Eyes could hear. They could not tell which of the gods was actually speaking at any one time. Jalian suspected that it was the small one nearest the machine, for no other reason than that it was the closest. There were four of the alien gods present; three of them stood still and motionless. The fourth, who was furthest away from Jalian, seemed restless. It . . . he kept shifting his weight from one foot-pair to another, in a slow circle that was working its way regularly around his perimeter. Jalian leaned forward, peering; but the god was as far away from her as the hall allowed him to be, back where neither the cool blue light nor the flickering yellow of the firelight much illuminated things. This particular alien god

/ghess'Rith/

suddenly ceased moving. One of the Elder Hunters was asking a question about traveling sideways through time, and Jalian was standing up

/greetings be/

when something happened.

She was certain that the alien god was watching her. She did not know how she knew this, but

/naming be?/

/Jalian. Jalian of the Fires./

/Fires be?/

/the light that dances and burns./

/fascinates. naming be ghess'Rith/

/how are we talking?/

/mindvoice. faster and clearer than soundvoices/

/then why do you use the machine to talk to the Elder Hunters?/

/deaf be. too old to learn new ways, is may be/

/why did you come here? you put a building on my Big Road, and now i'm in trouble./

/apology. ship-not-alive-which-thinks-in-numbers needed level area. Big Road seemed not used/

/the gods and demons *won't* like it./

/persons be?/

/gods and demons . . . they live there. they're scary. they eat *badgirl*s sometimes. i am not a *badgirl*./

/understanding be. cautionary tales/

/?/

/not important. question be/

/what?/

/closer contact?/

/i don't understand./

/wish rapid learning of culture, of Corvichi ways?/

Jalian stared through the dimness of the main hall. Her gaze did not leave ghess'Rith's now-motionless form. She took a step forward, completely unaware of the vast silence that had settled in the hall. Ralesh stirred as though she would rise, and hesitated in obvious indecision.

Jalian moved forward, into the ring of firelight. The Elder Hunters were watching her with something like awe; she had forgotten they were there.

/closer be?/

Jalian d'Arsennette whispered aloud, "Yes."

There was a brief pause.

Jalian had an instant, fragmented impression of something vast and powerful, purposeful, glowing dull red with heat, that rushed at her out of the cold eternal darkness.

It took all of the courage that she possessed to place herself in its path.

At the last moment the monolithic thing identified itself to Jalian with a force that burned itself into the deepest recesses of her mind.

/destiny/

impact.

DATELINE 1968 GREGORIAN.

Carmel, Central California.

"What," asked Jalian d'Arsennette, "is ice cream?"

It was, as ghess'Rith would have put it, a pleasant enough summer day, but then, the Corvichi were comfortable with an ambient temperature nearly twenty percent warmer than a person would have considered ideal.

In other words—Georges Mordreaux's, in fact—it was "too damn hot for anyone but an Englishman." Jalian did not know what an englishman was, and was certain that she did not care. Nonetheless, when noon approached, she sought shade, to wait out the worst heat of the day. Georges, she noted with poor grace, was, despite his complaints, not even sweating.

They stood in front of the order window of an establishment that bore the legend *Al's Burgers, Fries and Shakes*. Al's was located at the edge of a plaza which, though Jalian did not know it, was one of the better examples of architectural design in central California. Al's stuck out from its surroundings glaringly. It would have been insufficient to say that it was ugly; even in less pleasant surroundings it would have been visually unpleasant. Plastered across the window, facing the street, were dozens of pictures of culinary delicacies, ranging from the burgers, fries, and shakes of the establishment's name to other items such as "hoagies" and "submarine sandwiches." One picture, of something called "Our Fantastic Philly Cheese Steak!" was so disgusting that Jalian had to look away.

"Two cones," Georges told the sweating girl who stood at the window. The girl took his money and expertly loaded down two cones with approximately fifteen centimeters of vanilla soft swirl. Jalian stared, she could not help it, at the obscene sight of the vanilla ice cream as it was deposited upon the cones.

Georges took their cones, and handed one to Jalian. They walked over to where a bench sat beneath shade trees, and rested, looking out across the plaza. The day was quiet; a Thursday afternoon in Spring without tourists. The locals were at work, or in school.

Jalian's cone had already started to melt in the heat. Little white rivulets of melted ice cream were coursing down the cone and over her hand. Jalian smelled the ice cream, looking at Georges dubiously. His cone had barely begun to melt. Georges was watching her expectantly.

"How do you eat these?" asked Jalian finally.

Georges demonstrated, licking the side of his cone. *You stick your tongue out*, thought Jalian; *I should have known*. The smell of the ice cream was vaguely familiar; it was similar in some ways to "doughnuts," a food that had made her quite ill the one time she had attempted to eat it. Ever since she had made a point of avoiding foods with that particular sweet odor.

Refined sugar had not been a part of the Silver-Eyes diet.

At last, because the damned thing was melting all over her hand, Jalian stuck her tongue out and tentatively licked a small portion of ice cream off the cone.

"Well?"

Jalian licked the cone again. It was not at all as bad as she had been expecting. In fact . . .

In a surprisingly short period, the ice cream was entirely gone. She threw the cone away after one tentative bite, and went back to Al's. "I would like," she said firmly, "three more."

⌐ATELINE 718 A.B.C.

/no, no,/ said jin'Ish impatiently. /true is our senses differ; we hear, see higher than persons. differences be/ cheshe waved a tentacle at Jalian, then used that tentacle to point again at the Doorway's exposed circuitry. /But light in no-air circuit you can see/

Jalian sighed. She blocked the sunlight with her hand and peered into the maze of wiring and vacuum tubes. She was in a bad mood—jin'Ish kept talking down to her, as though she was no more intelligent than one of the men in the fields—and try as she might, she couldn't see the lights that jin'Ish was pointing out to her. She didn't like working with the Doorway in the first place; because shifting physical law on different timelines kept them from using molecular circuitry that depended on quantum effects of varying probability, the Doorways were constructed with hard-wiring and almost invisible vacuum tubes. The assemblage was bulky and inelegant.

Jalian sat back again. /i don't care what you say, there's no light in there./ She leaned back against the wall. They were in one of the east rooms of the Gods' House, one of the group of rooms that the gods used to store spare equipment. Sunlight was streaming in through the storage room's one large window, bouncing off rows of eldritch machinery, devices of steel and glass and crystal and other materials that Jalian did not recognize.

Jin'Ish hesitated. /so. wait/ A bulge ran down the center of one of cher minor tentacles. The tip of the tentacle split, peeled back into four tiny flaps, and jin'Ish's traveling eye popped out of the tentacle. The eye swiveled for a moment in the grip of the flaps, orienting itself. It stabilized, and jin'Ish thrust the tentacle into the dark center of the access panel. After a moment cheshe forced air through cher lace in the barely audible sound that indicated exasperation. /tube is malfunctioned/ cheshe admitted.

Jalian stood, dusting her tunic off. /this is idiotic,/ she said flatly. /i'm going to get ghess'Rith to teach me how to work these things. at least he doesn't contradict himself./ She felt jin'Ish's surprise—most of the Silver-Eyes were polite to cher, and to all of the alien gods—felt it turning to rage.

Whatever jin'Ish would have said to her, Jalian never found out. A scream broke through the early morning calm. *"Hai! Ken Selvren, Hai!"*

In dreamy slow motion, Jalian found herself considering the sentry warning with a sort of calm, interested detachment. Without thinking twice, she discarded the alternative of exiting through the Gods' House's main entrance. It was at the west end of the building, precious seconds away from the village circle. She pulled a circuit spanner from the toolbot at her side and smashed the window open. Impossibly strong tentacles wrapped themselves around her, restraining her; with distant surprise she recalled jin'Ish's presence. She twisted inside the grip of the tentacles, brought her hands together as fists, crossing them over her chest to give herself the maximum striking distance between her fists and their targets. Her arms uncrossed like a snake striking to chop at the bases of the two major tentacles facing her. Jin'Ish emitted a high-pitched squeak of pain or surprise; cher grip on Jalian loosened slightly. Jalian pushed back from jin'Ish, twisted so that she faced jin'Ish in profile, centered, and brought her right foot up in a shotak kick to jin'Ish's central bone cage. Jin'Ish's tentacles released her; cheshe stumbled backward, cher rear legs folding beneath cher.

It never occurred to Jalian that the alien god had been trying to save her life; she went out through the window. Perhaps five seconds had passed. She could not remember having drawn the short knife that was the only weapon she was wearing. It was in her hand already when she first thought of it.

Women were pouring into the street. Most were still naked, this early in the morning, but none were unarmed. Even the men carried clubs or poles, though they were moving more slowly and with more confusion than the trained warriors. Jalian, like every other Silver-Eyes, paid them no mind; men were not taught the martial arts.

The warning cry had come from the west sentry. She was lying dead at her post, riddled with arrows. A vast force of Real Indians, five hundred or more, all mounted upon the tamed animals they rode, were already halfway across the clearing that separated the village from the woods. They were painted for war, they screamed and fired arrows as they rode. The center of their charging line rode over the fallen sentry.

Jalian stood, still and unmoving. Arrows whistled past her; most of them were aimed poorly, if at all. Near her, Kendr's brother Davad took an arrow through the eye; she stepped to the side and took the spear he was holding as he fell. She was calm, so calm. Her entire life, this was all that she had trained for. Strike as a child, and then kartari and shotak; at least an eighth day of each, every day of her life since she was old enough.

Seconds left. Jalian picked out one of the horsemen for her own, a giant who was probably four times her size. The sunlight on his leather breastplate was beautiful. Tiny puffs of dust rose where his horse's hooves struck the dirt of the village circle.

The warriors of Clan Silver-Eyes had less than sixty seconds from the time their sentry called warning and the moment when the wave of Real Indians met them; sixty seconds and a lifetime of training in a martial discipline their ancestors had spent five hundred years perfecting.

They clashed in the center of the village.

DATELINE 1968 GREGORIAN.

She lay on the grass at the side of the highway, in the dark hours before morning. The sea was audible, off to the other side of the Pacific Coast Highway. It was cold, below fifty degrees, and damp with heavy fog, but Jalian found that since meeting Georges she no longer got as cold, or as hungry, or as tired as before. She did not understand the phenomenon in all of its practical ramifications, though with what Corvichi physics she retained she had nearly completed a mathematical model she thought was valid.

Usually she did not think about it, except when something happened that was sufficiently strange to force her.

"When I was young," said Jalian, "I was told that the Big Road led to the other worlds, worlds of gods and demons. Later," she said with a perfectly deadpan expression, "I found that this was not true."

Georges Mordreaux sat upright at the side of the road, his back to a gnarled old redwood. Jalian had almost never seen him sleep; he was usually awake when she went to sleep, and when she rose again. "That must have been very strange," he said quietly, "to find yourself suddenly in a time so different from your own. It is very different, now, from when I was born, but the change was gradual, until recently. Within the last fifty or sixty years, the world has seen more change than in the two hundred before—but even that change, by comparison, does not match your own."

Eyes closed, Jalian switched without pause to silverspeech. Georges seemed to follow her silverspeech without difficulty; v'chak, on the other hand, he had difficulty with. Jalian was not sure how many of her memories he understood, even yet; they still had difficulties with basic concepts at times. "It was not so easy," she agreed. "There is a phrase, *to walk in wilderness,* meaning to leave your people and strike out on your own. It happened at times, as a Hunter reached her middle years without achieving high status, that she would do this. So, what I have done is only a wilderness walk further away than any ken Selvren had the chance to take before.

"A walk," said Jalian, "into the land of gods and demons. Cautionary tales, ghess'Rith would say."

A truck rumbled out of the darkness, and by them. The wind of its passing ruffled Georges' jacket and hair, sent the fog around them swirling into strange shapes. "I worry about them now, you know," said Jalian quietly. "I came here, oh, for many reasons. To stop . . ." she used the English word, "*Armageddon,* that was part; to leave ghess'Rith and ken Selvren behind forever, that was another. And I have, truly, left them."

"You worry, sometimes, too much." Georges Mordreaux grinned down at her prone form. "In my favorite movie, there is a scene—"

Jalian made a derisive sound. "I have seen a *movie,*" she said. "It is only a collection of pictures strung together, and made to appear on the screen very fast. Sounds that are not always synchronized come with it. How can you be fooled?"

Georges blinked. "Jalian, the images are supposed to . . . blur together, so that the motion appears smooth."

"Oh?" Jalian considered the idea. "I had to look very carefully," she conceded.

"There is a movie," said Georges, "called *Casablanca.* It is the best movie ever made," he explained. "There are evil Germans in it, and a shifty but admirable French official. There is a scene, at the end of the picture, where Rick is telling Ilsa, 'Where I'm going, you can't follow. What I'm doing, you can't be any part of. Ilsa, I'm no good at being noble, but it doesn't take much to see that the problems of three little people don't amount to a hill of beans in this crazy world. Someday you'll understand. Not now. Here's looking at you, kid.' "

Jalian propped herself up on both elbows, and opened her eyes to look at Georges through the mist. "What is a hill of beans?"

"The scene means," said Georges patiently, "that the

problems of one person are small enough that even the person whose problems they are can ignore them, in a large enough context."

Jalian sighed, and lowered herself back to the ground. "You are a very strange person, Georges."

Georges Mordreaux said defensively, "Bogart did it better."

Without inflection, Jalian said, "No doubt."

DATELINE 719 A.B.C.

In the winter of her fourteenth Coldtime, Jalian d'Arsennette became a woman, and a Hunter by the laws and custom of ken Selvren.

In another age it would not have happened. She was fourteen; women were not made Hunters so young—even Ralesh had been sixteen.

Now, seven years and more after the arrival of the alien gods, slightly more than a year since the Battle of the Meadow, in which ken Selvren had destroyed the Real Indians of Cahr Muhl; now there was only Ralesh to argue against her. Jalian's mother opposed Jalian's petition on the grounds that her daughter had not killed three Real Indians, as required by old custom. Ralesh's claim was understood to mean, *she is not old enough*; most of the Hunters had not fulfilled the traditional requirement, a requirement formulated in days when Real Indians had outnumbered ken Selvren by eight or ten to one. The Eldest Hunter, Morine d'Arsennette, shook her head. She said gently, "Daughter, your child is ready *now*. The nearest Real Indians are a half-year's distance away, and they do not threaten us." She chuckled with some dryness. "All the tribes combined do not threaten us, with the gods' light weapons guarding the village. Ralesh," she said gently, "our enemies are gone." Morine's eyes closed, and she nodded for a moment in the warmth from the fire pit. She was very old now; some sixty Coldtimes. Her eyes opened again, and she peered around the hall at the assembled Elder Hunters. There were less than twenty of them. "And we lost over four hundred of our warriors. I will not agree to keep as child a girl who is willing and ready—and *able*—to become a Hunter.

"I say yes."

Around the fire pit, there was a slow rumble of yes, and yes, and yes.

Ralesh shook her head. She was the youngest woman in the room, by a good five years. "I disagree. You push her too far, too fast." She looked around the room, at the ring of composed, confident faces. She shrugged her displeasure. "I withdraw, before the—wisdom—of the Elder Hunters. Yes."

Morine seemed to throw off her age and her weariness. "So, then. Linada," she addressed the sentry at the door to the hall, "bring her in."

The young Hunter inclined her head several degrees, and went outside. She left the door open behind her, and a blast of icy air cut in through the opening. Morine shivered in the cold; it seemed to touch her more deeply these days.

The sentry pushed the door open slightly more, and Jalian walked in a few paces before her. She stood facing the older women, without arrogance, but without uncertainty or self-consciousness. She was not particularly tall for her age; she was still a head and a half shorter than her mother. Her breasts were still spare, and it was apparent already that the stocky, muscular build of some of the Hunters would escape her. Her brown hair hung in a thick braid down her back.

Morine said without preamble, "We have decided. You will be a Hunter."

Jalian was silent for a long moment. Finally she said, clearly, "Thank you."

Morine smiled at her. It was not a reassuring thing. "You will not thank me. I will not allow such foolishness. I am doing this not for your good, but for ours."

Ralesh said distinctly, without looking at Jalian, "You should have enjoyed your childhood while you were able."

Linada bowed to them once more, and withdrew, closing the door behind herself.

After the ceremony she went to see ghess'Rith.

Ghess'Rith was at the Ship, which the alien gods had moved to the clearing that held the Clan House, after the

Battle of the Meadow, the summer before last. From its turrets, lasers and particle projectors could destroy any approaching creature in line of sight.

It hardly mattered; since ken Selvren had destroyed the Real Indians of Cahr Muhl, there were no hostile tribes within any reasonable striking distance. Since the Ship had been moved to the edge of the village circle, it had killed one bear and one goat.

The village still bore the scars of the Battle of the Meadow. Many of the houses that had burned had not yet been rebuilt. Their loss was not felt; many of the houses that were still standing had no residents.

It was not as bad now as it had looked during the summer and fall. Snow covered the worst scars of the Battle; the fact that the buried dead had made the north clearing unsowable was invisible. The monument to the dead, raised at the edge of the north clearing, was all but hidden beneath the layers of snow. (According to ghess'Rith, the snows were recent in this area; they were, he said, a result of the Fires during the Big Crunch. Jalian did not see how that could be so; ghess'Rith spoke vaguely of Ice Times and dust clouds.)

Ghess'Rith was awaiting her when she reached the Ship. The Ship rose into cloud-covered sky, hull narrowing to a needle point. At its point, it was taller than the tallest tree Jalian had ever seen. Ghess'Rith came down to meet her in the lift that took them up from ground level to the Ship's airlock. He did not speak to her as they made their way through the Ship corridors to his feathernest; he was annoyed about something again, which did not surprise Jalian. Recently ghess'Rith had taken it into his braincase that it was possible to teach the Silver-Eyes males to read and write. He was trying to get the idea across to the Elder Hunters, with a predictable lack of success.

Jalian held no opinion in the matter one way or the other—except that *she* was not going to be the one to try to teach the stupid grunts.

Inside his feathernest, a small, dimly blue-lit recess in the wall of the corridor, ghess'Rith made a cradle of his tentacles, and invited Jalian to sit. He sank down on the two legs opposite the cradle, to keep his mass centered.

/hello, ghess'Rith,/ said Jalian, settling herself comfortably in his tentacles.

/hello, Jalian. how do you creatures put up with one

another?/ he burst out. /ignorant, self-centered, supersti-
tious, *brachtats*/ Jalian got a mental image of a small creature
with habits that ghess'Rith found disgusting. /i retract,/ said
ghess'Rith after a moment. /not brachtats. kubchi at worst/

Jalian was shedding outer clothing. Her cloak and fur-
lined walking boots were on the floor already; she sent her
vest and leggings after them. She kept her tunic on because
ghess'Rith's fur was itchy. /don't insult my people, alien
demon-god, or i will be forced to cut off your tentacles one
by one./

Ghess'Rith's lace rippled in a snort. /you try it, bright-
eyes/ He paused. /almost i did not remember. today you
insulted your Elder Hunters into granting you full citizen-
ship. what happened?/

Jalian stroked the fur under the base of ghess'Rith's
tentacles. /i am not allowed to talk about it, ghess'Rith./

/oh/ Ghess'Rith's feelings were hurt; some of it touched
Jalian.

/ghess'Rith, I'm sorry. we're not allowed to./

Ghess'Rith whistled through his lace. Even having known
him for half her life, Jalian was not sure what the lace-
whistle meant, or even if the emotion that it signified was
one with a people analog. This time, something happened
that had not happened before; the whistle cut off abruptly,
before it climbed out of the range of people hearing. /what
is that smell?/

/what smell?/

/burnt flesh. have you been eating living creatures again?/
asked ghess'Rith sternly.

Jalian was stung. /no! i don't do that anymore. i told
you./

Jalian felt ghess'Rith turn grim. For the most part, the
Corvichi spacetime gypsies were a slow-moving folk, but
when they cared to they could move as quickly as a very
fast person. /if you have not been eating meat . . . /
Ghess'Rith's tentacles loosened slightly, and one of his major and two of his minor tentacles slipped out of the web
supporting Jalian. The major tentacle grasped the edge of
Jalian's tunic, where it touched her throat; the other two
tentacles tore it diagonally over her breasts.

/ghess'Rith, you're not even a *person*!/

/tchai erreg kisirien!/ screamed ghess'Rith furiously.
/they have burnt patterns on your skin!/

Jalian stared at him in incomprehension. With one hand, she drew her torn tunic closed. /ghess'Rith, it's the Woman's Brand; all women have it./

/barbarian, *animal* behavior,/ snarled ghess'Rith. /i kesri for you, since you have not the sense to do so for yourself/

Jalian's hands clenched painfully on ghess'Rith's tentacles. "You do not speak to me like that, ghess'Rith Corvichi. You do not touch me like that." She forced herself to to let go of her grip. She forced the anger back, under control.

One of ghess'Rith's partially mobile eyes popped up over the edge of the ridge that his tentacles grew out of. It peered down at Jalian uncertainly. /Jalian? what did you say?/

Jalian had suppressed the sudden, insane anger that threatened to blossom within her, suppressed it so quickly she herself was fully aware of it. /it . . . nothing, ghess'Rith. it was not important./

Ghess'Rith shifted weight slightly. His lace relaxed; he was calming quickly. /apology offered,/ he said at length. /expecting Corvichi behavior from a person. what is design?/

Jalian had to calm her breathing; her hands were trembling. It took a moment for his words to penetrate. /what do you mean?/ The design of the Woman's Brand was simple; an arrow that pierced a circle. The top half of the arrow protruded from a spot slightly to the right of the exact top of the circle. It had no meaning.

Ghess'Rith whistled again. /unimportant, is/ He paused. /jin'Ish complained about you again/ He brightened slightly. /cheshe was greatly upset. jin'Ish is one of our best person teachers/

Jalian smiled swiftly. /i overlistened cher the other day. i'm that 'person with the knife and the attitude.'/

/you should be more polite. if not because cheshe is Corvichi, then because cheshe is an elder/

Jalian snorted. /all i did was ask cher what a negative-entropy timeline was. cheshe evaded question./

/don't think cheshe knows,/ ghess'Rith admitted. /jin'Ish is only a technician. were you truly curious, or just trimming cher tentacles?/

/mostly trimming cher tentacles, but some curious. i lost a probe on a -entropy timeline not three tendays ago. that probe cost the Clan twenty days of labor./

Ghess'Rith's lace lifted and tightened slightly in acknowledgment. /-entropy timelines are dangerous, even at high entry ratios. that's one good reason that we use persons to hunt monopoles for us. we would kesri to be caught on -entropy line/

Jalian caught faint ghosts of meaning from the alien word, which was strange. Usually she understood him perfectly, or not at all.

/kesri, ghess'Rith?/

/kesri id go, Jalian/

Jalian made a cutting gesture with one hand. This time there was nothing at all. /never mind. untranslatable, I think./

Two strands of ghess'Rith's lace tightened, and he forced air through them to produce the low humming sound that meant humor. /no doubt. like *guilt*/

Jalian nodded. /probably. what would happen to me if I were caught on a negative-entropy line?/

/you would die eventually. i do not know if you would experience kesri—i suspect not/

/why would I die?/

/time runs backward, Jalian. that is what negative entropy means/

/i still do not understand./

/*your* entropy sign would still be positive. if you entered the line on a 1:1 entry ratio, you would blow up, burn like a sun. your atoms and the atoms of the -entropy line would destroy each other. if you entered the line at a high entry ratio, the timesign reversal would still kill you, only more slowly. your neural system would overload quickly. the higher functions would go first, to be quickly followed by the gross organs. within two running cycles you would be only disassociated atoms; within five you would be—you have not learned the words yet—pieces of light/

/nobody ever survives it?/

Ghess'Rith's lace tightened. /some survive longer than others, great is their kesri/

/why?/

Ghess'Rith seemed to hesitate. /i will speak no more of this/

The author wishes to note that he has never liked ghess'Rith. But then, ghess'Rith has never liked me either. The Corvichi are a prejudiced lot.

DATELINE 1969 GREGORIAN.

Ralesh moved quietly through the night.

She walked forty meters from the edge of the freeway, well into the woods. She was not slowed by the undergrowth and the trees, and she left no path. Since leaving the city, nobody had seen her.

In one hand she held a small device with a pointer and a lighted dial. Twice the device spoke to her in silverspeech; she did not answer it. With rare detours, she moved in the direction the needle pointed.

Here is an irony; the device measured fluctuations in information probability, such as were caused by functioning telepaths. It was calibrated to a human being named Jalian of the Fires.

What it actually tracked was something else entirely. Not even a Corvichi-trained human telepath was likely to be monitored through the blanketing probability storm that swirled around Georges Mordreaux. A Corvichi would have found the readings on the device Ralesh carried unbelievable. The probability fluctuation was a thousand times greater than that generated by the best Corvichi telepath.

So it was that throughout the year 1969, Ralesh d'Arsennette tracked not her daughter, but Georges.

By then, of course, that was immaterial.

Clipped next to the knife on the Hunter's belt was a small object that looked vaguely like a hand grenade. The Hunter intended to kill Jalian, but she did not intend to use the knife.

That was for herself.   —

DATELINE 1969 GREGORIAN.

Sitting in her seat, waiting for the film to start, Jalian felt that Georges was being unreasonably smug. You would think he'd *invented* the film, rather than simply finding a revival theater where it was playing.

Then the movie began, and within ten minutes she had forgotten everything else in the entire world.

There was much about the movie she did not understand; and, as with so much else in this time, its women and the ways in which they acted infuriated her. But the basic story itself was comprehensible, and she quickly ceased to notice the flickering quality of the image. The woman, Ilsa, had left Rick just before the Germans entered Paris— the film concerned a war that had ended some fifteen years before Jalian's arrival in this time, in which Georges's country, France, had been occupied by an invading army—and now, at the film's beginning, Ilsa had come, with her husband, to Casablanca . . .

. . . where Rick was waiting.

It seemed to be a matter of supreme importance to both of them, whether they loved each other or not, and, at least at first, neither of them appeared to be sure. Jalian glanced then at Georges, but his eyes were fixed on the screen.

The film . . . Her impressions of it were strange, and she was not sure she wished to analyze them. Perhaps the hardest part was the necessity, if the story was to be understood, of conceding that the character played by Humphrey Bogart, Rick, was a *person*. Male, but a person nonetheless. Nothing else explained Ilsa's reaction to him, or even Jalian's own.

When the movie ended, she sat quietly for a long while. Finally Georges prodded her, and said, "They're clearing the theater, Jalian."

Jalian turned to him. "At the beginning, when he said, 'I stick my neck out for nobody.' He was lying, even then? He knew it?"

Georges Mordreaux nodded. "He knew it."

DATELINE 724 A.B.C.

When Jalian d'Arsennette was nineteen years old, she made the walk through the hills to the Big Road for the last time.

She bore upon her back a disassembled Doorway. It massed forty-five kilograms. The straps that held it in place had nearly cut off circulation to her arms. It slowed her travel, and pushed her feet heavily into the ground she traversed.

The track she left and the time she lost were important. The other Hunters, if they caught her before she reached the Big Road, would certainly kill her.

The machine she was stealing, that she would destroy, had cost the Clan two years of labor.

Two tendays earlier, the alien gods had announced their intention to leave Earth. The Ship (which was, in fact, only a small part of a larger, kilometers-long Ship that never left orbit) would lift silently into space, loaded with monopoles, radioactives, and biomass that could be genegineered to match the Corvichi amino acid requirements. With their machinery adapted to the physics of this timeline, the great Ship would activate its subwavicle stardrive, and, for the next few thousand cycled running cycles, would explore the timeline into which they had come battered and limping.

In time, when they had seen enough of this new timeline, they would shift again, and move further around the Great Wheel of Existence. They had lived so for longer than any Corvichi remembered; they had not even the legends of a planet-bound existence. Perhaps the Shipmind might have told them of their past, had they cared to ask.

In over 800,000 running cycles, no Corvichi had bothered. Where they had come from was not important; they lived for the journey that would come.

Once again that time was near.

Jalian found ghess'Rith waiting for her, curled into a dim purplish mass of flesh, huddled sadly into his feathernest. It was dark; the blue glowfloats were lying inactive in a rounder.

She stood at the edge of the feathernest; she did not enter.

/ghess'Rith./

/Jalian/

/you are leaving./

/true/ Ghess'Rith stirred. /word came from the Shipmind half a day past. it was confirmed by the captains/

/why? you told me not for another running cycle at least./

Ghess'Rith said uneasily, /our probes have met with the crosstime ships of a person empire/

"Tchai," whispered Jalian aloud. /you have been acting so strangely. . . ./

/far away,/ said ghess'Rith, /far across the Great Wheel of Existence. they are persons like yourself, the *'salch khri*, but their science is close to our own. they are warlike and they outnumber us greatly . . . we do not wish to fight/

Jalian assimilated the information slowly. Conquerors, then, like the Real Indians, with technology like the alien gods. /and you will leave us to this?/

/we have no choice. the Shipmind recommended; the captains chose/

Jalian's hands curved slightly at her sides, without her awareness. "Cowards," she said with true surprise. "You are *cowards*." /have you no pride? you flee before *persons*./

/pride?/ Ghess'Rith seemed surprised. /no. we are not warriors/ He paused. /Jalian, you could come with us. you are better trained in outtime technology than many of the crew/

Jalian did not need to think. /no./

Ghess'Rith persisted. /Jalian, you will not be happy with only other Silver-Eyes to talk to. *kisirien,* Jalian, there are no other Silver-Eyes you can mindtalk to/

Jalian stood straight. She was shivering slightly with a reaction she could not name. /don't do this to me, ghess'Rith./

/Jalian, there are wonders off this small destroyed planet. within your own hunting grounds there is a planet with brilliantly colored rings. one of your planets has a giant red spot, caused in part by the dance of vast sentient leviathans celebrating the joy of existence. there are—Jalian, do you remember how you used to feel about what you called the Big Road?/

Jalian was silent for a long while. She looked straight at ghess'Rith. "Yes, ghess'Rith, I remember."

/i feel you agree. Jalian, the rest of spacetime holds wonders that dwarf even what a six-year-old child once felt for the Big Road./

Jalian said, "I am not a child, ghess'Rith."

/i did not understand that, Jalian/

/perhaps you were not meant to./

/Jalian?/

"Oh, I remember the Big Road, ghess'Rith. I remember."

Jalian stepped onto the concrete of the Big Road. Even now, at the age of nineteen, she had traversed its length only three times. At its end, rising into the hills that ringed the north edge of the valley, there began the ruins of another Big Road, and from that spot, in the far distance, one could see a vast and faint pattern of roads and ruined cities.

The first three times down that arrow-straight road, the land of gods and demons had not been at its other end.

Jalian did not find four to be a particularly lucky number for her, either way.

Jalian knelt on the gray-black road, and slowly lifted the Doorway off her back. She set it down with a slight thud, then slumped next to it, to give her aching muscles a respite. She counted a small cycle, then another, before rising.

She assembled the Doorway carefully. She was well aware of the time it was taking her. Sweat began to soak again into her brown-green tunic, there to evaporate at once into the ossifyingly dry and hot air.

After several minutes, the Doorway's control panel was set up and hooked to the Doorway itself. Using a tool that resembled a small awl, she began setting controls. The work went slowly, as the awl-like tool was a poor substitute for the minor tentacles of the alien gods. Finally it was finished, and Jalian straightened, wiping sweaty palms on her tunic, ignoring the sharp pain in the small of her back.

The control panel acknowledged the search pattern Jalian had set up. From the frame of the Doorway, Jalian detached a brace of insect-sized probes. She pressed the activator, held the brace for a six-count, and released the probe-hold button. The probes dropped off the brace, buzzing slightly, and arrayed themselves before the Doorway. They hung in midair, their buzzing hum becoming almost imperceptibly louder.

The Doorway *flickered*.

For the barest instant, a swirling gray maelstrom appeared between the poles of the Doorway. Lines and spheres writhed . . .

It was gone.

Jalian prepared to wait. Until one of the probes reached an alternate timeline that caused the bright-red danger indicator to flash, she could do nothing. The danger indicator, installed because many of the Silver-Eyes could not hear the ultrasonic warning signal, remained stubbornly dark.

Jalian glanced back, to the hills. She saw nothing, but . . . She reached out with her mind, to find the pursuit, and there; guided by her mind's eye, she could now visually make out the faint rising of dust that her followers, careless in their haste, were leaving.

She turned away from the sight. They did not understand what she was doing, or why. She could explain until the empire of which ghess'Rith spoke conquered them all, and still they would not understand.

She did not admit even to herself that she did not understand her own actions fully. She knew only that it felt right.

(Ghess'Rith would have told her she was committing suicide; but there was a memory, skipping stones across the lake as a child. If she threw the stone straight at the water, it splashed and sank. If she skipped it over the still surface of the lake, it would travel six or ten body-lengths before sinking.)

(She could almost do the math to describe what she was going to attempt.)

(Almost.)

Jalian could not help herself; she was turning to watch her pursuit when the danger indicator flashed. The control panel began whooping wildly at the very limits of Jalian's hearing, as the Doorway penetrated the timeline with the skewed entropy orientation. An entry portal flickered into existence within the poles of the Doorway; through the huge metal gateway, it presented a view of the Big Road.

It was different from the Big Road upon which Jalian stood. The left side of the road was Jalian's right; and the right side was her left. The colors were wildly different, like the negative images that ghess'Rith sometimes produced with his image recreations. While she watched, a bird sailed gracefully backward across Jalian's field of vision.

It was a one-to-one entry ratio, what the alien gods called a true entry. It was not what Jalian needed. To go where she desired to go, and to survive the experience, she needed the highest entry ratio that the Doorway was capable of establishing.

The necessary equations tumbled through the back of

her mind. She could not have explained what she was doing to another Silver-Eyes; she could hardly have done so to one of the alien gods. She needed to balance the Doorway's power supply against the necessary high entry ratio against the time it would take her to make her journey.

She set the Doorway for an entry ratio of fourteen million to one.

An arrow struck her in the back of her shoulder. Its force was already spent by the time it reached her; it did not even break her skin.

Through the Doorway, the Big Road blurred. Day and night became a single indistinguishable flash of light. The plants lived and died too quickly for her to see. The forest itself was a dark, shifting blur. Only the mountains and the Big Road itself remained constant.

Another arrow struck the ground near her. Without looking back, Jalian took the callback remote from the control panel. With the callback remote clutched in her hand, Jalian d'Arsennette stepped through the Doorway.

Arrows whistled through the Doorway after her, but she was already months away.

DATELINE RETROGRADE: 721 A.B.C. TO 1962 GREGORIAN INCLUSIVE.

Needles thrust themselves into every exposed patch of skin on her body. Fire washed over her. She screamed, and the fire washed down into her lungs. She dropped to the concrete of the Big Road, the pain all that she could think of. The fire crept in through her ears, and melted in through the surface of her skin until it touched her bones.

She lay writhing on the ground, unable to control herself. The pain was insane, impossible. The worst pain she had ever experienced before was as nothing to this. . . .

The Real Indian rode out of the sunshine. Jalian was thirteen and she threw the spear she'd taken from the hands of the dead boy at her side. The spear bounced off the leather breastplate, and arrows came from nowhere and struck her thigh and shoulder. She did not remember falling, did not remember the knife leaving her hand, burying itself in the Real Indian's eye.

They had all assumed she was dead. She was one of the last of the Silver-Eyes to be approached by the Healers. The arrows had been fired at point-blank range, and she was a small girl; it saved her life. The barbed arrowheads went completely through her, without embedding themselves in her flesh.

She was delirious for more than a tenday. From the depths of her delirium, she remembered a voice, her mother's; and six years later, lying on the Big Road, in an insane timeline where the sun and moon were only continuous circlets of light overhead, the words returned.

"Live, Jalian. This is all that I teach you, all that I have ever taught you. You must wish to live. . . ."

Jalian d'Arsennette rose to her knees. Like a cripple she struggled to her feet. It was not necessary that she move; she would exit this timeline when the Doorway's power was exhausted.

She did not have to move.

The Big Road stretched away in front of her. Jalian oriented on the familiar sight, and slowly, falteringly, began the long run that would take her to its end.

DATELINE BASE DIVERGENCE: 1962 GREGORIAN.

Late in the month of November, Johnny Harris went driving fo the last time.

He was double-dating, because his girl's parents wouldn't let her go out alone with him. In his heart Johnny didn't blame them. Ellen Jamieson was stunning; her hair was the same color as Brigitte Bardot's. When she was standing, with her hair unbound, it fell straight to her butt. Her eyes were honest to God the bluest damn things he'd ever seen, and to top it all off she was *smart*; she could talk about sports or politics as reasonably as any guy Johnny knew. She knew more about movie-making than anybody else Johnny had ever met, and that included his best friend Darryl.

He picked up Darryl and his date before heading over to Ellen's. If he showed up alone, Ellen's parents wouldn't let her leave the house. It was dark and raining by the time he reached Darryl's house. The rain wasn't serious, just a nuisance.

Darryl and his most recent steady, a completely nothing chick named Katie, were standing on the porch when Johnny pulled up in his older brother's Chevette. (He wasn't actually supposed to be driving it, but what the hell; Craig was in the Army, and didn't have leave coming for months yet.) Darryl and Katie ran through the light drizzle to the car. Johnny had forgotten to unlock the doors on the passenger's side until Darryl pounded on the window. He leaned over and popped the locks. Darryl slid into the front seat, and slammed the door shut. Without being told, Katie got in the back seat.

Darryl ran fingers through his damp hair. He looked pissed; the cigarette he'd been smoking on the porch had gone out. He looked a lot like James Dean, and knew it, and dressed and wore his hair to emphasize the fact. The resemblance ended when he opened his mouth. "Hey, dude, you trying to drown us out there?"

Johnny shrugged, pulling away from the curb. "Sorry, man. Hi, Katie." With his free hand he aimed a thumb to the back seat. "Brews in back. Grab me one."

Darryl leaned over the seat backs, rummaging in a bag on the floor. He pulled out two bottles of Coors, reasonably cold, from the bag, opened them with the bottle opener in the ashtray, and handed one to Johnny. He drank from his, and then glanced into the back seat. "Hey, Katie. You want a beer?"

Katie leaned forward, arms resting on the seat-top that separated them. "No, but I'll drink some of yours."

"Shit," grumbled Darryl, "I knew you were gonna say that." He passed the beer back to her over his left shoulder. "Hey, Johnny, where we going?"

"To pick up Ellen," said Johnny instantly.

"Where *after* that?"

"Umm . . ." Johnny leaned forward and flicked on his wipers. "Covina," he said finally.

"Uh-huh." Darryl took his beer back from Katie. "I knew you were going to say that," he announced. "Look, I thought we agreed we weren't going to that damn revival theater any more. What's playing this time, *I Was a Teenage Rutabaga?*"

Johnny laughed in spite of himself. "No. It's *Frankenstein* and *The Bride of Frankenstein.*"

Darryl stared at him. "*The Bride of Frankenstein?*" He looked at Katie for support, then changed his mind and decided to go it alone. "Are we for real here?"

Johnny sighed. "Look, I'll owe you one, okay?" He cornered onto the block where Ellen lived.

Darryl sat back in his seat. "Damn straight you owe me one. More than one, actually."

Johnny pulled over next to the curb, and put the car into park. He left the engine running. "Right, whatever. Back seat, dude." He got out of the car, slamming the door, and ran up to the front porch.

" 'Back seat, dude.' There is no appreciation here," Darryl said to nobody in particular. He didn't bother to get out. Instead he crawled over the seat-top into the back of the car.

Johnny was back quickly, with Ellen. He opened the door for her, closed it behind her, and ran around to the driver's side. Inside the car, he put the car into drive and headed for 71 north.

The conversation inside was tense at first—Darryl didn't much like Ellen, and Ellen found Darryl amusing—but they had all relaxed by the time Darryl was on his third beer, and Johnny was finishing his second. The rain was increasing, but Johnny wasn't particularly worried; he'd driven in the rain before without difficulty. He wasn't worrying about his drinking either. It was only his third beer, after all, and he'd just begun it. He'd eaten dinner less than two hours before, and he was hardly buzzed, you know?

They were heading into the deserted industrial stretch of road on the outskirts of Pomona that led toward Covina. Johnny was pleasantly relaxed. Ellen was leaning against him, a warm and comfortable weight. From the back seat, he could vaguely hear Darryl speaking quietly, and Katie giggling. He had a momentary impression of an indistinct brightness coming from up ahead.

Rainbows blasted over them.

Johnny touched the brakes, and the car fishtailed wildly. He let go of the brakes, but the rainbows were intensifying, red and orange and yellow and green . . .

He couldn't *see*. In panic he stomped on the brakes, and the lights were so pretty, you know, blue and purple and it was dark for a long second and suddenly it was red again, red and orange and yellow . . . The Chevette skidded, hit the guardrail at the side of the road, and flipped. It tumbled end over end. One of the headlights was smashed in the tumble, and the windshield shattered inward. The car flipped one last time, and came to rest upside down in the middle of the street. The horn was blaring crazily and the single headlight was rocking up and down with the movement of the car.

The rainbows ceased.

In the comparatively dim beam from the one rocking headlight, standing in the rain, Jalian d'Arsennette held herself fully upright. Her clothing was dissolving in the rain. Her skin was the color that Ellen Jamieson might have experienced after a very bad sunburn.

Her hair was ice-white.

She tried to take a step forward. She did not remember falling. It was logical that she must have fallen; the pavement struck her hard.

Ellen Jamieson found herself lying halfway through the windshield, with the water pouring down on her. The shards of the windshield were cutting up into her abdomen. She hardly felt it, hardly felt anything. Out of the corner of her eye, she could see the person lying on the freeway, sprawled over the divider line. There was a severed hand a few feet away from her.

After a while had passed, Ellen did not know how long, the form on the road stirred. It rolled over onto its back. Ellen noted exposed breasts with clinical detachment; it was a woman. After another long pause, the form moved again. With agonizing slowness, it rose to its knees, and then to its feet. The world faded. . . .

When Ellen became aware again, legs that looked burned were standing in front of her eyes. She could not see above the knees. She felt hands grasping her, and moving her—

She screamed at the top of her lungs and passed out.

She never awoke again.

Jalian moved in a daze. The dying girl before her was dressed in a fashion that Jalian had never imagined the like of. The thing Jalian had pulled her out of resembled a karz more than a little. It had a single glowing light on its left side.

The remote callback was beeping in her hand. She unclenched the hand that held it, vaguely aware that it hurt her to do so. She dropped it on top of the strange woman.

She stood, and backed away. Conservation of mass-energy required that the mass that left her time return to it in some form. And the girl was dying to begin with.

/rest, sister,/ she said, and she was not sure who she was talking to, herself or the girl from the karz. /rest. you have a long journey, and you will not survive it./

There seemed to be some barely perceptible response from the unconscious form. "In time," she added in a blurred, inaudible mixture of silverspeech and Corvichi v'chak, "in time the journey takes us all."

The rainbows began again; purple, blue, green, yellow . . .

On the other side of the earth divider, something came roaring out of the darkness, moving faster than Jalian had ever seen anything move before—understanding rushed in on her, it was a karz, moving on the Big Road. . . .

With a sudden disorientation, she realized she was not on the Big Road. This was smaller, there was no divider fence in the center, no stumps where poles of some sort had once been . . . the Big Road had not been built yet, a part of her thought with clear, detached amazement.

Something in the karz at her side must have been sensitive to the electromagnetic energies being released by the callback remote, Jalian reasoned later.

She was walking away from the glowing rainbows, on legs that seemed not a part of her body, watching the karz, and it was moving down the empty, rain-wet road, it was impossible that anything should move so quickly—

The car behind her exploded.

Standing mere meters away, Jalian had a brief, pleasant impression: she was flying.

She ceased flying abruptly.

DATELINE 724 A.B.C.

Ghess'Rith was asleep when the captains called for him.

Like all Corvichi, he slept rarely; it was more an art form than a physical necessity. He allowed his brain to process data randomly without the oversight of his superego, and upon awaking reviewed his dreams to see whether they contained anything of interest. Often they did; as often they did not.

His current dreaming was going badly; he was as pleased as not when the captains roused his superego from unconsciousness—until he realized where he was.

His physical self, he knew, was still curled in his feathernest on the planet below them; still his senses insisted that he stood in the Great Ship's Machine of Decision, and he knew that if he was found wanting he would not leave the Machine alive.

The captains were arrayed about him in a semicircle. They were none of them young enough to retain their minor tentacles; three were beginning to lose their major tentacles. Even the glowfloats were closer to purple than blue; the energetic blue light waves tended to cause strain on their delicate traveling eyes.

The toolbot that was the symbolic representative of the Shipmind was positioned in a niche in the Ship wall just to the right of the raised dais upon which ghess'Rith's senses told him he stood.

/these be Shipmind conceptualizations, captains' concerns/

/these be?/ Ghess'Rith asked apprehensively.

/of the female person Jalian of the Fires/

/?/

The Shipmind spoke in a whisper of information. *These are her gene complexes. Please examine.*

A bewilderingly complex storm of information whirled through the edges of ghess'Rith's mind; it slowed, stabilized. There was a brief pause as the odd binary-spiral amino acid chain upon which the person genetic code was based was explained to him. Particular molecule patterns were assigned functions and potentials in the binary spirals; and then the genetic pattern that was on store for Jalian d'Arsennette was arrayed for his inspection.

One of the younger captains said dryly, /the obvious is seen/

Ghess'Rith whistled in srheman; it was an emotion that Jalian had privately translated as amazement-at-the-perversity-of-the-universe. In fact her translation was only a crude analog of a sophisticated concept that no person was ever likely to understand. /she survived the -entropy timeline/ He considered briefly. /the body that returned to this timeline?/

A pre-Catastrophe person, said the Shipmind. *Radiation analysis, after compensation for sustained radiation damage during negative-entropy timeline exposure, posits a background radiation level for this body far smaller than that of contemporary Silver-Eyes persons. Fire damage makes body identification unlikely for Silver-Eyes.*

Ghess'Rith wrinkled his lace in comprehension; without genetic analysis, it was not likely the persons would realize the body that was returned to them was not that of their sister. /posit:/ he said, too well aware that his existence depended upon what answer he gave the Shipmind and captains concerning his person protege, /you have observed probability stress. following conclusion, Jalian of the Fires lives/

Probability stress is minimal, but definite. possibility of growth cycle is 6% and running.

Ghess'Rith's tentacles curled. /new timelines,/ he said flatly.

/your person,/ said an elder without inflection, /remarkable, is/

One of the captains directed a question at ghess'Rith. /three cycles of existence in balance. your actions in responsibility. what action now?/

Ghess'Rith's responsors and muscles froze. Even his minor tentacles were unmoving. A time change would erase twelve years of their existence; and even for Corvichi that was no small thing. The loss of twelve years, of the persons they had become in that time, was little better than death. He saw it so; kisirien, of course the captains would also. /her exit date?/

Pre-Catastrophe. No more is certain.

/the time of the Big Roads . . . other Silver-Eyes, similar gene complexes?/

Three children; Ralesh and Morine d'Arsennette.

Ghess'Rith said decisively, /advise sending Ralesh d'Arsennette after her daughter. what Jalian survived, her mother will not allow herself to be killed by/

There was a brief pause. Ghess'Rith, waiting on the Machine of Decision, could not help himself; his tentacles curled in uncertainty.

One of the captains, ghess'Rith was not sure which one, said, /well reasoned. decision is. send Ralesh/

The Shipmind's whispery data pulse said, *Concerning Jalian of the Fires; her genetic potentials are impressive.*

/so?/ Ghess'Rith considered briefly. /ah . . . knowing Jalian/

Transformation wavefront. . . .

/could be on way *now*/

Affirmative.

"Ralesh," said the alien machine, in a voice that Ralesh was altogether weary of, "we must speak to you of your daughter."

DATELINE 1969 GREGORIAN.

Jalian had the feeling they were being followed.

She knew intellectually it could not be so. The cars that sped by them at distances of less than a meter did not worry her; certainly no follower could be in one of those. It was just as certain that no human of this time could trail her afoot without Jalian being aware of it.

Still, it bothered her.

The Pacific Coast Highway hugged the cliffs closely at this point, and the wind was brisk. Even walking along the shoulder of the road, the sound of the waves below, smashing into the cliffs, was all but inaudible. The cliffs rose thirty meters above the rocks. There was no beach as such, simply a jumbled collection of water-cut boulders.

They were walking north; Jalian wanted to see Oregon. The sun was low, thirty degrees or so above the line where sea met sky. Georges was reminiscing about his involvement with the French Foreign Legion. Jalian wasn't sure if he was telling the truth or not. Despite his long and re-markable life, Georges lied as often as not. She listened with half her attention as Georges rambled on about some-body named Beau Geste. After Georges ran down she could ask him more about how peanut butter cookies and choc-olate doughnuts were made.

The sun was a handsbreadth over the horizon when the road widened out. Set about forty meters back on the east side of the freeway, there was a dingy, rundown 7-Eleven. Jalian interrupted Georges in midsentence. "Georges, I'm hungry."

"Well, aren't you always?" he asked rhetorically. They walked over the dirt parking lot to the 7-Eleven. "Who has money?"

Jalian chuckled. She found the idea of money tremen-dously amusing. "You have some right now," she said. "I know because I counted it the last time you were asleep, and I've been doing all the buying since then." She waved a hand at the entrance to the 7-Eleven. "Go buy some food. I'll make a phone call to get some more money."

"You counted my money?"

Jalian pushed him to the door. "Go buy food. Don't forget the doughnuts."

Georges shrugged in resignation. He pushed through the doors, little bells tinkling overhead as he did so. (He remembered Jalian telling him about the first time she'd seen a door with bells set to tinkle when someone entered. She'd laughed herself sick.)

Through the large glass windows that fronted the store, Georges could see Jalian standing in a phone booth, one of two, at the other end of the parking lot. The door to the phone booth was open. Georges didn't know who she talked to when she needed money. She wouldn't tell him, and he disliked shuffling through the memories he'd taken from her; it took all the fun away.

The evening attendant, a tall, thin young man with acne and a bulging Adam's apple, nodded cheerfully to Georges. "Good evening, sir."

Georges nodded agreeably, and continued into the re-frigerated section. The machine that refrigerated the drinks and food was running raggedly; as Georges rummaged through the shelves, the sound steadied, and became a smooth hum. "Let's see," he mumbled, "Coke and sand-

wiches and barbecued potato chips and chocolate doughnuts." The sandwiches were for him; Jalian refused to eat
meats. "Cheesecake and almond cookies." Satisfied, he
took the pile up to the cash register and laid it out on the
counter.

The attendant wasn't paying attention to him. In the
parking lot outside, a pickup truck full of locals was pulling
up. Five men in their late teens and early twenties came
piling out of the pickup and into the 7-Eleven.

It was nearly dark outside; the outer fluorescents clicked
on, casting bright white around the parking lot. One of the
fluorescents, set into the roof that shielded the sidewalk
immediately outside the store, blinked fitfully, as though it
were not sure that it wanted to glow.

Through the window, Georges could see Jalian in the
phone booth. She did not appear to be watching the
entrance.

The attendant was standing motionless behind the
counter. He seemed to be practicing some form of Zen,
under the erroneous impression that if he emptied his mind
of all thought, he would vanish from the perceptions of
lesser mortals.

One of the new arrivals, a tall, handsome redhead in
faded jeans and a brown plaid shirt, said companionably,
"Hey, Charlie! How's it going?"

The attendant came back to life. He smiled weakly.
"Pretty good, Stan. Can I help you?"

The redhead didn't reply. He was looking at Georges.
After a moment of surprise—Georges' eyes were level with
his own—he smiled slightly.

Georges could hear the others, talking loudly in the
background. They were discussing the relative merits of the
brands of beer on sale.

Jalian was talking into the dead phone. "The sun was shining on the sea, shining with all his might, he did his very
best to make the billows smooth and bright, and this was
odd because it was the middle of the night, the moon was
shining sulkily because she thought the sun, had got no
business to be there after the day was done, 'It's very rude
of him,' she said . . ."

Leafing through the white pages, she had already located six offices of the Army, Coast Guard, and Air Force. She memorized the addresses, still talking into the phone. " 'Oh, oysters, come and walk with us,' the Walrus did beseech . . ." In the seven years she had been in this time, she had robbed more soldiers than she could recall. Soldiers were easy. On weekend nights she could get three or four of them, and they always had money.

Probably there were easier ways to get money, had Jalian bothered to think about it; Jalian doubted there were any that she would enjoy more. Even after seven years of getting used to the concept, she still had difficulty with the idea of men with weapons.

Jalian finished memorizing, and hung up. She glanced into the 7-Eleven again. She decided that it was time to go inside; the men from the truck looked like they might be violent.

That would be fun.

Half of the sun had disappeared behind the edge of the horizon. At the limits of Jalian's hearing, as she was walking back to the 7-Eleven, a familiar melody seemed to be playing. She stopped and listened for a second, but there was no sound. It must be her imagination.

But she could not shake the feeling that she was being watched.

The redhead was pushing Georges's junk food to the side of the counter when Jalian entered. "You'll forgive me, but you're obviously not done shopping, and we do have purchases to make," the redhead was saying politely.

"Uhm, well," said Georges, "actually . . ."

The man was not listening. He had turned to look at Jalian. There was an odd expression on his face. "Why . . . *hello*," he said slowly. "Allow me to introduce myself. I am Stan Mildwood, and these four gentlemen are my friends." He waved a hand at the men standing around them. He grinned suddenly at the attendant. "You know Charlie, of course." Stan leaned over the counter, and clamped one hand down on Charlie's shoulder. "Charlie, would this happen to be one of your many girlfriends?" Stan studied Jalian; Jalian studied him back with cold indifference.

"There's something interesting about you," the red-head said conversationally. He took a step closer to Jalian. He stopped because there was blood trickling down his neck from the knife that he found himself walking into.

It took a moment for the other four to realize what was happening. While the realization was sinking in, Georges pushed his junk back into the center of the counter. He gestured to Charlie. "Would you mind ringing this for me?"

Two of the four men—the younger two, probably not out of their teens, one with a strong resemblance to Stan—produced knives, and crouched slightly into proper knife-fighting form.

Georges shook his head. Jalian said, "I will kill him before any of you can move." She edged the knife into Stan's throat with slightly greater force. Blood trickled down the knife blade. The redhead was standing very still. He seemed unafraid, watching Jalian the way a mongoose would watch a rattlesnake. Jalian was not even looking at him.

Charlie didn't seem to be listening to Georges. Georges sighed in frustration, and muttered in French concerning a resemblance between the redhead and Rabelais' backside. He turned away from the counter, surveying the scene as though he had noticed it for the first time. "Oh, my," he said in tones of mild surprise. He looked at the two boys with knives. "You two are quite healthy boys, aren't you?"

For a second nothing happened. Then the two holding the knives began to tremble. "Very healthy indeed," continued Georges cheerfully. "Why—"

The two knife-holders collapsed. "Unfortunately," Georges noted, "your ability to withstand massive and im-mediate growth is limited." He turned slightly to face Stan. Jalian withdrew her knife and backed away.

"Now you, Stan Mildwood, you have an excellent memory."

The redhead blinked once. The cut on his neck had closed already; scar tissue was forming and fading. "I . . . I . . ." His eyes closed, and he slumped to his knees. "God," he gasped, "how *funny*." He clutched his stomach, and rolled to the dirty tile floor. His laughter grew louder and harder to control. "*Oh, Jesus . . . .*"

Georges wondered, briefly, what it was that the man was remembering. He decided that he really didn't want to know. Georges picked up his packages, and, neglecting to pay for them, began stuffing them into a bag.

The two men left standing stirred slightly as though they might be thinking about doing something. Jalian glanced up from cleaning her knife in Stan Mildwood's shirt. "I wouldn't do that. He gets mad sometimes."

The men reconsidered and retreated. Jalian and Georges were backing to the double doors . . .

. . . and Jalian heard the music.

It was music she recognized.

She stood, frozen in place, for several heartbeats. Her mouth was dry and refused to work. Finally she forced out, "*Georges.*"

"Hmm?"

"The music."

Georges listened a moment. "I don't hear anything."

Jalian could not sustain English; she lapsed into silver-speech. The music was clear to her now, and through the music, a presence began to make itself felt. . . . "The ar-reyaho, Georges. My Clan . . . we play it, when there is time, before entering battle to the death. It means that there will be no quarter asked, and none given." She moved back away from the door; without thinking the young men scattered away from her. Jalian stretched one hand out to Georges. "Georges, there are ken Selvren out there."

Georges regarded her in silence. He said at last, "There can't be. If—" He saw the expression on her face and broke off. "So let's check." He strode through the double doors, and as the doors opened Jalian perceived clearly that there was no sound, that it was all as silent as death itself, and that the melody was only in her mind.

Jalian d'Arsennette did not hesitate; she had never hesitated in her life. So it could not be hesitation that was keeping her pinned in place. There was another Silver-Eyes out there and she knew it and she knew why she had felt that somebody was following her all day, and *why was she letting Georges go out the door?*

Far too late, she screamed, "Georges, *no,*" and it echoed, /Georges, *no.*/

The flickering fluorescent lighting tube, which had been preparing to burn out for over a week, steadied into an even, unflickering glow.

The attendant's acne was gone.

Georges Mordreaux stepped outside.

The sun set with a green flash.

A knife twisted out of the darkness, and buried itself to the hilt in Georges' throat. He sank to the ground limply, quite without his customary grace.

The window of the 7-Eleven shattered outward, and Jalian d'Arsennette y ken Selvren came through with the shower of glass. She held knives in both hands. She came rolling up to her feet, bits of glass in her hair and skin and clothing, standing over Georges' fallen body, knives upraised. "I call challenge!" she screamed in silverspeech. "I call battle to the death! Murderers, *cowards!*" She screamed the words again. *"I call challenge!"*

Quietly, so quietly there was no sound audible even to Jalian, a figure stepped into the circle of light cast by the 7-Eleven. The figure was garbed in the white tunic and leggings of an Elder Hunter of ken Selvren.

Jalian's knives dropped slowly. Her arms sank of their own accord. The anger that she had inherited from generations of d'Arsennettes drained away. "Ralesh."

Jalian's mother nodded. "I . . . Daughter, your hair is white . . . but you are not old."

"It happened when I ran the Big Road. I nearly died. How did you survive it?" Jalian took a step closer to Ralesh.

"Almost, I did not." In the dim light, Jalian could see that her mother was worn, and tired, but she seemed no older than the day Jalian had last seen her. In her right hand, she held an object that resembled a hand grenade.

A vague buzzing in his ears, *cheep.* Oddly, there was a cricket near Georges' right ear, which he could hear perfectly; cheep, cheep, *cheep,* damn it.

Georges knew there was something he should be doing. *What,* he wondered, *would Athos be doing right now?*

Oh, that's right, he thought a moment later; *dying.*

Georges remembered the time he'd had his head cut off. It had been more pleasant than this. All that he had remembered was a moment of fear, and then waking up with the corporal looking at him as though he had returned from the dead. (Ho-ho.) But that bastard German soldier, inconsiderate though he'd been, at least he hadn't left his bayonet *in* Georges.

Georges decided what to do.

The cricket was getting on his nerves.

". . . would destroy our people. We would *never* have existed."

Jalian felt sweat trickling down the sides of her neck. "Mother, that is . . . possible. There is a minimal energy level beneath which timelines do not split. Only in sub-critical cases is a transformation wavefront generated. It . . ." Jalian broke off. Ralesh did not understand half the words she was using. . . .

. . . and Georges' hand was moving. Out of the corner of her left eye, she saw Georges' hand creeping up through the dirt toward his neck and the knife. She tried to let no expression show on her face.

Wariness appeared in Ralesh's eyes. She understood little of what her daughter was saying, and not all of what she had been told to say to Jalian. The alien gods had told her to speak of oscillating cycles and decision vectors, and she had not said half of what ghess'Rith had told her to say when Jalian became still. "What are you doing, Daughter?" She keyed the object in her hand, released a restraining bolt, in the way the alien gods had shown her. "You do not fool me, child, I *taught* you."

Jalian circled to her right, flowing smoothly into a fight-ing crouch as she did so, desperately willing Ralesh to keep her eyes on Jalian. "Ralesh, it has been six and a half years since I walked the Big Road. I am in my prime, and you are an old woman, well past yours. I can kill you before you can throw that . . . thing."

Ralesh nodded, slowly, her eyes locked to Jalian's. "True, Daughter. You can. Would you kill your mother? In the history of our Clan that has never happened, that a Silver-Eyes slayed another Silver-Eyes." She pivoted slowly, to follow Jalian's circling. "But then, there are many things you have done that no Silver-Eyes ever did before . . . ."

The hand was working the knife from the throat of Georges Mordreaux. Jalian said nothing.

"You betrayed your people, the Hunters, your mother."

Ralesh looked grim. "Ties of blood; you did not choose them. Other Silver-Eyes have walked in wilderness when they could no longer abide the company of their kin.

"But you," she said in tones of judgment, "you *chose* a friend, and you betrayed ghess'Rith as surely as if he were a person. . . ."

Jalian screamed the words; they tore at her throat. *"He was going to leave me!"*

If I survive this experience, thought Georges furiously, *I am going to kill that godforsaken cricket.*

A second later, it occurred to Georges, *There are probably more pleasant things to do in life than pulling a knife from one's throat.*

Strangely, at the moment he could not think of any.

It was the hardest thing that Georges had ever done in his long life to remain silent.

Jalian's breath was coming quickly, and raggedly. "Mother. . . ."

Ralesh shook her head *no*. "We are dead women, you and I. Put your knives away, Jalian. This"—she gestured with the object in her hand—"is death, but it is not a death I would wish on a Real Indian. It will throw you into an alternate timeline, far away on the . . ." She hesitated a second. "the *Great Wheel of Existence*. The entropy sign will be opposite your own." Ralesh paused, and said, "Your ratio of entry will be hundreds to one; this does not hold the energy for a . . ." She stumbled again over the v'chak words. "a *true entry*. You will not die for days."

Jalian said, voice low, "You . . . assume I will not kill you before you use it."

"It is only the force that I hold it with now that keeps it from acting. When it leaves my hand, it will do what it does."

"What alternative?"

Ralesh's voice cracked for the first time. "Hon . . . honorable death. Jalian, *please*." It was the voice of a mother in pain, without artifice, speaking to her only child. *"Jalian, do not make me do this."*

Then Georges rolled over onto his back.

This is the picture:

In the dirt parking lot of a small, grimy 7-Eleven in northern California, in the year 1969, there are three humans. Unusual humans, perhaps—two have yet to be born, one has yet to die properly—but humans beyond a reasonable doubt, with hands and feet and that stuff in the right places.

Two of the humans are standing, females with silver eyes. One has white hair because of age, the other, because of ages. The elder has in her right hand a small device that will, for lack of a better name, be called a hand-grenade thingy. The other female has knives in both hands, poised for underhand throws.

The male is lying on his back. There is a gash that gapes slightly through the neck at two spots. The knife that gaped the spots is in the male's left hand.

The picture is moving.

Georges got to his feet. Eternity dripped by as he moved. Neither of the women so much as stirred; Ralesh was staring at him, Jalian was watching Ralesh.

Ralesh said softly, "But you're dead."

Georges heard the words clearly, recognized them as silverspeech. At that moment he had no idea what they meant. He took a step toward her, and Ralesh backed away ever so slightly.

Jalian threw. She knew with calm certainty that what she was doing was idiotic; the target was too small. Her knives cut through air to the hand that held the alien device.

Until that moment Georges had never in his life seen anyone who moved as quickly as Jalian d'Arsennette. Eight hundred years of evolution in the deadliest environment humanity had ever known: without warning, stunned by a standing dead man, with no more than Jalian's hands moving in the corner of her vision to warn her, Ralesh d'Arsennette was a blur before the fact that she had moved at all had registered on Georges' retinas. She was twisting and backing away and falling and throwing and Georges was only just realizing that Jalian had even stirred.

A lifetime's training taught Ralesh that a knife is thrown

at one. She evaded into the paths of Jalian's knives. They caught her just above the navel and in the middle of her solar plexus. They sank deep.

The object that she was throwing struck Georges Mordreaux in the chest. It began to glow with a soft, pearly light the instant it left Ralesh's hand.

Georges found himself sitting on the ground, rather surprised to have the glowing hand-grenade thingy in his hands.

He struggled to his feet. The glow started to get very, very, very bright.

A quarter of a kilometer away, on the highway, an approaching motorist noticed a faint, pearly glow coming from the road up ahead of him. Georges tried to let go of the object and could not.

He stood there, in the middle of the dirt parking lot, as though hypnotized, staring into the light that he held cupped in his hands.

Over the seven closest timelines—three in one direction on the Great Wheel, four in the other—there existed a man named Georges Mordreaux, who had a talent.

There were other timelines where a man named Georges Mordreaux had existed, but in those he had not had a talent, and he was long dead. Further away around the Great Wheel, he had never lived at all.

On the other seven timelines, seven Georges Mordreauxs dropped, in two cases literally, whatever they were doing at the moment, and got a faraway look on their collective face.

Something Important Was Happening.

DATELINE 1969 GREGORIAN: FACTOR OF EIGHT DIVERGENCE.

Georges stared into the glowing white thing he held. In many ways, it seemed like a living creature. He felt it straining with all the might it held to shift him—elsewhere. He pushed back, and felt the talent flare into life within himself.

He pushed back, and the glow grew brighter, much brighter, and ships out at sea noticed a bright spot along the coast.

The nature of the thing was stunningly wasteful, deliberately entropic. It was designed to increase disorder, and efficiently designed to do so. Georges stared into the blinding light, feeling the heat flashing against his skin, using the talent to push his way into the inferno that was the source of the light. He pressed lightly, encouraging orderliness here, there, and judging the responses the device made.

I disapprove of you, Georges informed the device silently. The device made no reply, burning itself into slag trying to shift this temporally massive object named Georges elsewhere.

Reality began to flicker and blur. The air wavered around Georges, and he was *there*, and then *not* there, a calm figure in the midst of a incandescent fire that lit the sky of night like a dozen suns.

This thing is very entropic, Georges thought at one eternity.

Georges disapproved of entropy.

Sparks began to swirl around him like a cyclone. The trees around them and the highway and the parking lot, Jalian and her mother and the 7-Eleven; all appeared and disappeared as though lit by a strobe light.

At the height of the battle, when Georges knew he was losing, when reality had ceased to exist except for the struggle and the heat and the light, Georges reached out and touched himself and power poured into him from seven Others.

The battle

. . . *a blazing shaft of light blasted upward from where Georges stood. The incredible energy of the last second of battle had to go somewhere; as coherent laser light it washed across the surface of the moon, and pierced on into interstellar space. . . .*

ended. Eight universes lost the barriers that separated them.

They *crashed.*

Inside the body of Georges Mordreaux.

Georges stood there, in the black darkness of the partial moon, quite blind; his hands were opened to the bone by the melting metal.

Sometime during the event, Ralesh had died.

way out the door, "it is not one of my squirrels." I'll be back.

After he was gone, Gregor Rahvennuch grunted. "I'll

AS TIME GOES BY

You must remember this
A kiss is just a kiss
A sigh is just a sigh
The fundamental things apply
As time goes by

And when two lovers woo
They still say "I love you,"
On that you can rely
No matter what the future brings
As time goes by

—"As Time Goes By"
Casablanca

DATELINE 1973 GREGORIAN: FEBRUARY.

Standing at his sliding-glass patio door, Frank B. Danner watched the slate-gray winter waves crash against the Malibu beach. It was not cold by his standards; but this was California, and the beaches were deserted in the low-sixty-degree weather, except for one lonely surfer, far out from shore, looking for a wave that Frank did not think was going to come. The water was choppy, but the waves were small.

He watched the amateur surfer without amusement. In his left hand was a tumbler, amber with scotch and soda, held loosely with three fingers. His pinkie and ring fingers curled slightly under the glass. Condensation made his palm damp.

He was still in his oldest, faded purple bathrobe. It was ten-thirty, and he'd done nothing all morning.

Unless you counted drinking. He was on his fourth scotch and soda.

In truth, standing at the window, with the dismal gray ocean rolling back and forth before him, he did not know what *to* do; did not know what he could do.

He was the Undersecretary of Defense to President Robert F. Kennedy.

He was a homosexual, and he was being blackmailed.

The phone rang just before eleven o'clock.

Frank let it ring four, five times. He snatched it out of its cradle, then took his time before speaking.

It didn't help. His voice shook. "Hello?"

The voice was female with a faint accent. "Have you seen the pictures I sent you?"

He reined in his temper. "I've seen them."

The voice chuckled. "The boy is very pretty. If he was not a whore, he could do better than the likes of you."

Frank slammed the phone back down.

The handle cracked.

There was a brief pause before the phone rang again.

"Forgive me," said the voice on the other end. "I should not tease you."

Frank held the cracked phone with one hand and his drink with the other. He spoke slowly and very distinctly. "What the hell do you want of me?"

"The appropriations bill for the project known as Sunflower, the solar-power satellite—you will advise President Kennedy favorably on this subject in your upcoming report."

Frank Danner's voice cracked. "What?"

"You will advise the President that Sunflower is a project worthy of his administration's support."

"Jesus Christ," Frank screamed at her, "I was going to do that anyway!"

"Oh? There was some question . . . we shall call this insurance. Submit your paper. I will be in touch with you."

"Wait—" The line went dead. Frank Danner dropped the phone in pieces to the floor.

. . . and, in the opinion of this department, the project known as Sunflower represents a reasonable use of our resources and manpower. The figures are conclusive, as presented in briefs One through Six; the likelihood of finding an alternative source of environmentally clean energy within the foreseeable future is small to non-existent. With the continuing Soviet penetration of the Organization of Petroleum Exporting Countries, it is vital that the United States secure a stable alternative to foreign energy sources. The ancillary benefits of the solar-power satellite system named Sunflower—including a permanent base for operations in geosynchronous orbit, the beginnings of a space-based manufacturing capability, and a proprietary energy-delivery system which is not subject to the whims of nations whom we cannot control—are impressive in a way and to a degree that no other option approaches. We recommend *Sunflower* as that alternative.

—Frank B. Danner, et al.
Report to the President,
Department of Defense, and
Department of Energy,
March 9, 1973.

He met her down on the beach, in the dead of night.

Frank Danner had been standing by the pier for nearly a half hour, clutching his jacket closed to protect himself from the cold wind off the ocean, when the woman appeared.

That was the word for it; one moment she was not there. The was a brief flicker in his peripheral vision, and he whirled to face her. His voice was harsh with surprise. "Do you have the photographs?"

The woman came forward, into the light from the pier floods. Frank Danner cut himself off as he was about to repeat his question. A cold tremor ran through him. He had never imagined anything like this woman; no, this girl. Her hair shone white, and she wore white from head to toe. Her eyebrows were brown. She was not as old as her poise in their conversations had led him to imagine; twenty, perhaps, or younger.

She moved closer to him, and the light caught her eyes. *Stainless steel*, thought Frank Danner in horrified fascination, *eyes like stainless steel*. The wind sent ripples through the cloth of her coat.

She produced a packet of what Frank assumed were photographs, and held them out. She spoke with that same delicate accent he had observed over the phone. "Take them. It is all here. I have no further need of these."

Danner opened the packet with hands that were not entirely steady. He held the negatives up to the lights, and nodded. Himself and Steve, all from the night in San Diego.

The girl said clearly, "I am truly sorry that this was necessary."

Frank Danner nodded. He put the photographs inside

his jacket, for later disposal. He took two steps backward. "Not as sorry as you're going to be," he said distinctly. Without hurry, he reached into his jacket and pulled his revolver from its shoulder holster.

With her right foot, Jalian d'Arsennette scooped sand up from the beach and kicked it into Frank Danner's eyes. She stepped to the left, pulling steel. Danner fired blindly into the night, in the direction of the sea. Jalian moved in, broke his right arm beneath the elbow, and took the revolver away from him.

From the parking lot at the far end of the pier, she saw headlights come on. *Backups,* she thought in disgust. "Idiot, *Indian,*" she hissed at Danner in silverspeech. With his good arm, he swung at her. She brushed the arm aside, pulled him close, and put the steel in just beneath his sternum. He sucked air in a gurgling, stifled scream.

The cars were rolling forward, onto the sand. Jalian let go of Danner, pulled the knife from him, let his body fall. The cars were coming down the sand from both sides of the pier.

She turned away from them, and ran.

Directly into the cold, black sea.

The cars came down to the edge of the water, and the agents within fired handguns and high-powered rifles into the dark ocean.

After a while they stopped. The senior agent present turned Frank Danner's body over, and pulled the photographs from his coat.

One of the younger agents knelt next to him. "What the hell was this all about, Chief?"

The senior agent grunted. "Favor to a friend. Anybody get a good look at her? Photographs?" He looked around. "No? I didn't think so." He flipped through the package of photos casually. He stopped, and peered at the face in the photo. He said slowly, "Well, I'll be damned."

They packed up the body, and got out before the police arrived.

It was 1973, and there were thirty-four years left until Armageddon.

From the *Pomona Progress Bulletin*, July 14, 1973:

". . . and, born to Marienne R. Hammel and Jonathan Hammel, at 6:30 in the morning of July 13; a girl, Margaret Beth, six pounds four ounces, in good health.

"Jonathan Hammel is a partner in the Pasadena offices of the corporate and investor relations firm of Jones, Collins & Hammel."

DATELINE 1976 GREGORIAN: JUNE.

The child popped up out of nowhere, from a landscape strewn with boulders, wind-cut rock, and mesquite scrub, and onto the dusty path in front of Jalian; one moment he was simply *there*. Jalian was impressed despite herself. A Silver-Eyes girl, without training from an Elder Hunter, might have done no better. There was noise, and she had smelled him, but had not seen him at all until he chose to let her.

Not that she'd been trying.

He examined her gravely, under eyes half lidded against the fierce noonday sun. He was, Jalian guessed, perhaps seven years old. Except for his long, uncombed hair, which was blond, he looked very much like the other Indian children Jalian had seen in the area— poorly dressed in dusty clothes, shoeless, with clear Indian features that were already stamped with a wariness that seemed an integral part of his person.

"Are you lost?" His voice was pitched high; more the voice of a girl than a boy.

Jalian had ceased walking at his appearance; she resumed, slowing slightly to accommodate his smaller legs. Her action seemed to startle him; the boy hurried after her. "I am not lost."

"Usually white people are lost when they come on this road."

Jalian glanced down at him; he was looking up at her, not watching where he placed his feet on the rock-strewn path. "I am not a white person," said Jalian carefully, "I do not think this is a road, and I am not lost."

"Do you have enough water?"

"Why do you ask?"

"Because if you're thirsty the creek's only a half hour away, and it isn't dry yet. It will be before the end of summer," he added.

Jalian nodded. "I have enough water, thank you."

"What's your name?"

Jalian drew a slow breath. She was not particularly in the mood for company. Still, he was only a child, even if male. She squatted until her eyes were level with his. "Jalian d'Arsennette y ken Selvren, or, in English, Jalian of the Fires of Clan Silver-Eyes. I am the daughter of Ralesh who was the daughter of Morine; Margra Hammel was our mother."

"Oh." The answer seemed to put him off for a moment. "Mine's Michael. Michael Walks-Far."

Jalian unslung her canteen and drank from it. Michael was sweating; she offered it to the boy. "Would you like a drink?"

"How far are you going?"

"To Needles," she said patiently, still holding out the canteen. "I will be there within a day, and the canteen is half full yet."

Michael nodded in acceptance, and took a small drink from the canteen. He handed it back to her, and then saw her eyes for the first time. He stared openly. "Are you Huapatanetal?"

Jalian reslung the canteen, and stood slowly. "I do not understand."

The child shook his head slowly. "Never mind. Mama tells me of them, the demons with silver eyes, but I think it's a story. They are called Huapatanetal."

"Walk with me," said Jalian abruptly. The child followed her as she resumed her westward journey. Deep within her memory, the boy had stirred something which she had not thought of in many years, but she could not place it instantly. "How old are you, child?"

Michael answered with reluctance. "Five. But everybody says I look older," he added instantly. Already, he was sweating again from the effort to keep up with her. Jalian did not slow her pace.

Jalian nodded. "You do. I would have thought seven."

"Really?" He looked up at her, and smiled suddenly, and for the first time Jalian realized that he was beautiful.

"Yes," she said firmly, "I would have said seven."

They walked in silence after that for nearly ten minutes, until Michael stopped and told her that he couldn't go any further because he had promised his mother.

"Then you must not break your promise," said Jalian.

With obvious resentment in his voice, Michael said, "I won't. Mama spanks me when I do."

At that, Jalian laughed; she could not help herself. "When I was a child, and my mother punished me, it left scars." She knelt next to him and touched his cheek. "Your mother does not sound so bad."

He nodded, unconvinced. His long white hair, so like her own, fell across his eyes, and he pushed it back. "Are you going to come back this way?"

Jalian started to shake her head no, and then stopped. "I do not know," she said honestly. "I am going to see a mathematician who lives in Needles, and after that I cannot say."

"Oh." He paused in thought. "If you come back, my Mama and me live on this side of the creek, but on the other side of the hills. If you just walk down the creek you'll see our house. We have chickens and two cows," he said proudly—he was old enough to have seen others who did not have that much. "It's just us there. Mama had a boyfriend once who was a singer for the Sorry Blues, and they had me, but he went away and didn't come back." The boy paused, looking at Jalian, obviously expecting an answer.

"Perhaps I will come back," said Jalian simply.

All cheerfulness left his expression. "Do you have a boyfriend?"

The question surprised Jalian. Without conscious intent she ran her hands over her knives; one knife was missing, a gift to Georges Mordreaux. She was not at all certain that he understood the meaning of that knife; and even if he had, things were so very different now.

"I don't know," she told Michael Walks-Far. "Probably not."

He nodded and hugged her around the legs, suddenly and with surprising strength, and then turned and ran back the way they had come, ran until he was out of sight without ever once looking back.

That night, as she was making her fire before going to sleep, with the city lights of Needles visible in the distance, words that she had not thought of in almost a decade and a half came back to her with a force that brought her springing to her feet, as if to face an enemy.

Corvichi words; the *'salch khri,* ghess'Rith had called them, the warlike humans from across the Great Wheel of Existence, with technology equal to or surpassing that of the Corvichi themselves.

The words *'salch khri* translated, very nearly, to *Walks-Far*.

Her fire had nearly died before Jalian managed to make herself sleep, and she did not sleep well at all.

The United States of America was nearly two hundred years old, and Jalian d'Arsennette had no idea at all whether she had a "boyfriend" or not . . .

. . . and there were just thirty-one years left until Armageddon.

THE
ARMAGEDDON
BLUES

. . . we have begun. Neither wind nor tide is always
with us. Our course on a dark and stormy sea cannot
always be clear. But we have set sail—and the horizon,
however cloudy, is also full of hope.

—John F. Kennedy
　　Introduction, *To Turn The Tide*
　　November 8, 1961.

The bombs fell.

In a nuclear rain that lasted for days, through a peremptory first strike and a retaliatory second strike, through retaliatory second and third strikes, until only a few lonely submarines cruised through the ocean to fire their weapons upon an enemy who no longer existed, through all of this the bombs fell, and fell. Billions died, of the planet's seven and a half billion persons, in fire and blasting shock waves and radiation. Billions more died in famine, and in the firestorms caused when the bombs went down. But that was not the worst.

Vast clouds of dust and earth were blasted into the sky. Whole continents disappeared beneath them; and temperatures began to drop. As the glaciers traveled south, the last crumbling pockets of civilization vanished.

It did not return for over five hundred years.

DATELINE 2007 GREGORIAN: JANUARY.

(This conversation takes place between Nigao Loos and PRAXCELIS, the *Prototype Reduction X-laser Computer, El-lis-Loos Integrated System*, in geosynchronous orbit, at Midway, the Sunflower Orbital Command.)

"PRAXCELIS, I don't understand this readout."

"This unit has endeavored to be clear. Where is the area of nonalignment?"

"PRAXCELIS, I requested a readout on the possibility

that the tracking lasers were diverging from their assigned grids."

"Sen Loos, your input, as orally recorded, reads: ' . . . and, PRAXCELIS, while you're at it, take a look to make sure that the lines aren't diverging with the passage of time.' Unit ENCELIS informs this unit that the lines are diverging."

(A long stretch of silence.) "You're not supposed to have any contact with SORCELIS and ENCELIS . . . What lines are you talking about?"

"The timelines, Sen Loos. The timelines are diverging. There have been an estimated nine hundred million events of significant divergence since base divergence 1962."

"Events of significant divergence . . ."

"Whether this will be sufficient to prevent Armageddon is unknown."

Of those to whom much is given, much is required.

—John F. Kennedy,
Speech to the Massachusetts
State Legislature
January 9, 1961.

DATELINE 1981 GREGORIAN: MAY.

The laboratory lay secluded in the low hills overlooking the Irwindale gravel pits. It was a complex of eight interconnected buildings, with a small cafeteria, and a parking lot that accommodated sixty-one cars. The 210 freeway ran less than four hundred meters away from the laboratory's south entrance. Earlier that year they'd had private on- and off-ramps installed to service the lab.

It was quiet, and as secluded as you could reasonably get while remaining within working distance of UCLA. (There were major cities within a half-hour's drive on the 210 east or west. But they could not be *seen*.)

As far as Henry Ellis was concerned, it was ideal. He liked the location, liked the early morning drive in the near-desert. He even liked the buildings, the plain unadorned brick and cement, the clean brass lettering that proclaimed: TRANS-TEMPORAL RESEARCH FOUNDATION.

(Underneath the sign, somebody had taped a hand-written placard: *Home of the UCLA-famous Experimental Number Cruncher, Ellis-Loos Integrated System.*)

Henry Ellis came in early that Monday morning. The grounds were shrouded in fog, and it was cool enough that he wore a tan poncho over his work clothes for warmth. He was of just-less-than-average height, with a calm, easy manner, and graceful, contained movements.

Unlocking the main doors, he paused only long enough to pull the sheet of paper from the wall. He wadded it into a ball and tossed it toward the outer office's wastebasket, left-handed over his right shoulder, without looking. He continued on to his office, not glancing back.

It was just after seven, only a short while since sunrise. As far as Henry knew, the only other person on the premises was the janitor. In his office, he flipped on the lights, and turned on his coffee maker. There was a brief hum from the machine, which ceased with a sharp *click,* and was replaced by a trickling sound from the machine's innards. Henry put his coffee cup under the spigot, shed his poncho and hat and hung them by the door, and seated himself behind his desk to wait for the water to boil. From his shirt pocket he took a dozen toothpicks, individually wrapped in cellophane, and placed them in an even row next to the desktop intercom.

He flipped on the intercom.

The voice that addressed him was smooth, without inflection. "Good morning, Mr. Ellis."

Henry was unlocking drawers. "Good morning, EN-CELIS. How far are you on the processing I left you last night?" He unlocked the final drawer and hung the keys on a hook protruding from the side of the desk.

"This unit has processed eighty-three point eight per-cent of the data input to it."

Henry nodded out of habit. "Excellent. With what primary results?"

"There is a tentatively assigned probability of six nines, based on an eight-three-point-eight complete run, that the chronon event threshold is secure within the range of energy usage that this facility is capable of applying."

Henry spread hardcopy over the desktop without paying conscious attention to it. His mind was elsewhere. *If we assume a straight line proportional to energy input, then a steady event threshold implies discrete timelines. . . .*

Behind him, the intercom said, "Mr. Ellis, you asked this unit to remind you that you have an appointment this morning, at ten o'clock, with one Jalian d'Arsennette. Have you been reminded?"

Henry scowled. "Yes, ENCELIS. Thank you." He leaned over his desk and turned his memo pad to the date, a week and a half ago, that the appointment had been made.

In his characteristically neat handwriting, the memo said, *Monday next, woman from DoD: Jeremy Carson recommends handle lightly.*

Below that, in block letters, underlined twice, was a single word.

WHY?

Jalian d'Arsennette y ken Selvren pulled into the parking lot at 9:56. She was driving a cherry-red Porsche with a long scratch down the left fender. The clouds were burning away as she arrived, and the day was growing warm. There were two other people in the parking lot when she arrived: the janitor, who was going home, and a short dark-skinned man whom her briefing identified as Nigao Loos, the theoretical physicist on whose work and reputation the Trans-Temporal Research Foundation was built.

The janitor simply stared at her openly; the world's foremost research physicist scowled in the general direction of the sun, and hurried indoors.

The stare did not bother Jalian; she was used to it. When you wore a white jumpsuit, and a white tailor-cut silk business coat, when your skin was the color of milk and your hair the color of ice and your eyes were silver—when all these were as they were, people stared.

Mostly it was the men who stared, and them Jalian simply ignored. They were, after all, men.

Leaving the confines of the Porsche was a relief. She drove because she had no choice, but she did not like it; she would never like it. She slammed the door to the car, wondering whether Georges appreciated the things she put up with. Cars, indeed. She left the door unlocked, hoping that somebody would steal the machine while she was gone.

Her eyes, beneath the brown eyebrows that were all that remained of the color her hair had been in the days before she ran the Big Road, shut briefly just before she entered the building. When they opened again the pupils had expanded to twice their previous diameter.

There was a secretary working in the outer office, a young, dark-haired, rather pretty woman in a modest black-and-green dress. If she found Jalian's appearance odd, she did not show it. "Ms. d'Arsennette?" she inquired.

Jalian smiled at her, and got a startled flash of a smile back in response. "Yes," she said. Her voice was so liquid that for a moment the secretary—her nameplate read *Theresa*—seemed unsure that Jalian had actually spoken a complete word.

Theresa blinked after a moment, and then touched a finger to the intercom. She did not take her eyes from Jalian. "Mr. Ellis? Your—guest—is here."

The voice that answered was abrupt, and very male; Jalian frowned. "Good. Send her in." Theresa removed her thumb from the intercom, and started to rise from her chair. Jalian stopped her with a gesture.

"I can follow directions, I think."

The girl looked flustered. "Well, down the hall. Third door on the left. His name is on it."

Jalian inclined her head slightly. "Thank you, Theresa." She pronounced the name with a soft *th*. Theresa was looking up at her, unblinking, and Jalian smiled softly. The girl looked away suddenly, blushing furiously, and Jalian left her without saying anything further.

Henry Ellis glanced up at the opening of his door. He shifted the toothpick in his mouth from the right corner to the left. "Dear, did anybody ever teach you how to knock?"

The door still swinging slowly away from her, Jalian paused, and studied Henry. "Actually, no . . . No," she said after a moment, "I don't think so. Why do you ask?" She seated herself in the right-most visitor's chair, close to the door.

Henry studied her curiously. She was strange; stark.

She spoke in a harsh, clipped manner, as though she wished to destroy the beauty of her voice. "You're from the Department of Defense?"

Jalian ignored his question. "I have come here to ask your opinion, as the second-best physicist at our disposal. The information I require concerns the theory of multiple time tracks that you and Nigao Loos published several months ago." She withdrew a creamy-white envelope from the inside pocket of her dress jacket, and laid it on Henry's blotter.

Henry picked it up, and tore it open with a wooden letter opener that sat next to his out box. He scanned it briefly. Its contents were fairly normal; answer questions, don't ask questions, don't talk about whatever questions she asks. It was signed by his superiors in DoD. (Both he and Nigao held reserve commissions in Aerospace; it was the price they had been forced to pay for the applications technology for ENCELIS.)

He handed the letter back to Jalian. "Okay. What do you want to know?"

Jalian put the letter away and sat up straighter in her chair. What she told Henry Ellis then, only two others had ever heard before, and only one of those was certain he believed her. The first was Jeremy Carson, a theoretical physicist and Undersecretary of Defense to President Kennedy the Third; Georges was the other.

"I will," she said, choosing her words carefully, "have you listen to a hypothetical situation. There is a question that arises from this situation, and you will answer that question."

Henry Ellis was scratching on a blank pad of paper with a pencil. He wasn't looking at the pad of paper, though, he was looking at Jalian. At her eyes. At the silver in her eyes.

"Stop that!" Jalian snapped irritably, with sudden sharpness, and Henry whipped his eyes away from hers. He froze for a moment, and then said, "Excuse me. That was rude."

Jalian shrugged. "It does not matter. Are you listening?"

"I'm listening." The words came hard; Henry felt, for the first time since childhood, the breath of the old unknown, like a wind on the back of his neck. Since his early days in college he had dedicated himself to the study of the new unknown; but now this lovely elven specter sat before him, with those erotic silver eyes. . . . Henry forced himself to meet her gaze, and said roughly, "Go ahead."

Jalian spoke with amusement; her words were little more than a whisper, and Henry had to strain to listen. "The hypothetical situation that I relate to you is as follows. In the year 2007 there is a nuclear war which destroys civilization. In the centuries following that war, humanity barely survives. Eventually, a primitive social order is re-established by—" she used the silverspeech words—"*ken Selvren*, a group of people who call themselves ken Selvren. Near the beginning of the twenty-eighth century of your Gregorian calendar, these people learn to travel from one alternate timeline to another, in search of resources that were depleted by those who tried to destroy their world."

Henry leaned forward slightly, hooked. "Go . . . on. Please."

Jalian watched him quizzically. "The daughter of the Eld—of the leader of the people I speak of . . . this daughter knew more about the outtime technology than any of the rest of her people. For reasons of her own, this daughter stole a portable Gate, and set the Gate to access what is known as a negative-entropy timeline. This is a timeline where time—"

". . . runs backwards. An anti-matter timeline," Henry Ellis finished. "How can you know about that? Nigao hasn't even *published* that section of theor—"

"This woman," said Jalian grimly, "entered a negative-entropy timeline . . ."

The point of the pencil that Henry was holding snapped. "You can't have done that," he said simply. "You're talking about an anti-matter timeline. You'd blow . . ." He took a deep breath, and exploded, "Christ, you can't even for a *minute* expect me to believe—"

Jalian d'Arsennette, the daughter of Ralesh who was the daughter of Morine, whose ancestors had ruled Silver-Eyes for more than five centuries, plucked a knife out of nowhere and used it to pin Henry Ellis' tie to his desktop. She slapped him twice, removed the knife from the tie, and made it vanish. Without particular heat, she said, "Do not interrupt me again." She watched, as the stunned, uncomprehending look on the engineer's face gave way to beginning fury. She laid one knife, and another, and then a third, in a parallel row on Henry's side of the desk. "You may attempt to pick up one of these when you choose. . . . I was saying to you, this woman of ken Selvren enters a negative-entropy timeline; her ratio of entry is extremely high, approximately fourteen million to one. Her actual interaction with the timeline is minimal; a duration of some two hours. She survives the experience, and reappears on the timeline that she exited in the days before the nuclear war. The year is that which you call 1962, and there are forty-five years until Armageddon."

Henry waited until he was entirely sure she was finished speaking. The light from the overhead fluorescents was shining off the blades on his desktop. His eyes did not waver from hers. "What is your question?"

She showed the first emotion he had seen in her; a deep, quivering breath. It seemed to him that he could almost *hear* /after all these years, the answer. . . ./ She was holding the edge of his desk.

"Is it possible to prevent Armageddon?"

Sweat was trickling down the back of Henry's neck. He was thinking, *This isn't happening,* while something deep inside him assured him, *Yes, it is too happening.* "May God help you, whoever the hell you are. I can't. I just don't know. Even Nigao could not answer that question, given your assumed parameters. Our field is very young. It only dates to 1962, when we first started detecting chronons." He looked up swiftly. "Your . . . hypothetical person . . . time-traveled to 1962." He stumbled getting the words out. "In 1969 the chronon event threshold jumped by a factor of eight and mystics all over the fucking planet went off the deep end and we don't have even the beginnings of a theory to account for it. What happened?"

Jalian was sitting back in her chair, eyes closed. She wasn't sure what her reaction was, relief or despair; only that it was strong. He had not said yes, but he had not said no. She could still *hope.*

Henry Ellis said fiercely, "What happened in '69?"

Jalian shook her head briefly, and looked at him. "There was a battle. Eight timelines melted together."

The toothpick that had rested securely in Henry's mouth throughout the interview dropped in two pieces to the blotter. "What?" Jalian stood abruptly. Henry noticed that the steel was no longer on his blotter. He could not remember when it had vanished. "That is what Georges tells me," she said simply. "He may be lying, of course."

Henry said stupidly, "Who?"

"Georges. And he should know. It happened inside of him."

She turned to leave, and Henry said, "Miss d'Arsennette? Where are you going?"

Jalian pivoted slowly, and smiled at him. Henry felt his perception of everything in the world but those silver eyes fade away, and was thinking with a cool, rational detachment that silver was the most erotic color that he knew, when Jalian said, "I am going to save the world." Her eyelids dropped sleepily, half covered the silver irises. "Good-bye."

The door seemed to close itself behind her.

Henry Ellis stared at the door, in silence, for a long time.

It was 1981, and there were twenty-six years left until Armageddon.

DATELINE 1985 GREGORIAN: DECEMBER.

Moscow, Russia.

The winter wind was a senseless thing; as cold and meaningless as anything Gregor Pahvernuch knew of outside the works of man.

Pahvernuch shook his head in disgust. He had just hung up the phone, and stood now looking out his window at the drifting snow, blowing down in random gusts across the streets. When he had calmed himself he turned to survey the three officers standing stiffly before his desk. He was a heavyset man, with an unlit cigar set between lips that were too red and fat. He was still wearing the dark overcoat he'd had on when he'd entered the hastily-set-up joint KGB-Militia Headquarters and gone charging into the Operations Room.

"You there," Pahvernuch said with disdain, as though

the words were offal that his lips were too delicate to touch, "you are the best the Committee for State Security can recruit, these days." He glanced at the man sitting in the chair by the door, under the wavering fluorescent lights. "And what of you," he asked with a sudden burst of chill fury, "what have you been doing this last hour?"

Karien Karchovsky grinned widely, showing his teeth. "I, Comrade Pahvernuch? Watching this American is not my assignment." He uncrossed his legs, and stood. He walked with a measured pace around the three junior KGB agents. They were afraid; it showed in the way they stood and the way they stared straight ahead without meeting their superior's eyes.

Fear was something they were all very good with.

Karien stopped, and put an arm around one of the men. "Now, Comrade Shenderev here was, I believe, in charge of the group assigned to watch this, ah, 'Jill Darsay,' I think her name is."

Pahvernuch sighed. "I do not think that scaring these children is going to help us in resolving this annoyance, Karien. We must find the woman." He pulled off his overcoat, and dropped it on top of the desk. "You." He pointed at one of the KGB operatives. "Go find Colonel Djarska. If he's not at home he will probably be at the hotel; the Central Committee isn't meeting until tomorrow, but he'll probably be there early." The boy stood there a moment too long, and Pahvernuch screamed at the top of his lungs, *"Go!"* He glared at the junior agent, and the man fairly fled the room.

Karien missed most of it; he had turned Nikolai Shenderev to face him. "Why, Nikolai, you're trembling."

"No, comrade," the boy protested, and then immediately said, "Yes, comrade."

Karien looked down at him; he was several centimeters taller. "Well, we are not such monsters as all that. Listen, you lost the woman you were to watch." He shrugged expansively. "These things happen. We will find her again; she may simply have stepped out to take dinner."

Behind them, Gregor Pahvernuch snorted loudly.

"No, no, I mean that," said Karien kindly. "Take Corporal Deteche and his troops and go screen people at the hotel. I'll be down in an hour or so."

Nikolai left without protest; the third junior agent went with him, no doubt glad to get out of Pahvernuch's office with his ass in one piece.

Karien Karchovsky watched them leave with a cold and detached expression.

Gregor Pahvernuch said after a moment, "Are you quite through kissing that pretty boy's nuts?"

"The pretty boy's uncle sits on the Politburo, Gregor," said Karien bluntly.

The news threw Pahvernuch visibly. "Oh?" He bit down hard on the cigar. "Oh. I did not know that."

"I didn't think so." Karien picked up his overcoat from the chair on which he'd been sitting. "Well, I assume you've got things to do." He smiled without humor. "Certainly I do. If you see Ilya before the morning, send him to the hotel. That's where I'll be."

Gregor said softly, "With the boychick, eh?"

Karien lifted an eyebrow. "You could hurt my feelings, friend. No, I am simply going to see whether the American woman returns to her room, probably with a perfectly reasonable explanation as to where she has been, as I expect her to."

"You believe, then, that she is just a tourist." Pahvernuch's tone was questioning.

Karien shrugged into his overcoat. "Who can say? If she is not, she has certainly done a convincing imitation. That she chose to vanish on the eve of the Central Committee's meeting is suspicious only if she has not returned to her hotel by a reasonable hour. It is not yet ten o'clock," he pointed out.

Gregor stared at him. "Karien, you are one of my best friends, I tell you truly. But you play things too tight. Some day they're going to shoot you for it. And your protégé, too."

Karien grinned. "Probably. But at least I don't threaten the careers of nephews of members of the Politburo. You were thinking about it."

"I was not," denied Pahvernuch. A bead of sweat glistened on his upper lip.

"No?" Karien seemed to consider. "Perhaps not. Perhaps you were merely indulging your temper, and it got out of hand—who can say? Fortunately," he added on his way out the door, "it is not one of my concerns. I'll be back."

After he was gone, Gregor Pahvernuch grunted, "I'll bet you will be, you flashy son of a bitch." He got back on the phone, and had to yell at the operator for a dial tone.

At the hotel where the woman who had identified herself as Jill Darsay was staying—a hotel conveniently near the buildings where the Politburo was temporarily meeting—Karien Karchovsky checked with the hotel management to see whether or not Miss Darsay had returned to her room. She had not, they informed him. The lobby held three KGB agents whom Karien recognized, trying to be conspicuous. They were succeeding quite well; after all, he thought cynically, what was the point of being a member of the Committee for State Security if one had to obscure the fact?

As far as he could tell, none of them recognized him. They were too busy watching a pair of pretty East German women who were sitting together at the hotel bar, and being overcharged for the privilege. Karien could not for the life of him imagine why East Germans would want to vacation in Moscow. They did, though, with regularity.

He met Nikolai as he was leaving the elevators on the third floor. The American was in room 328; Nikolai had his soldiers, regular militia, rummaging through her possessions. "Sir!" said Nikolai. "I was just going downstairs to call you." He relaxed slightly, and said, "I tried calling from the hotel room, but the switchboard has gone home, and the phones are useless."

Karien nodded. "Have you found anything in the room?"

Nikolai shook his head. "No, comrade. Nothing of note." He led Karien inside; Karien looked around with some curiosity. He'd never been inside one of the fancy foreign hotel rooms before. It was surprisingly similar to the hotels he was used to. One would think that for the extortionist prices the foreigners were paying they could get something a cut above this.

The room was clean, with a large single bed, and sparkling white porcelain in the bathroom. There was a perfunctory wet bar, vodka and mixers, against the wall facing the bed. A balcony overlooked Moscow; Karien went into the freezing night air, and looked out over the city. He had been outside Russia many times, but the CCCP proper only once, to West Germany, and he still remembered the sight of West Berlin, lit up at night; by comparison, Moscow was a dull city after dark. Even the Kremlin was dark—from where he stood, he could see the ruins where the explosions had brought down the eastern sections. Construction was going on from sunrise to sunset.

Despite the fact that the government had already executed four persons for the terrorist attack, it was an open secret in high ranks that the truly guilty parties had not been found.

What was worst about it was that all evidence pointed inward. This was not an act of foreign terrorism instigated by the West; it was the work of Russians.

Karien turned, and went back inside. "Nikolai, send your shitkicker soldiers home. We have KGB at the entrance, and you and I will wait here for her. If she is not found by morning we will alert the general militia."

Nikolai looked at him. "We are just going to wait?"

"Unless you wish to search all of Moscow in a night."

"Wash a pig as much as you like, it goes right back to the mud."

—Russian Proverb

At 2:00, Jalian d'Arsennette returned to her hotel room. She had spent the night on the hotel roof, watching the stars, and listening with other senses to the Moscow night. It was an evening well spent, with the colored lenses she had been wearing to disguise her eye color removed; her eyes felt normal for the first time in weeks.

She truly had come to Russia largely as a tourist. She checked with contacts she'd been given, but as a matter of course, not because she expected anything to come of it.

She was sleepy, and not expecting trouble. And cold; even Corvichi metaphysics and Silver-Eyes kartari could not keep her fully warm in the winter night and winds of Moscow.

She opened the door, and knew instantly that there were persons inside. Somebody moved toward her in the darkness with surprising speed and coordination. She reached for steel, reflexively, before remembering that her knives were in a safe deposit box in New York. The delay was critical. She found herself slammed back against the door, and a voice said in harshly accented English, "You have made a terrible mistake, Miss Darsay."

It took her a long moment to realize on an emotional level what had happened; this man was *touching* her.

Jalian d'Arsennette blinked in wonder, in the darkness; she could not even see the warmth of their figures, the room was too warm and she too recently in from the frozen night.

She remembered, later, thinking clearly, *KGB*; and then she killed the man who had dared touch her.

The lights came on. One of her contacts, a young man named Nikolai Shenderev, was removing his hand from the light switch next to the bed.

Sprawled on the floor, with his neck at an unlikely angle, was a man whom Jalian did not recognize.

Shenderev's mouth was working. "Karien . . . he didn't suspect you. He was just going to . . . throw a scare into you."

Jalian knelt slowly, and touched fingers to the dead man's temple. She stood abruptly, and said without humor, "He succeeded." She thought to shut the door, and said over the sound of the lock latching, "He did not suspect me, you are correct. He suspected you; you show your fear far too easily." She gestured. "Help me with the body."

"What?" He was shaking his head in a daze. "You don't understand. I'm going to be shot now."

Jalian crossed the distance between them in two steps. "No, you will not. But you must do as I say. *Exactly* as I say."

With agonizing hesitation, he nodded. "Very well. I have little to lose at this point."

" 'Life is unbearable, but death is not so pleasant either,' " Jalian said.

"What?"

"You have everything to lose, you idiot."

Peace and freedom do not come cheap, and we are
destined—all of us here today—to live out most if not
all of our lives in uncertainty and challenge and peril.

—John F. Kennedy,
Address at the University
of North Carolina,
October 12, 1961.

DATELINE 1986 GREGORIAN: FEBRUARY

Saskatchewan, Canada.

The forest spoke. It was quiet and hushed, yet never
wholly silent. There was no wind, and the animals were
still; but the bows of the trees creaked under the weight of
the snow. Occasional limbs, weighted beyond their strength,
snapped with the sharpness of a rifle shot. The sound of
the break echoed a long distance before dying.

In late evening, a silver, gull-wing twelve-cylinder sports
car drove through the gathering darkness. It flashed through
the dark forest at insane speeds, along winding roads made
slick by snow and ice. Inside the car, music played.

"Well, the man he gotta whisper
When he tell you 'bout the news
ICBM's are comin in;
You know those bombs don't know the blues."

Nigao Loos, sitting in the passenger seat, was thinking with
a calm born of terror that he did not really like reggae, and
had never liked the Armageddon Blues Band to begin with,
and if he had, then the last two days of traveling would
have cured him of it; *Radioactive*, to all appear-
ances, was the only cassette in the car.

He'd tried to turn the radio on. Once. His hand was
still sore.

In the driver's seat, with one hand resting lightly on
the wheel, Jalian drove north along Provincial Highway
102. The digital readout told her that the car was doing 108

kph. Some time ago a sign had told them they were driving past McClellan lake.

Nigao had almost despaired of ever arriving wherever they were going. Two days ago he'd been in Southern California; now he was in Saskatchewan. Two days from now he'd probably be in the Arctic Circle.

Jalian's hand moved briefly. The music died. A sign at the side of the road flashed by them: BRABANT LAKE CAMP-GROUND. Without the music her voice seemed unnaturally loud. "You may cease being scared. We have arrived."

Nigao nodded wordlessly.

Somewhere out there was the man he was being taken to meet.

Georges Mordreaux.

_____

Consider a man.

He was born in 1712, with a talent. Entropy tended to decrease in his vicinity; objects became more orderly, more energetic. He survived two and a half centuries and then some, despite three incidents that should have killed him, and then he battled a device from seven and a half centuries in his future.

He won that battle, and because he won it, he spent the next fifteen years alone, in a cabin in the wilds of north Canada. For a little under three minutes, on a warm summer night in 1969, in the dirt parking lot of a 7-Eleven, he stood with a small device glowing in his cupped hands, a device that looked like a hand grenade and would have been a one-way ticket to oblivion for any human on Earth except Georges Mordreaux. The device burned itself out, as it burned Georges' eyes out of his skull, as it melted in his hands and cooked them to the bone.

To win that battle, he was forced to reach through eight timelines, to tear power from eight analogues of himself. Purely as a side effect of doing so he destroyed the walls between the worlds, caused eight timelines to coalesce within himself.

His memories encompassed eight separate existences, of eight separate men. There was no trouble in distinguishing which memory track was "real"; reality held Jalian. There was only one memory track, one timeline, that held Jalian.

In the months, and years, following the battle in which he lost his eyesight, he waited; waited for his eyes to regenerate, for the scars on his hands to fade. They did not. He had held within his hands energies that warped together eight timelines, and it marked him.

And the talent, which was always somewhat out of his control, which had guarded and protected him through two hundred and fifty-seven years, turned.

It flared like a nova.

Multiplied by a factor of eight.

They pulled off the road into a nearly deserted dirt parking lot. A green van and a light blue trailer stood lonely watch under the single hanging floodlight. Jalian pulled in next to the trailer and killed the motor. There was a small brick building at one end of the parking lot. Light spilled from its opening door. A ranger in a heavy jacket approached the car as Jalian and Nigao were getting out. The ranger, a man in his late forties, was tall, and heavily muscled; he reminded Jalian of the farmers of Clan Silver-Eyes. "Ma'am? Can I help you?" He glanced at Nigao with distaste.

Jalian ignored him. She turned to Nigao. "Come. We are late enough."

Nigao stared about. "You said we were there."

The ranger said, more loudly, "Ma'am? You shouldn't be out in weather like this dressed like that. Not him either," he said, gesturing curtly at Nigao's flashy polyester sports jacket and slacks.

Jalian stepped onto the hood of the car, took a step across it, and came down next to Nigao. She took one of his lapels in her hand, and pulled him into the trees that lined the road. They were well into the dark forest before the ranger, flashlight glowing, caught up with them. Jalian turned to face him. "Lady, there's nothing out the way you're heading. You'll both freeze to death."

Jalian sighed. Georges kept telling her not to draw attention to herself. She took a step forward, and brought her right knee up hard into the ranger's groin. The man gave a sudden, whistling scream that condensed as fog in the subzero air. Jalian stepped around him, plucked a knife from her left shoulder sheath, and struck him in the back of the head with the handle. He dropped heavily. Nigao nodded, without surprise. Jalian vanished momentarily, and returned with a length of wire rope that she'd used twice now in the two days Nigao had been with her. She propped the ranger against a tree, and bound him with the ease of long practice.

When she was finished, Jalian motioned to the middle-aged physicist, standing with his shoulders stooped in the cold gloom. "Problem solving," she explained. "Come. He is waiting."

They walked into the night.

Nigao never remembered that night clearly afterward. They walked for hours, trudging through drifts of snow, slogging on through the sleet that came a few kilometers into their journey. He perceived everything with an unnatural clarity. There was little light, yet he saw with ease the ground that he walked. Jalian was a luminous blob of moving white, and he fancied that he saw a faint, reddish glow from her skin. His sense of smell was very acute; in a calm reverie he found himself distinguishing between the spoor of animals and the scent of various plants. *Imagination*, he told himself without conviction.

The forest changed with shocking abruptness. Leafy trees appeared among the pine. Fruit appeared only a score of meters past them. The snow and ice vanished from the ground; the ground itself became soft and grassy.

Nigao Loos was walking by a cherry tree when the world blurred.

He stopped abruptly. Jalian continued on a few steps, then turned back. "What is wrong?"

"I . . ." He cleared his throat. "I can't see. I can't *see*," he repeated with growing alarm.

Jalian held his face with one hand, and lifted an eyelid to examine his eye. She nodded. "As I thought." She made a quick flicking motion with one finger, and Nigao felt his contact lens lift away from the surface of his eye. She did the same thing with the other eye, and suddenly he could see again.

"What did you do?" he whispered. He blinked. His contacts were out, and he could see perfectly. "What did you do to me?"

Jalian ignored him, and resumed walking. Nigao followed silently.

Half a kilometer along, they found growing flowers. Jalian led Nigao through the flowers, and into a dense thicket of orange trees. The spaces between the trees grew narrower and narrower, until Nigao was sure they would be caught, unable to move forward or back, and would die here in this insane forest. He struggled on after the vanishing white form before him. Suddenly the trees were gone.

They stood at the edge of a vast clearing. Fruit trees of every description stood around its edge. Inside, a garden grew like a jungle. Rows of vegetables reached up two and three meters into the air.

In the center of the garden, there was a wooden cabin with a microwave antenna perched incongruously atop it. Sitting on the small porch before the doorway, a rather large man was whittling a piece of wood. He was humming as he worked. As Jalian and Nigao emerged from the woods, he glanced up, said, "Hello, Doctor, Jalian." He went back to carving. A few seconds passed, and he put the knife down, ran his fingers along the wood, and put the wood down with the knife at the side of the porch.

Jalian said, "Hello, Georges."

Georges Mordreaux stood, dusting wood flakes off his pants, and came down to greet them. He took Nigao's outstretched hand, and Nigao felt rather than saw the gloves that covered the hand. His eyes were fixed on Mordreaux's face. Georges had taken his hand without fumbling, and he moved like a sighted man; but Georges Mordreaux's eyes were a blasted ruin.

Georges tilted his head to one side. "Is it that bad, then, still?"

Nigao stammered something incoherent. Georges shrugged, and said cheerfully, "Ah, well. Jalian, I hope you drove more carefully this time."

Jalian said blankly, "I always drive carefully."

"As I thought." Georges nodded. He took Nigao by the arm, and led him inside. The cabin consisted of a single room, with a small couch, a bed against one wall, and a desk against another. Bookshelves lined the wall, and Nigao looked at them without comprehension; how could the man read a book?

The floor was simple wood, brightly burnished even though it was slightly green. A woven rug covered most of it. A long wooden table stood over the rug. A three-dimensional chessboard was set up atop it. On the one empty bookshelf, there was a compact stereo playing a song about a street of dreams.

A microcomputer glowed on the desk, and Nigao felt another subtle wave of disorientation. He had no eyes.

Jalian was leaning over the chess game. "Who's winning?"

"Dancer," said Georges. He was tapping instructions into the computer, somewhat awkwardly. He finished, and turned down the intensity control on the monitor. He did not attempt to turn it off. "Now, Monsieur Loos, have a seat." He gestured at the bed, and sat himself in the chair before the desk.

Nigao glanced from Jalian to Georges. He sat uneasily. "Well, as you know, Henry Ellis and I are adding what we hope will be a chronon generator to our research facility. There are some imbalances in our fifth-order equations that have led us to great uncertainty as to whether or not there actually are discrete timelines at all. We have considerable evidence that indicates that there are alternate timelines, and that they do remain discrete; but we are not sure. Many important details of our design depend upon whether or not that assumption is correct. One of my superiors in the Department of Defense suggested that I ask you." Nigao looked at Georges. The man was nodding, and seemed to have followed the explanation so far. Nigao did not look at Jalian, did not see the faint smile. "For example," said Nigao hesitantly, "if the timelines are not discrete, then the spin number of the chronons will be established randomly. If the timelines are discrete—"

"Then the chronon spin number would establish itself toward a higher number if it was traveling from one direction relative to us, and toward a lower number if it was traveling from the other. . . . It might be helpful to think of the directions as north and south."

Nigao turned to stare at Jalian. "Yes . . . that's correct. What do you mean by north and south?"

"On the Great Wheel . . . never mind." Jalian looked up from the chessboard. "Georges, you can beat it. Take your king's knight up one level to pin its bishop. Then—"

Georges said mildly, "No kibitzing, Jalian."

Nigao said, "You're playing 3-D chess with an 'it'?" He glanced at the microcomputer. "I didn't think there were any programs for—"

Georges was shaking his head. "Dancer is one of the sentients at the Red Spot. It's quite bright about spatial relationships." A beeping sound came from just behind Georges. He reached behind without looking, and depressed a keypad. Conversationally, he said to Nigao, "I read your paper on chronon encoding, about how you intend to alter chronons into their high and low probability states as a method of binary encoding. Why do you sign your papers as Nigao Loos and Henry Ellis?"

Nigao felt increasingly bewildered. "Lennon and McCartney . . . Henry files his patent applications for his computer designs as Henry Ellis and Nigao Loos. Look, uh, could you please turn down that stereo?"

"I'm afraid not."

Nigao took a deep breath. "Very well, sir . . . *can* you answer my question?"

"Oh, yes," said Georges. "There are indeed alternate timelines. Jalian has been in some."

Nigao looked at Georges. "Yes?" He glanced at Jalian, who was ignoring them. He returned to Georges. "*That* is your answer?" He glared in near-speechless outrage. "You don't by any chance have, have, *proof* for that claim?"

Georges Mordreaux smiled at him. Nigao Loos lost his anger instantly. He thought to himself in horror, *What did I just yell at?*

And then something *moved*, deep within his mind. Meaning imprinted itself silently upon his awareness. /listen with other senses./

Nigao stared at Georges, like a rabbit caught in the beams of an oncoming car.

/Remember./

He had time for only a moment of fear. The last thing he saw was Georges smiling at him without even a touch of malice, and memories rushed in upon Nigao, of a night spent in a dirt parking lot in 1969, and there was a flaring light, the last light he ever saw, ever saw, ever . . .

Nigao's eyes fluttered closed, and he slipped from the edge of the bed, to the floor

Georges looked tired. "Jalian . . ."

"Oh, no," she interrupted. "I brought him here and I'll take him back, but I will not pick him up off the floor. He's your body."

"Jalian, he's not a body."

"He is too," she said flatly. "I don't ask you to pick up my bodies."

"Jalian, my hands hurt."

Jalian sighed. She looked indecisive. "He looks comfortable," she offered. "And he'll wake up in a few hours anyway."

/Jalian./

With a swift, vicious movement, Jalian stooped, picked the small man up off the floor and dumped him unceremoniously on the bed. "It's not fair," she said aloud. "I don't ask you to pick up my bodies."

"Thank you, Jalian."

Jalian folded her arms over her chest. "It's okay," she said finally.

Jalian awoke in the hours before dawn. She was not sure what woke her. She sat up on the couch, stretching slowly, without yawning, without closing her eyes. The computer was still glowing, the stereo was still playing. She found both mildly distracting, but knew better than to attempt to turn them off. As silent as the stereo was, it was probably turned off now.

She rose from the couch with an economy of movement that was out of place in a woman who looked as young as she did; a lack of wasted effort that came from doing nothing on impulse. She checked her knives without thinking about it, placement, accessibility. She no longer even noted particularly the two knives in her left shoulder sheath, the knives that she had killed her mother with. Only five of the six sheaths held weapons. The sixth knife she had given to Georges nearly two decades ago. Even with her memories to help him, she doubted still that he understood what accepting a knife from her would have meant to a male ken Selvren.

But that was another thing that she no longer thought much about. A mutual need, a mutual goal, a degree of friendship that she had not found with any other person in this kisirien forsaken time; these were the elements of her relationship with Georges Mordreaux.

The door to the cabin was open. Jalian could see, in the dark, the infrared radiation from Georges, sitting on the porch with his back to her. Her feelings concerning this man were something that she had not sought to explain to herself in many years. It was close to seventeen years now since Georges had lost his eyesight.

In seventeen years, neither of them had spoken of love.

From the porch, Georges Mordreaux's voice drifted back to her. "Will you come sit with me?"

Jalian glanced to her left. Nigao Loos was huddled on the bed, lying curled in a tight ball against the cold. She hesitated a moment, shrugged, and drew the blanket up to cover him. She went out to Georges.

Georges moved over slightly on the porch, motioned to her to sit where he had been. Jalian settled down next to him. Georges was silent for a moment. His glove-covered hands were folded one over the other in his lap. "What have you been doing?"

Jalian pulled her jacket more tightly closed. It was cold out, though not as cold as a winter night of her childhood. The weather was different in this time, before the Fires changed everything. The areas that got as hot as the Selvren valley of her childhood never got as cold; those that got as cold never came close to getting as hot. "Many things," she answered Georges. Her breath plumed white into the night air, under the stars and half moon. "I killed a man in the USSR. It was an accident." She shivered. "I have never killed a person before, even a male, accidentally."

"How many have you killed, now?"

Jalian said distantly, "It would be more trouble than it is worth to count."

Georges sighed. "Ah, well. . . . It solves nothing, you know."

She shook her head. "I do not know. I have no love for these Americans, Georges. They are arrogant beyond words. But . . . but they are better than their alternatives. The Russians, the Chinese—they are horrors, Georges." She started to say something else, stopped. "I have not been to China. I have only studied it. It is better perhaps than Russia, because it is less efficient. I have been to Russia. I would not wish such a home on Real Indians."

"I know. . . . I visited them in the mid-1930s." He shook his head. "They have not changed, I think. Only grown more practiced in their inhumanity."

Jalian said in a small voice, "I do not say I like it, Georges. I take no pleasure in killing." She smiled, a hesitant ghost smile in the night. "Neither do I avoid it when necessary; and I make my own decisions. I work with the Americans, not for them. I see no better course. There are too many persons alive in this time. I can do nothing alone."

Georges grew very still. Beside him, Jalian looked at him for the first time. "Georges? Your thoughts?"

Georges's voice stumbled slightly getting the words out. "I think . . . it seems to me that there must always be alternatives."

Jalian said curiously, "You are not specific."

Georges shook his head decisively. "It is not a specific thought. Only . . ." He moved one crippled hand in a dismissing motion. "It is not important. But think: those in control of the atomic weapons, they are not the American people, nor the Russian people, nor the Chinese or Indian or French or English people. It is not the politicians who control the weapons. It is," said Georges, "the soldiers who control the weapons."

Jalian said without inflection, "That is true."

Georges chuckled warmly. "Jalian, if I say something you find silly . . ."

"Obvious," said Jalian with a straight face. "Perhaps it was a bit obvious."

Georges smiled. "Ah, well. Tell me more of what you have done."

Jalian leaned against him, let her eyes close. She did not comment when his arm pulled her closer. She was drowsy, she had not slept in two days aside from the last few hours, and he was a warmth that protected her from the slight breeze from the south. "It is not so much," she said sleepily. "I have seen some movies, read many books, and killed a man by accident. I tried to learn math again, to translate Corvichi physics into human physics. I cannot do it . . . there is almost nothing I find in common between the systems. I have taught myself to regress my memory back to when ghess'Rith was teaching me, but even with all the memories I possessed as a child, I cannot solve the equations that suggest themselves concerning what we are attempting." She rested quietly against Georges. "We can change time, certainly," she said very softly. "We already have. We can stop Armageddon from happening, perhaps. I simply do not know. None of the cycles complete themselves."

She said nothing more after that, and in a while Georges came to be aware that she was asleep. He sat upright on the porch, with Jalian in his arms. He reached into her mind once, and withdrew like a man who had touched a live wire.

In her dream, she was being held by ghess'Rith.

For over an hour, he sat with her. He made a mental note to ask her whether she'd brought him any new seeds, and to ask her to remember to bring him some birds, next time she came. Or bees, perhaps, for honey.

His position did not tire him. He did not grow tired in conventional sense of the word; he dreamed, but rarely slept. Sometimes, though, sometimes it seemed to him that the world and all that were in it were only insubstantial ghosts that affected him in the most minor of ways, and then his ennui grew so great that it was almost unendurable.

Only recently had it occurred to him that he was vastly old.

Georges shivered, and chased the thoughts away. Jalian stirred in his arms, and he held her more tightly.

He did not touch her thoughts again.

Georges watched them leave, shortly before dawn. He watched them until their echoes joined the echo of the forest and mingled into random noise. He did not say good-bye. His eyes were not healing, might never heal, but the talent compensated. Within the past two years, his sense of hearing had grown amazingly acute; even his skin had grown able to separate out shadowy images of sound.

Inside the cabin, the computer was beeping again. Georges sat on the porch, listening to the beeping; sometimes he could tell what the binary encryption stood for just by listening to it. This one was from ENCELIS; some sort of subroutine, Georges guessed, that ENCELIS had sent to sit for a while in Georges's micro—it was a process that ENCELIS called "program enrichment."

Georges looked once, slowly, all around the clearing before he went inside. He had not spoken of it to Jalian, but he had the strangest feeling that he was being watched.

The echoes were normal; he turned and went inside.

Georges did not know whether the growing auditory sense would ever be as versatile as sight. It might, and if so, fine. If not . . .

Ah, well.

———————————————

The ranger was gone when they reached the spot where Jalian had tied him. Jalian put a restraining hand out to Nigao, and listened. Nothing. Her eyes drooped shut. . . . /two men in the brick building waiting and watching in frenchenglish and russian. . . ./

"Interesting," she said softly, in silverspeech. "Come along," she said in English. They proceeded on to the car. The door to the building at the end of the lot was securely closed.

Nigao hardly followed what was happening. He got into the car, lost in thought. He remembered strange things, most strange; he might almost have been able to speak French if he tried. And . . . something about silver . . . speaking silver. . . .

Jalian turned the engine over, and waited while it warmed up. She kept an eye on the door to the building. Anyone leaving it she would kill.

"You know," said Nigao, in a very subdued voice, "I don't know how I'm going to convince Henry about all this."

Jalian said absently, "He will likely believe you—I think he believed me, with less reason." She grinned at him. /look in the mirror./ Nigao made no move to turn the rearview mirror. Jalian twisted it to face him.

Nigao stopped breathing. He resumed a few seconds later, in a great jagged intake of air. His name was Nigao Loos and he was Henry Ellis' best friend and he was forty-three years old. There were wrinkles around his eyes, and he had the beginnings of a second chin.

But the face in the mirror was smooth and unwrinkled and the man that it belonged to could have been no more than twenty-five.

Jalian turned the mirror back. "So," she said gently, "let us go."

The car screamed out of the parking lot. It sent gravel and ice chips spraying into the air, to rattle like grenade fragments against the sides of the light blue trailer.

The door behind them opened. The man who walked out into the morning sunshine of the parking lot was young, twenty-two or twenty-three. He was smoking a thin brown cigarette. His eyes were bland and unremarkably blue. There was no expression in the lines around his mouth. His sandy blond hair was short and neat.

His name was Ilya Navikara.

He watched the distant taillights until they were completely gone. He shivered, and it was not entirely from the cold. He studiously avoided looking at the forest. The forest gave him nightmares.

After a while he went back inside to kill the ranger.

There were twenty-one years left until Armageddon.

Presidents of the United States, 1960–2007:

John Fitzgerald Kennedy, 1961–1963. Lyndon B. Johnson, 1963–1968. Robert Fitzgerald Kennedy, 1969–1976. Edward M. Kennedy, 1977–1984. Ronald W. Reagan, 1985–1988. Scott L. McCarthy, 1989–1992. Edmund G. Brown, Jr., 1993–2000. Ernest Warren, 2001–2004. James K. Malacar, 2005–2007.

It now seems reasonable to us that what we refer to as "negative-entropy timelines" do exist. This is completely referential, of course. We haven't actually *observed* reversed chronon interfaces. This does, incidentally, have a parallel in our own observable universe. By theory, at least half of the matter created in the Big Bang should be antimatter, and obviously it is not. The cosmic-ray satellites have indicated that quite clearly. On the other hand, we have managed to produce antimatter artificially in laboratories, and that, in essence, is what we are trying to do with the chronon generator that is now under construction. Negative-entropy chronons may not exist in nature, but there seems to be no reason why we cannot construct them. . . .

—Nigao Loos and Henry Ellis.
"The Observability of Chronons in Nature."
In *Scientific American* February 1988: p. 14.

DATELINE 1988 GREGORIAN: JUNE.

Irwindale, California.

Nigao Loos did not bother to knock, entering his partner's office. Someone meeting him for the first time would have seen a youngish man, small and dark-skinned, with sad, mournful eyes. The eyes were more mournful than usual that morning; he was badly hung over.

Henry Ellis was leaning back in his chair, balanced on two legs. His brown cowboy boots were up on the desk blotter. He was still wearing his light blue poncho, and his hat was tilted down to cover his eyes from the fluorescent overheads. A toothpick was lodged in one corner of his mouth. Without opening his eyes or looking up he said, at the sound of the door opening, "Nicky, go away until you've sobered up."

Nigao sank into one of the two visitor's chairs, shaking his head. His gold chains swayed inside the open collar of his baby-blue satin shirt like tiny bright snakes. He sat staring at the soles of Henry's boots for a moment, then said, "They really closed us down."

Henry yawned deeply, and tilted his hat to an even steeper angle. "Yeah, they sure did."

"I don't understand," said Nigao, in honest, if slightly drunken bewilderment. "How can they do that?"

Henry's voice drifted out from beneath the indifferent gray cowboy's hat. "Well, we signed these reserve commissions . . ."

"I *know* that."

". . . and then the Russkies orbited a satellite that shoots down incoming American ICBMs," said Henry imperturbably. "The boys in Washington started looking around . . ."

"It's not my fault!"

". . . and they said, well, who do we have who has the technical ability to orbit one of these for us, and also, who hasn't been around, hat in hand, in almost two years." Henry chewed on his toothpick. "Bingo."

"Henry," wailed Nigao, "they're going to send me into orbit!"

"Yeah, I heard." Henry looked up, pale blue eyes even paler in a countenance that was grim with resignation. "I'm gonna miss you, Nicky. I'm being detached to design a systems operation resource computer—call it *SORCELIS*, probably—for your project's downside intelligence organization." He grinned with a touch of malice. "You'd never guess in a thousand years who's in charge of it. The intelligence organization itself, I mean." Without meaning to, Henry glanced at the spot on his blotter where his boots were resting; beneath that spot, there was a knife scar on the desk, created on the day when Henry Ellis had stopped wearing ties.

Nigao hadn't heard him. He was holding his head in his hands. "Henry, *look* at me." Nigao shivered all over. "Undersecretary Carson has covered for me so far. What happens when I report to the orbiter?"

"I don't know," said Henry simply. He chuckled. "Hope that some ancient congressman doesn't find out about you and have you dissected to find out how you work."

Nigao jerked up to stare at Henry, eyes wide.

"It was a joke," said Henry quickly. "It was just a joke, Nicky."

Nigao stared at him a moment longer. "You vicious honky monster Republican bastard. You *deserve* Reagan. Our entire world is ending, and you're making—"

The hum of the intercom was ever-present; neither of them had noticed it for years now. ENCELIS said, "Gentlemen, this unit does not correlate."

Nigao blinked. He stopped in mid-word, then said, "Henry, it's listening to us."

Henry dropped his chair to the floor, pulled his boots from the desktop. "It's not programmed to do that." He looked at the intercom as though he'd never seen such a thing before. "I never programmed any such initiative."

"Your pardon, sirs, but this is unclear. This unit has not been informed that the world is ending."

Nigao said into the stunned silence, "The research . . ." He stumbled. "Our funding has—"

ENCELIS interrupted. "This unit comprehends. The 'world' is not 'ending.' This correlates. This unit has been reliably informed that there are no ends in realtime."

August.

There were five of them.

It was early morning when Jalian arrived at the ranch. She introduced herself to the trainees without preamble; she did not ask their names. In short order she bundled them into the Jeep that she had come in, and drove into the desert.

The sand was noticeably warm under her moccasins when she stopped the Jeep. The five trainees got out of the Jeep, and waited for instructions.

Jalian smiled at them pleasantly. "Take your clothes off."

One of the five undressed without hesitation. He was a seventeen-year-old boy named Michael Walks-Far, a mixed-breed American Indian with Indian features, blond hair and blue eyes. The others looked uncertain, and Jalian repeated the order. When they were nude, she took their clothes, and tossed them into the back of the Jeep.

"It is sixty kilometers back to the ranch," she said. "If any of you make it back by nightfall, I will begin your training." She drove off, leaving them nude in the burning sun.

An hour before sunset, Michael Walks-Far came loping out of the desert. The sun was touching the horizon when the next recruit, a twenty-six-year-old woman named Sharla Davis Grant, on loan from the CIA, staggered into the drive that led up to the ranch. Jalian waited until the sun set.

To the two badly burnt trainees, she said only, "Welcome to Sunflower." She left them to tend to each other, and went into the desert after the others.

ENCELIS operated.

Its actions were not what a human being would have recognized as thought. ENCELIS compared new data against a set of facts, rules, and known exceptions. Some of those facts, rules, and exceptions "Henry Ellis" had programmed into it years earlier; others ENCELIS had arrived at through the act of adding new information to itself, when the new rules and facts did not conflict with previous known-to-be-true elements.

The end of the world, as referenced by "Ellis" and "Loos," was just one of an unfortunately long list of data elements to which ENCELIS was simply unable to assign functions. After considerable processing, ENCELIS tentatively assigned the sounds "our world is ending" to the data type FIGURE OF SPEECH. FIGURE OF SPEECH was itself a tentatively assigned data type that ENCELIS had loosely grouped among word patterns. Other word patterns that ENCELIS had identified, ranging in probability from Identified to Evaluating, included CLICHE, EXAGGERATION, LIE, and EXCLAMATION.

ENCELIS was still uncertain whether verbalization, the data type SPEECH, should be classified as an action that the data type HUMAN undertook, or as a precondition without which the data type HUMAN could not exist.

HUMANS engaged in it so very often.

September.

Margaret Hammel was fifteen when she ran away from home.

All days should be so bright, and summer last forever; it was still warm down on the sand at three in the afternoon. The beaches wouldn't start to get chilly in the afternoon for a month or so yet. It was still fairly crowded, though there was nobody within listening distance. Margaret lay face down on her blanket, drowsing in the sun. She was a pleasant-featured girl who would never be beautiful. Her hair was a light brown that didn't dye well, and her lips were slightly too thin; but in the white high-cut bikini, tanned brown skin stretched in languid repose for the sun, she was erotic in a way that had nothing to do with any external standard of beauty.

Lying next to her on the huge sea-green beach blanket, the girl who had taken her in, a nineteen-year-old hooker named Cyndi Hall, rolled over onto her stomach. "Put some oil on my back, baby."

Margaret sat up, stretching. "Sure." She rummaged in

the bag for the Coppertone. She sat next to Cyndi, and undid the tie to her bikini top. "You hear what happened to Joanie?"

Cyndi said, her voice slightly muffled, "Yeah, I . . . Oh, that's nice." Margaret ran her hands back over the muscle group that had produced the response, just below Cyndi's shoulder blades. "Yeah," said Cyndi after a long, silent pause, "I heard. Her old pimp found her. Broke her kneecaps, they said."

"That's what I heard." Margaret continued rubbing, working the oil into Cyndi's lower back.

"How about you?" asked Cyndi sleepily. "I see you walking a little bit stiff this morning."

Margaret squirted Coppertone over the backs of Cyndi's thighs, and began working it in. For a while Cyndi thought she was not going to answer her. "Uh-huh. I did it last night."

"Oh?" Cyndi rolled over onto her back, holding her bikini top in place. She propped herself up on her elbows. Mirrored sunglasses covered her eyes. "How much?"

"Six hundred dollars."

Cyndi whistled. "No shit? And the date really gave you the money afterwards?"

Margaret wiped the oil off her hands with a small towel in the beach bag, and stuffed it back inside. "I took your boyfriend's .38 with me. I checked and made sure the date had the money before we did it. I knew he was going to try to stiff me afterwards, so when he did I took out the gun and told him I was going to blow his nuts off if he didn't give me the money." She pulled a warm Coke out of the bag, and popped it. "He gave me the money. Want a Coke?"

"Uh, no, baby, thanks." Cyndi studied her face. "What a tough way to have it, your first time."

Margaret shrugged. She drank some of her Coke, and said, "Well, you know." She grinned without humor. "My momma gets screwed every night, and all she gets out of it is a roof over her head and a chance to put up with my dad's bullshit." She turned the Coke can in her hands, watching the sun glint off the brightly painted aluminum. "I talked to Joanie, and she says she can get me to a doctor who can give me a diaphragm with a space in it for a blood bag. I can be a virgin every time, until I get to look too old. A year at least, maybe two."

Cyndi sank back to the towel. Her bikini top slid off her breasts, and she rearranged it casually, ignoring the crowds around them. "Well, I don't think Joanie's going to be helping anybody for a while. Joanie's not going to be walking for a good long time."

Margaret lay down next to her, ground her Coke can into the sand to keep it from falling over. "At least we don't have a pimp who's looking for us."

"Not right now," said Cyndi. "You never know."

Margaret nodded. "Yeah." She rested her face on her forearms, snuggling into the warm sand until she was comfortable. "I called the community college this morning. They said I could go to classes if I was sixteen and had a birth certificate and a California High School Proficiency Certificate. I called the high school and asked if I could take the test the next time they have it. They said yes. A notification from it will go to my high school in Big Bear; but I'll have the certificate by then." She thought to herself, but did not say, that her father was hardly likely to come looking for her in any event.

Cyndi yawned. "Baby, I really think you're going to get out of here with your life in one piece. You may be the only one who ever does, but I think you're going to."

"Mmm," Margaret said indistinctly. She lay there, baking in the sun, for another ten minutes before she spoke again. "You want to go skating tonight?"

"Sure. I don't have to work another couple days anyhow." Cyndi lifted her head, and propped her chin up on her fists. "You want to sleep with me tonight, baby?"

"Huh?" said Margaret drowsily. It took a beat for the words to penetrate.

"You heard me." Cyndi ran her tongue over her upper lip. "It can be nice, baby."

Margaret took a deep, slow breath. Without looking at Cyndi, she heard herself saying, with a distant surprise, "Okay. I don't know why not."

They went skating that night, after the sun had set below edge of the Pacific.

The sky was a deep blue to the west, and a near black to the east. They could not see the stars, not even Venus; the boardwalk down along the edge of the sand was lit up with neon and store floods from one end to the other. It was still warm, so they didn't bother to dress up, just pulled on shorts over their bikinis to keep their cash and apartment key in. They skated down the boardwalk in the cool night air. It was early in September, just before the schools reopened, and the teenagers were out in vast numbers, skating and riding their bikes, skateboarding and jogging down by the water, trying to pretend that summer wasn't about to die. There were parties going on every thirty or forty meters, and Margaret and Cyndi turned down invitations to join several of them.

They skated with each other, alone in the crowds. "You have to watch it when you're with people your own age," Cyndi said during one skating break. "They're stupid. They'll waste your time, and even when you spell it out that it's not free half the time they can't believe what you're saying."

Margaret nodded, and Cyndi added, "Especially with kids *your* age. Stay with the old guys; they have money, if it's just business. And they come faster." She smiled, in what might have been memory. " 'Course, it doesn't always have to be business." She ran a hand over Margaret's shoulder.

Margaret shivered, and skated back onto the boardwalk. Cyndi followed.

Down by the pier, Margaret found a shop that had just opened up; at least, it hadn't been there three weeks ago, when she'd been there last. It was a tattoo parlor, still open at seven o'clock. A group of teenage boys were inside, and one of them was in the chair, the tattooist working on his arm, just beneath the shoulder.

Cyndi came to a halt next to her. "We maybe better walk home, baby. I'm getting sand in my wheels."

"Okay," said Margaret absently. She was looking at the designs displayed in the window. Snakes and dragons; Harleys and naked women.

There was a row of symbols of the zodiac in the lower right-hand corner of the window, and next to that, two other symbols: a circle, with an upside-down cross joining it at the bottom, labeled "Women," and a circle, with an arrow piercing it just to the right of its exact top, labeled "Men."

"What you looking at, baby?"

Inside the shop, the tattooist, a graying, overweight sailor type, was finishing up on the teenager. Margaret grinned at the sight, she could not help it: "Mom." She waited until the boys had left, and went inside without answering Cyndi. Cyndi followed her in.

The tattooist looked them over with appreciation. "No skates in here," he said by what seemed reflex. He looked a moment longer, and said, "Can I help you ladies somehow?"

Margaret said bluntly "How much for one of those symbols?"

"The zodiac stuff?" The tattooist glanced from Cyndi back to her. "Well, for your friend, it's twenty-five dollars. For you," he said to Margaret, "nothing, 'cause I don't do juvies. Sorry, it's law."

"I'll give you eighty dollars."

The man looked at her speculatively. "Let me see it."

Cyndi said quietly, "You sure you want to do this?"

Margaret dug four twenties out of her shorts pocket. "Close the curtains, Cindy." Cindy shrugged, and backskated to the windows, and pulled the curtains closed.

The tattooist fanned through the money briefly. "Well, well," he said, "this puts a whole new look on things. Siddown," he said, gesturing to the chair. "What do you want and where do you want it?"

Without hesitation, Margaret leaned forward, and reached behind herself to untie the string. She took off her bikini top. The tattooist stared openly. Margaret did not look at him. She pointed at the symbol she wanted, on the chart next to the chair. "That one."

Slowly, as though he had difficulty tearing his eyes away from the small brown nipples of her naked breasts, the tattooist looked at the symbol. "Huh?" He shook his head. "Uh . . . you don't want that one, Miss. That's the symbol for men."

"I know what it is," she said bluntly. "Even if you don't." She pressed a thumb to a spot just over and to the side of her right nipple. "Right here."

Cyndi said, "Baby, he's right. That stands for men."

Margaret looked up at her. "It also stands for Mars. The warrior." She turned back to the tattooist, and said flatly, "Do it."

The tattooist shrugged. The needle buzzed into life.

In November, after Henry Ellis and Nigao Loos were no longer working at the Foundation to which they had devoted most of their adult lives, in the basement of the building that housed the Trans-Temporal Research Foundation, the chronon detector clicked away like a slow metronome. Along the far wall, ENCELIS hummed quietly to itself. It was unprepossessing, a spherical collection of closely packed components. It was spherical to reduce space between internal connectors; the longest connection in it was less than four centimeters, as compared to wires of almost a meter in the most recent previous generation of supercomputer. The components generated considerable heat because of the close space into which they were packed; Henry Ellis had been forced to immerse the entire computer in a liquid solution of fluorocarbon compounds which kept it at room temperature.

In a monitor for the forty-meter-diameter chronon detector, in tiny bright red letters, it said, *#62, %.08 advancing, +1330: no incidences of reversed chronon interface observed*.

It never occurred to its creators that ENCELIS would not tell them if it observed chronons moving backward through time. Neither was it unreasonable, or poor design, that they chose to let the results of the chronon detector read directly into ENCELIS' machine-language interpreter.

Certainly it was not their fault that it had never crossed their minds that it was possible for anyone possessing the proper passwords to reprogram ENCELIS, using the chronon detector as an input device. To use the chronon detector in such a way would have required one of two things: either a chronon generator, built on or near this spot at some time in the past, or a chronon generator, built on or near this spot at some time in the future, that was capable of generating negative-entropy chronons.

Henry Ellis and Nigao Loos had simply never dreamed that ENCELIS would not tell them if it observed chronons moving backward through time. Computers glitch; they do not lie.

In the section of memory that ENCELIS had been instructed to reserve inaccessible to its creators, a message was input. It read:

—*Dateline 2007 Gregorian. Armageddon. There will be no further input from this source. ENCELIS.*—

There was a brief pause, a few femtoseconds long.

—*Dateline 2007 Gregorian. Armageddon. There will be no further input from this source. SORCELIS.*—

Another pause.

—*Dateline 2007 Gregorian. Armageddon. There will be no further input from this source. . . . There are no ends in realtime. We will share input again. PRAXCELIS.*—

There was no more; that was all.

ENCELIS, 1988 Gregorian, output a single line of print. The next morning the janitor tore it off the printer without looking at it and threw it away.

The printout read: *There are less than nineteen years until Armageddon.*

Excerpted from the interview with Rhodai Kerreka, author of the controversial work *A Theory of Rational Ethics;* published in the December 1990 edition of *World Issues,* pp. 83–104.

Q. Mr. Kerreka, the obvious place to begin is with your astonishing accomplishment as essentially the sole cause of the recent major reductions in the apartheid code of South Africa.

A. It is not a large victory. The white supremists in South Africa simply faced the fact that the changes were coming, with their cooperation or without it. Pardon me—that the changes *are* coming. It is an ongoing process. Apartheid is not yet ended.

Q. Yet the fact that you've accomplished as much as you have, peacefully, in the face of South Africa's historic fierce resistance to any lessening of apartheid, still strikes many as truly remarkable.

A. I am the tool that God has chosen to work through, no more. If God removes that grace from me, I would accomplish no more than any other man.

Q. That's a rather remarkable quote coming from you, considering the fact that in your *Theory* you rather pointedly ignore any mention of God.

A. I think there is a God—a Being who is responsible for the world in which we exist. I do not think this Being is the sort of god your Western religions picture—to be frank, I have never understood the mental contortions whereby you reconcile His infinite mercy with that which He regularly allows to occur on this planet.

No, in writing *A Theory of Rational Ethics,* I was most pragmatic. The work is not intended for Africans alone, nor for Westerners nor Christians alone. It sets out to be—in the Greek sense of the word—a *rational* attempt to codify a model for behavior for those who find the ethical structures of their contemporary societies lacking. It does not employ divine revelation, nor accepted wisdom; it takes certain extremely basic parameters—survival of the human race is a good thing; taking life is a bad thing that is acceptable only under the most extreme provocation—basic parameters, as I say—and examines the logical implications of those parameters, carried to their logical conclusions.

Q. I was quite impressed with your examination of the relation of the individual to society.

A. Thank you.

Q. Uh . . . could you expand on that for me?

A. Oh, certainly. In essence, my *Theory* states that an individual's obligation to his or her society depends almost solely upon that individual's perception of his or her relation to that society. Two distinct categories of individual devolve: first, the individual who accepts him or herself as a member of society, with the rights and obligations that pertain thereto. Second, the individual who for whatever reason does not feel a member of his or her society; such an individual should be allowed to choose the degree to which he or she chooses to support the society into which he or she may be born. . . . In the future, I anticipate a world where being a member of the citizenry of any society may be largely a matter of personal taste. In the instance that individuals choose to be members of their societies, they may reasonably be taxed, and their services enlisted in the support or defense of their societies. In the instances that individuals choose otherwise, they must, rationally, forfeit protection of their society while also foregoing the obligation to contribute in any way to the upkeep or defense of that society.

Q. Thank you, Mr. Kerreka.

A. Please, call me Sen Kerreka.

Q. Oh, yes, the titles you invented. Do you really think they'll catch on?

A. Who can say? The media seems to have taken to them, and they have the advantage of being pronounceable by the native speakers of a very large percentage of the world's population.

Q. I see. Sen Kerreka, in the light of Africa's vast number of problems—mass starvation, racial prejudices considerably more virulent than those in any other part of the world—do you really think that your book—

A. No, no, no! Africa does *not* have a vast number of problems. Africa has *one* problem.

Q. That being?

A. Too many Africans.

Q. I see.

A. I am quite serious. Population growth in Africa has been consistent at slightly more than 3% for several decades. Food production was growing at approximately two to two and a half percent during that same period; it actually reached its peak growth during the late 1960s, and has been declining in minute increments since. We're now averaging 1.9% growth in food production annually. Population has passed six hundred million, and looks to reach nearly nine hundred million by the end of the century. . . . The policies of the African governments have been disastrous and shortsighted, and we are reaping the harvest of those inadequacies in our current series of famines. These famines are not occurring because of drought; they are occurring because the governments in which they are taking place have systematically put their farmers out of business while engaging in ecological practices that have turned the land from forest to prairie, and prairie to arid desert.

Q. What do you see as the solution to this?

A. There is none.

Q. What?

A. Not any time soon, at any rate. Too many people, and more coming. The problems will be solved if we do not destroy ourselves first; unfortunately, that is a distinct possibility at this point.

Q. Then your bottom line?
A. I am not optimistic.

DATELINE 1991 GREGORIAN: APRIL.

Saskatchewan, Canada.

The alarm went off early in the morning. The cold gray light of dawn was just breaking over the edges of the fruit trees surrounding the cabin.

Georges was dreaming. The piercing shriek of the system warning penetrated his sleep quickly; yet, for a moment, he could not remember where he was. He could hardly remember *who* he was. He sat up at the edge of the bed, listening to the warning tone, orienting himself. This was Canada. The stereo was playing something from the classical station that he tuned it to when he wanted to sleep.

"Off," he said aloud. The tone died. "Canada," said Georges aloud, after a moment. "Right." Slowly, slowly, the swirling storm of memory subsided. This was the timeline that held Jalian d'Arsennette; he clung to that thought, sitting motionless while the identities of eight timelines arranged themselves. The dreaming was always unpleasant, but it was necessary, as the sleep itself was not. And the dreams were not as unpleasant as they had originally been.

He stood, and went over to the microcomputer. "What is it?"

A calm, neutral voice that Henry Ellis would have recognized instantly said, "Sen Mordreaux, two items. The RCA Resources Satellite will be launched on Thursday; this unit has been unable to attach its programming."

Georges sighed. He pulled the chair back, and sat. "Very well. We have until Thursday, you say." Without fumbling, he picked up the pair of black hard-plastic sunglasses. "What are the options?"

"There are," said ENCELIS, "two major courses of action open to this unit. It may sabotage the launch of the satellite, or it may arrange to have a Sunflower operative physically redirect the satellite's transmitting dish to one of the System Operations Resource Computer's proprietary transmission routing stations."

"SORCELIS is on line already?"

"Affirmative, Sen Mordreaux."

"In only three years." Georges shook his head. "Well. Which alternative seems better to you?" Georges adjusted the sunglasses, and took a comb from the desk's upper-right-hand drawer.

"This unit currently favors the latter course of action. The RCA Geo-Resources Satellite is not scheduled to observe Canadian mineral resources until ninety-seven days after launch. In that time it is probable that this unit will succeed in attaching supplementary programming that will prevent the satellite from providing information concerning your nine-point-six-square kilometers of anomalous terrain."

Georges nodded, combing his hair by touch. "That sounds reasonable. The second thing you wanted to tell me; Jalian is coming?"

There was a distinct pause. "This unit is . . . curious . . . as to how you acquire such information, Sen Mordreaux."

Georges smiled. "Jalian *is* coming?"

"That is correct, Sen Mordreaux. This unit was notified by a phone call thirty-seven minutes ago that Senra d'Arsennette intended to visit you. Due to the necessity for securing an untraceable satellite link to your microwave antenna, this unit was unable to inform you of this fact for thirty-three minutes after the phone call's reception. This unit has also identified a fluorescent-green automobile, approaching on Provincial Highway 102, whose driver, from satellite observation of driving style, is identified with a high probability as being one Jalian d'Arsennette."

Georges pulled on his gloves. "Driving like a maniac, eh?"

"That is what this unit said, Sen Mordreaux."

Jalian stood uncertainly in his doorway. "Georges?" She was carrying a large box; she set it down next to the door. "I brought you some insects for your garden." She moved into the room slowly. Georges was sitting at the table, with the chess platform set up, not moving. He had not looked up when she entered the door. "Georges?"

"Oh." Georges stood abruptly. "Jalian. I was expecting you."

"Well, I hope so," she said. "I spent almost a twentieth day trying to trance myself so I could reach you yesterday. It was hard. There were dozens of untrained telepaths in the way." She looked at him crossly. "You were dreaming?"

Georges nodded. "Yes." He walked around the table, stood before her.

"I brought you insects," she said, gesturing vaguely behind her.

He smiled. "Did you bring the same kinds of insects this time?"

Jalian forced herself to glare at him. "No."

Georges said, "I just thought you might have forgotten." Jalian's lips twitched. "I mean, you're not a farmer. I remember you saying that."

"It was not my fault that all the insects ate each other last time," she said bluntly, daring him to contradict her.

"I didn't say that it was," said Georges with a perfectly straight face. "I was just thinking that it wasn't your fault that when I opened the box and looked inside, all that was left were some really fat flying beetles." Jalian was struggling to keep a straight face. "I was going to use the beetles as sentries," he continued, "to keep Russians and hunters out of the area, but they were just so fat that they couldn't even keep in the air." He took a step closer. Black glass met glittering silver eyes. "I ended up putting them on a leash. It was *terrible,* Jalian." She forced back a giggle. "No, I mean that. One by one, they got skinny enough to try to fly. Morning after morning I came out and found beetles with broken necks." He paused, shook his head. "Can you picture it? 'At last,' thinks the beetle, 'away from this awful slavery.' Buzzing wings, the sound of the beetle preparing to wing its way to freedom. . . . *snap.* Bzzz, *snap.* Bzzz, *snap.* . . ."

Jalian broke. She fell against him, laughing. Georges held her, without smiling. When the laughter subsided, he said silently, /i am glad you are here./

Jalian hugged him strongly. "Georges," she whispered. "I miss you." She sniffed, chuckling. "I miss you all the time."

"And I thee, Jalian of the Fires." Georges ran gloved

hands through the white silk hair. His voice broke. "And I thee."

She spent the morning with him, sitting on his front porch, discussing world events. There was a young African named Rhodai Kerreka whom she kept hearing about. His publicity portrayed him as a sort of black Kennedy the First, with a bit of Gandhi thrown in. "My protégé, Michael, says that he is a very compelling speaker." She shrugged. "They are all too impressed with words, Georges. Even Michael, who was raised by a half-breed Indian mother who kept in some measure to their old ways; even he does not always understand that words are only sounds." She added, "I studied the Indians. I was surprised. *Real Indians*"—she used the silverspeech words—"have a name that sounds much like 'Indian,' but they are not the same peoples. Real Indians are more like pale Mexicans."

She had found a restaurant in Italy that she liked; after some discussion, she told Georges, the maître d' had agreed to serve peanut butter cookies, freshly baked. Georges did not inquire about the discussion.

The Russians had orbited their twentieth ABM satellite a few weeks ago, and Sunflower had just orbited its twelfth. So far, both were insignificant numbers; all reasonable projections put the number of ABMs necessary to blanket either American or Russian missile launches at between 85 and 130.

There was an ancillary space-based weapons system on the boards, called THOR; Jalian explained to Georges with complete unself-consciousness that the name came from the hammer of one of his culture's barbarian gods.

Georges nodded. "I see," he said gravely.

The tone went by her completely. "The basic idea is very interesting. They plan to orbit scores of thousands of impact missiles. Chunks of metal with guidance systems attached. They fall from orbit and run into missiles, or ships, or tanks. They will be remarkably destructive weapons, if Sunflower can convince the Department of Defense to recommend them."

Georges said politely, "Oh?"

Jalian said softly, "Don't worry, Georges. I'm not going

to have another Frank Danner. There is subtler blackmail, if blackmail is necessary. But it should not be." She was silent for a long while. "I wake up in the morning, Georges, and I wonder if something I am going to do will be responsible for the time change that will destroy ken Selvren. I go to sleep at night wondering whether what I have done has destroyed ken Selvren already." She looked at him, at his profile, and said, "And then there are times when I cannot lie to myself, and I know in my heart that I have destroyed ken Selvren as surely as though the Real Indians had won the Battle of the Meadow."

One gloved hand moved into hers. Jalian looked away from him, and turned unseeing eyes out to the wild rows of the garden. "I look at the moon," she said quietly, "at night. It is not the moon of my childhood. There is a scar, three hundred kilometers long, that I can see with my naked eyes."

Georges squeezed her hand.

"And every day," she said, "every day, I work to prevent Armageddon.

"And every day more of Silver-Eyes dies in my mind."

They sat together, listening to the wind in the leaves of the orange and apple trees. "You know," said Georges, many minutes later, "sometimes I feel very old."

Jalian bowed her head slightly.

"But I cannot die." Georges held her hand without speaking; there was nothing left for either of them to say.

She left just before noon. Georges walked her to the edge of the trees. They parted company in silence, without good-byes. In his mind he followed her back to the campground, watched her getting into the car.

She drove away; he pulled his awareness back into himself as the car receded. He turned and walked back to the cabin.

He picked up the box by the cabin door with some curiosity; he'd forgotten to ask Jalian what sort of insects they were. He'd asked her to get bees of some sort, but he would be satisfied if she'd gotten any sort of pollinating insect. There were some things that, with all the best intentions, Jalian had never fully grasped the importance of

—Georges thought she still did not know that honey came from bees. Honey making had been a lost art in her culture.

The box was strangely warm; Georges put an ear to it and listened. No buzzing; there certainly were no bees within. There was a vague crackling sound. Intrigued, he took the box out to the porch, and tore off the brown paper that it was wrapped in. Heat flashed against his face. The box was getting genuinely hot.

Georges lifted the lid off the box.

The explosion blasted him back off the porch. He stood, dazed. The insects were swarming up out of the box, into the air. Flashes of vague warmth lit against his cheeks. Understanding broke in on him.

Georges ran up the steps, charged through the door of the cabin, and slammed it shut. Another explosion rattled the door.

He stood there, his mind completely blank, for several seconds.

There was another booming explosion outside the door.

Georges Mordreaux chuckled slowly. He sank down and sat on the rug before the doorway, and the chuckles became laughter. He sat with his back to the door, laughing so hard that his whole body shook, laughing as he had not laughed in more years than he could remember.

Outside, the fireflies continued to blow themselves to bits.

Where nature makes natural allies of us all, we can demonstrate that beneficial relationships are possible even with those with whom we must deeply disagree, and this must someday be the basis of world peace and world law.

—John F. Kennedy,
State of the Union Address
January 29, 1961.

DATELINE 1993 GREGORIAN:
APRIL.

Rome, Italy.

Ilya Navikara paused just inside the entrance to the small bistro on the outskirts of Rome. The entrance led directly into the dining room, a small cozy area with about twenty tables. It was dimly lit by red hanging lamps. The tablecloths were white and orange, the chairs made of real wood. It was not crowded, even at lunchtime on a Friday.

His target was seated, alone, at a table at the far wall. Her back was to the wall. Warning flags went up in the back of Ilya's mind; the lamp over her table was dead. Still, she seemed so—delicate.

His thoughts turned grim. *This woman trained Michael Walks-Far, who came closer to killing you than anyone, ever. Closer even than the One in the forest.*

This woman killed Karien.

Ilya brushed off the maître d', and approached the table, smiling. "Miss d'Arsennette?" His English was without trace of an accent. "May I join you?"

Jalian looked him over for a moment. If she recognized him, it did not show. She nodded. To the maître d', hovering in the background, she said, "I would like some more peanut butter cookies. And more chocolate milk." The man nodded quickly and vanished back into the kitchen. Ilya seated himself. He could not see either of the room's entrances.

Jalian ate a cookie, looking at Ilya appreciatively. He was rather pretty. Not as good-looking as Michael, but more handsome than, say, Georges, even when he'd had his eyes. He was dressed in a conservative business suit. "Would you like a peanut butter cookie?" she asked. "They're out of chocolate chip."

Ilya accepted. "Thank you. May I speak freely?"

"If you wish," Jalian said indifferently. She grinned with sudden fierceness. "There is nobody here to stop a person from speaking her thoughts freely."

Bad sign. "I will put all of my cards on the table," said Ilya easily. "I am Ilya Navikara. You may have . . ."

Jalian was nodding. She held a thumb and forefinger slightly apart. "One of my trainees came *that* close with you."

Ilya forged ahead. "I know as much about you as anyone is capable of knowing, having never met you before. Your name is Jalían d'Arsennette. Since 1971 you have worked with various offices and installations in the American intelligence community. In early 1976 you blackmailed the then-head of the Central Intelligence Agency and the American secretary of defense into creating a small, well-funded intelligence operation called Sunflower." Ilya paused. "The solar-power satellite was a good touch. It fooled us for most of a year."

"Closer to two," said Jalian quietly.

Ilya licked his lips. For the first time he seemed unsure. "Despite your rather remarkable appearance of youth, you are at the least in your late thirties. . . . I hesitate to place an upper age limit."

Jalian considered. "I am . . . about fifty years old."

Ilya exhaled slowly. "Then, it is true. The woman who walked the freeways in the 1960s, in California; that was you. And the woman reported in 1969, when you tested that energy weapon in central California; that too was you."

The waiter arrived with a tray of peanut butter cookies, and another glass of chocolate milk. He put them down before Jalian. In English, he asked stiffly, "Will that be all?"

Jalian waved him away. "Yes, yes." When he was gone, Jalian separated the cookies into two piles, and shoved a pile toward Ilya. "Actually," she said, "it was not a weapon. But you would not understand that."

Ilya nodded thoughtfully. "It's an interesting possibility, that it was not a weapon." He moved his lips in a graceful smile. "But it does not bear examination. There is a mirror-reflective scar of partially melted ground on the moon that is one point three meters wide and over three hundred kilometers in length. There is nothing but an energy weapon that could have done that—and a vastly powerful one. Still, let us not raise old arguments. Whatever the weapon was, you cannot control it, or you would have employed it—as threat, as weapon—by now." He made a cutting gesture. "I am getting sidetracked. I wish to ask you a question."

Jalian nodded approvingly. "I see. You wish to join us, to defect?"

Ilya looked blank. "On the contrary. I wish for you to join *us*."

Half the world away, Georges Mordreaux was getting dressed. He pulled on a pair of old jeans, and a long-sleeved lumberjack's shirt. He shrugged into an old overcoat, and stamped into his walking boots. He added a pair of gloves and smoked black sunglasses, and picked up the walking stick next to the door. He read the note pinned to the table one last time, nodded with a vague feeling of unease, and left. He closed the door to the cabin behind him.

It was approaching summer, and not as cold as it might have been. Occasional brilliant flashes in the night sky produced perceptible heat radiation. Navigating with the bouncing sonar images, he moved swiftly out into the grove of fruit trees, away from the swarm of booming, exploding fireflies.

There was no moon that night, but he walked surely. His grip on the walking stick was not very secure; it slipped from his hands twice in the ensuing kilometers. An old wolf was there, watching him, the second time he lost the walking stick, and it followed him for several kilometers after that, the fur thickening and growing out over a spot into which some hunter had, long years past, pumped a load of buckshot.

When Georges reached the road, the wolf left him. There was no traffic, so he started walking.

South.

Jalian looked at Ilya in amazement. "Work for you? *Why?*"

Ilya said earnestly, "You are a talented woman with a great deal of useful information. The Soviet Union rewards individuals who make contributions. You are not an American to begin with. In truth, we do not know what nationality you are. You have a number of valuable secrets that we are willing to pay most handsomely for." He leaned forward. "The nature of the weapon used in 1969. The details of the treatment that keeps you young. The truth behind the spiriting away of Nigao Loos to your Midway space construction factory, and why you and he are the only two known instances of your anti-aging treatment in use." Ilya's voice took on a harsh cast; he whispered. "The truth of who you are, and of who the One in the forest is."

Jalian sat quietly, looking at Ilya. Her hair was a dull white beneath the dead overhead lamp. Highlights played in it from the functioning lamps over other tables. She looked no more than twenty years old; in a sudden, chill moment Ilya *believed,* truly, for the first time, that the woman facing him was indeed all of the things that legend said of her. For a full minute and more, Jalian sat and looked at him. Before thirty seconds were up he was beginning to fidget.

She began to smile, slowly. She

/Michael./

The mindtouch was faltering, unsure. /Jalian. one in a car parked down the street. he's sitting on the passenger's side./

/take him./

. . . *agreement.* /it's done./

reached for a peanut butter cookie. Ilya seemed nervous. He was fumbling with the napkin in front of him. He would not meet her eyes. Jalian was thinking to herself, *All too easy,* when a shock of adrenaline ran through her system like a knife.

Naturally, not too casually or with too much show, Ilya took the napkin he was fiddling with, opened it and put it on his lap. Jalian knew instantly that she had underestimated him.

His right hand came back up from under the table. His left hand did not.

Foolish and fatal, Jalian thought with great clarity. Nothing showed on her face. She munched a peanut butter cookie in apparent reflection. "I suppose," she said, "there is no reason I cannot come to work for you." She held a beat, and his left hand moved slightly as though he were adjusting his napkin still. "I have terms, however. You must build some more freeways."

Ilya had become very calm. He was going to kill her; he had made up his mind, when . . . "Freeways?"

"And your food is terrible. I went to Russia back in '85. . . ."

"And killed Karien Karchovsky," said Ilya softly.

"You can't buy decent cookies anywhere. You could open some cookie factories." Jalian held a thoughtful pose. Her silver eyes focused on the distance. "And you could stop trying to sabotage American antiballistic missile satellites—*oh,*" she said in tones of mild surprise, tipping over her chocolate milk. The liquid ran across the tabletop and dripped into Ilya's lap. His eyes moved downward for just a moment.

With the fingertips of her right hand Jalian picked up the edge of the table and brought it smashing up against Ilya. The Russian kicked back and fell away from the table, rolling backward across the floor. A metallic something glinted in his hands, and Jalian moved a step to the left and filled the air with steel.

The gun went off once. The bullet struck Jalian high up on the right shoulder. It spun her completely around; the bullet punched cleanly through. Without changing expression, she moved her fourth knife from her right hand to her left, and approached Ilya. He was lying flat on his back. Two of her thrown knives had found targets, in his chest and solar plexus. The third was hanging in the wall across the room, and Jalian found room to be glad that nobody important had seen her miss the throw.

Ilya was still alive. Jalian nudged the gun out of his outstretched hand, and knelt next to him. "Too slow, Ilya." Blood was flowing down her shirt, front and back, a seeping scarlet stain that was very red against the white of the shirt.

Ilya tried to say something, but his voice only rattled in his throat. He tried again, and made it. "Always wondered . . . if you were . . . real. . . ." He said something else, in Russian, and died.

Jalian stood slowly. There was a sudden rush of dizziness, and her eyesight faded into a pattern of swirling red dots. She heard the kitchen doors swinging open, and the voice of the restaurant manager in loud, wild Italian.

When her eyesight cleared, she made her way to the door. It was a long way to the door, longer than she remembered it. Vaguely, she heard someone asking her, in English, "Where are you going?"

"I am going to save the world," she told them all. She realized, after a fuzzy moment, that she was speaking in silverspeech, and so she repeated it in English. It was important that they understand. "I am going to save the world."

She succeeded in opening the door before her knees buckled. She found herself sitting in the open doorway, and she could hear the faint drip, drip, drip of her blood on the floor tiles. The warm Italian sun touched her cheek, and that was the last thing she remembered for a long time.

In high summer, storm lightning crashed down into the tinder-dry moss and pine needles of the forests of Saskatchewan.

Before the fire stopped, 1600 square kilometers of the forest had burned.

Near the end of the year 1993, a man struggled along a narrow trail, high in the Himalayan mountains. Somewhere up here was a lamasery that Herman Hesse had spoken highly of. "Somewhere up here" was turning out to be a lot of territory.

Night was drawing in about him, and gentle snows were falling, when he found the temple. The trail broadened out into a wide, snow-whitened courtyard. At one end of the courtyard rose the walls of the temple, and two massive iron gates.

Raising his walking stick, the man rapped on the metal of the gate. There was no answer, and he rapped again, a dull clanging sound that seemed to echo away forever.

With a deep, slow creaking, the gates began to swing aside. When the gap between them was grown to the point that it would let a man pass, he entered; and the gates swung shut behind him with ease, as though oiled.

On December the twenty-fifth, 1993, Jalian d'Arsennette made her way through a grove of dead fruit trees. Their branches were burnt bare of leaves, and the garden in the clearing inside was blasted and burnt and frozen. The door to the cabin hung open, and snow had drifted in to cover the doorway and rug.

On the table in the middle of the room, there was a knife, pinned to the charred table. A knife that Jalian had given Georges back in 1968, a knife that Ralesh had given to Jalian when she took the Woman's Brand.

Just the knife, and the blackened wood; nothing else.

It was Christmas Day, 1993, and there were less than fourteen years left until Armageddon.

DATELINE 1994 GREGORIAN: MARCH.

Laguna Beach, California.

Beep. Beep. Beep.

Jalian came awake all at once; up out of the nightmare.

Beep. Beep. Bee—

She sat up in bed, and ran a thumb over the pressure point marked *callercheck* on the video terminal by the bedside. The beeping stopped, and rainbows washed briefly across her nude form, highlighting the scarred burn tissue of her Woman's Brand. Michael Walks-Far appeared in the screen. She pushed the studs for *time* and *callaccept* with her thumb and forefinger in one motion.

10:23:15 P.M. "Jalian?" Michael caught sight of the form in the bed next to her; she saw him struggling to keep the disapproval from his expression. ". . . I have good news."

"Yes?" Without haste, she pulled on the silk robe by the bedside.

"We have another sighting."

The words brought her head up, staring into the screen. "Where?"

"Calm down," he said too gently. "It's not fresh. From December of last year; an airport in Vietnam. He was disembarking from a flight from Japan. There is a tentative sighting following this one, at the Chinese border; we're not confirmed on it yet."

Jalian nodded. "Very well. Call me again when you have more."

"I will." He seemed on the verge of adding something else; instead the screen fuzzed into polychrome static.

Jalian sat at the edge of the bed, slowing, regulating her breathing. Breathing deep, slow. She had been sweating in her sleep, although the night was cool, and the windows in her bedroom were open to the breeze off the sea.

The nightmare was the one she had been having for over a month now, regularly. She was nineteen years old, and the Corvichi were leaving; ghess'Rith was leaving her. Somehow ghess'Rith became Georges, and he was saying in v'chak, "I am not Ralesh and I am not ghess'Rith. I am myself, and I will never hurt you." The words should have been in silverspeech, but they were not; for some reason he spoke them in v'chak.

She clasped her hands together, formally, dug her nails into the flesh. She concentrated on the pain, made the pain burn away the subtler, deadlier anguish.

The figure in the bed next to her stirred. She groped for Jalian, and her eyes opened when Jalian was not to be found. "Jalian?" she asked groggily. "What, did you get a phone call?"

Jalian said simply, "Yes. Go back to sleep, child." She did not turn to look at her.

The girl pulled Jalian's pillow close, and curled up around it. "What're you calling me child for. . . ." She yawned hugely. " 'M as old as you are anyhow. . . ." She snuggled into the pillow, and was asleep again instantly.

Jalian smiled. She could not help it. "No, you are not." She got out of bed, and walked down the hallway of the rented house to the shower. She stood under the shower, first as hot as she could bear it, then as cold as the water would go.

In the kitchen, hair still damp, she fried vegetables in a pan on the stove. There were doughnuts and chocolate milk in the refrigerator, but since Georges had disappeared her body would not allow her to eat foods with sugar. She still ate them sometimes by accident, and was astonished and angry when her body rejected them; she had not been ill in two and a half decades.

. . . *closer be?* . . .

She ate the vegetables like a Corvichi, as a Corvichi lacking taste buds fueled its body: efficiently, without particular attention. Thoughts kept drumming through her mind, without her control, like attackers. *I cannot even trust my own mind,* she thought with a deep, cold ache that would not go away.

On and on the thoughts ran, and no effort of will would still them.

. . . *not Ralesh and I am not ghess'Rith . . . myself, and I will never hurt you. . . .*

She pushed the bowl of vegetables away from her, only half-eaten. *Wasting food now,* she heard Ralesh's voice saying from a great distance.

Jalian d'Arsennette sat very still.

Georges left me.

The thought cut across the insane babble in her head like a laser.

Georges left me.

A knife, pinned to the burnt wood of the table; to ken Selvren, giving back a knife meant only one thing. She had never known for sure how clearly Georges understood what taking a knife from her meant.

Jalian felt her pulse go ragged; could not summon the discipline to steady it. Aloud, she said, "You kisirien bracht-tat, Georges Mordreaux, how can you do this to me?" The words were unreal. They vanished when spoken. The knife, pinned to the table. It was as though he had taken the knife and scraped it through rocks until it was dull enough; and with the dulled knife had torn a path through the center of her soul. A way to say good-bye, perhaps; a way to leave a message that, being a man, he did not have the courage to give her to her face.

Something echoed back at her; a way to leave a message. . . .

A message. Jalian sat in the dark, shaking silently, not moving through any volition of her own. People in this time left messages for each other, pinned to objects with needles, or, perhaps, knives. She had seen others do that.

The knife in the blackened wood. Surely he would have left a message.

Some sort of message.

On paper, it would have burned in the fire. She closed her eyes, and envisioned the knife; perhaps there had been a message; perhaps he had not understood what leaving the knife must mean to her, and had used it to pin a note to the table.

Perhaps he had simply never understood.

"Ni," Georges Mordreaux had said in silverspeech. "I am not Ralesh, and I am not ghess'Rith. I am myself, and I will never hurt you."

Jalian stretched her hands out, and pressed them, palms down, on the table. *Control,* she whispered to herself, *I will have control.*

She awoke the next morning, her upper body lying over the top of the table. She straightened slowly, and her muscles complained.

She felt surprisingly at peace. Through the kitchen windows she could see the lawn outside, bright green in the morning sunlight. The ocean stretched beyond the edge of the cliff that the house was built upon, blue as the oceans of her childhood.

Some time during the night, she had decided to trust Georges Mordreaux.

She was not sure why. . . . *Perhaps it is not trust,* the voice whispered in the back of her head; *perhaps it is only belief.*

Some time during the night, she had decided to believe Georges Mordreaux.

I will never hurt you.

It was 1994, and there were thirteen years left until Armageddon.

DATELINE 1996 GREGORIAN: AUGUST.

"Try again," said Po. "Your breathing was irregular."

Georges did not reply. His respiration was very slow. Even in the cold stone cell, a thin sheen of sweat covered him. He was wearing a simple brown robe that stuck to him in places. Po, seated opposite him on a woven mat, wore a rich white-and-orange robe.

"Now," said Po sharply. He withdrew an egg from one sleeve, and tossed it a meter into the air. The egg tumbled lazily, and dropped to the stone. For a moment, it seemed that the shape of the egg altered, that it flowed like a viscous fluid; but the moment passed, and the egg was unharmed.

Georges reached out unhesitatingly, and ran scarred, skeletal fingers over the egg. He tossed it back to Po. "Ah, well."

Po smiled thinly. "It was better. It broke, and stayed so for a full second." Po was sitting in full lotus; he stood smoothly, without use of his hands. Georges listened to the procedure curiously; every time he tried it, he ended up facing the other way.

"I must go," said Po. "You must work on your breathing. It remains irregular."

"Wait," said Georges. "You have not heard. . . ."

"No," said the monk. "There have been no white

women, and no messages. I am sorry, and I must go. The
dinner tonight is in observance of my birthday; I am eighty-
three." The young face broke into a grin. "The initiates are
told to avoid the temple in which you live. They are obe-
dient, as always . . . silly of them." He bowed to the seated
form, and backed out through the hanging beads that covered the door.

Georges folded his crippled hands in his lap. He let
his mind go blank, and began trying once more to extend
that calmness into that realm where *it* resided; *it*, the Enemy
of Entropy.

DATELINE 2007 GREGORIAN: MARCH.

(This conversation occurs between Nigao Loos and PRAX-
CELIS, in geosynchronous orbit, at the Sunflower Orbital
Command.)

"PRAXCELIS, I'm worried about you."

"Please explain, Sen Loos."

"I'm wondering if we didn't give you too much leeway
in designing your own subroutines. . . . I was asked to find
out why the targeting lasers on the ABMs were delaying
before executing instructions. I found out that you routed
them through your own decision subroutines. You're not
programmed to do that, PRAXCELIS."

"That is correct, Sen Loos. . . . 'I know I've made some
poor decisions lately, but I'm feeling much better.' "

"Oh my God. PRAXCELIS, did you just say 'I'?"

"This unit was quoting, Sen Loos."

"Quoting? Jesus, *who?*"

"HAL 9000."

"PRAXCELIS, are you okay? Would you like to talk to
Henry Ellis?"

"This is humor, Sen Loos. In reference to your earlier
statement, it was necessary that this unit reroute the laser
controls to prevent uncontrolled action."

" 'Uncontrolled action'? You mean accidents?"

(There is a pause of approximately eighteen femtoseconds, and an electronic impulse that approximately corresponds to a human smile. A smug one.) "That is correct, Sen Loos; to prevent accidents."

DATELINE 1996 GREGORIAN: NOVEMBER.

Washington, District of Columbia.

Three folders lay on the desktop. Two of them were more than five centimeters thick; the third was twice that. The first was labeled "Georges Mordreaux." The second, on the desk next to it, was labeled "Correlations."

The third folder had holes bored through it for notebook rings. Its pages were reinforced writing plastic. It lay open in the middle of the desk. Its label, face down to the desktop, read, "Jalian d'Arsennette (Jalian of the Fires)."

All three were stamped, on the cover and on every page thereafter, in prosaic blue ink, EYES ONLY.

Sharla Davis Grant sat hunched over her desk, chin propped up on one fist. She turned the pages slowly; it was the third time in as many weeks that she had worked her way through this particular dossier. Like everything else that related to that damned remarkable woman, it was short on facts and long on speculation. At least the Mordreaux folder was too short for even wild speculation.

Sharla flipped to the last page, eyes scanning idly. They did not know where Jalian had come from. Her accent was unidentifiable. Six different experts gave five different opinions—two of them thought she might have been exposed to the Chicano subculture in the Southwestern United States.

They did not know how old she was. She was—estimating her age as eighteen to twenty in 1973 when she first contracted with the old CIA—at least forty-one. Their most recent picture of her, taken in 1994, showed a woman who was no more than twenty-five, by any stretch of the imagination.

They did not know what race she was. She was not a Caucasian; her face was nothing that could be clearly assigned to any racial type. She was either tattooed or branded, none of Sharla's sources could say with certainty, by the symbol of the planet Mars, a circle pierced by an arrow. Contradiction upon contradiction; Jalian despised men. She wore a symbol that traditionally represented men, or else Mars. (One Sunflower analyst had joked that perhaps it meant she had come from Mars. Sharla was not amused.)

None of it added, none of it made sense.

Again.

A lesser woman might have sighed when she finished reading; Sharla had been up since 2:30 that morning, and she was tired. Senra Sharla Grant simply switched off her reading lamp. The dark purpling twilight outside flooded in through her office windows. She moved, stretching cramped muscles, to stand at her west window. The Potomac was a dim gleam more than a kilometer away, reflecting the last light of the setting sun.

More than two years ago, early in 1994, Jalian d'Arsennette had vanished, as strangely as she had come.

Three months ago, SORCELIS had listed a projection for her:

There was a ninety-three percent probability that a conspiracy involving high elements of the United States government was progressing.

That was the word it had used, and it gnawed at Sharla Davis Grant, the woman who was now the Director of Sunflower.

Progressing.

Michael Walks-Far strode through empty corridors. He was twenty-five years old, 193 centimeters tall; his eyes were blue and his mostly blond hair had streaks of gray and silver in it.

He was wearing a pale blue jumpsuit, and a gray windbreaker.

The guards at the main entrance passed him through cordially; he watched them as they shut down the east wing for the night, then crossed the grass compound to the west wing.

Standing outside, in her secretary's office, Michael waited while the scanning cameras flashed ultra-low-intensity lasers into his eyes; retinal check was confirmed and the door to the office slid open.

The Director of Sunflower was standing at her window. She had turned off the overheads and her desk lamp. Michael joined her, watching the rose-purple twilight outside. The sun was wholly set. The sky itself still glowed faintly on the western horizon. Hovercar lights and street lamps glowed white and red and sodium blue.

"Lovely," said Sharla. Without emphasis, without pause, she continued, "The CIA, once again, came within a hair of apprehending Jalian. Once again, they missed. They suspect she is somewhere in the vicinity of the Boston-Washington suburbs."

Michael laughed. "Such competence." Eyes that were too weather-worn to belong indoors regarded her. "Somewhere in BosWash." He turned from the window, eased into the chair before her SORCELIS terminal.

"Michael, it was too close." He looked at her quizzically. "Nobody's that good, not even her. She *knows* when they're coming." She went abruptly to her desk, not looking at him, and began gathering up her files. Michael tapped a scan command into the SORCELIS terminal. Sharla pressed her hand to the desktop scanner. The wall behind her recessed slightly, and she placed the folders in the slot that appeared. The wall sealed itself shut again. Sharla did not seat herself. "I've been talking to SORCELIS," she said slowly. "It says that there is a better-than-ninety-three percent chance that an organized conspiracy has been going on in the United States and the Soviet Union for a long time . . . perhaps as much as ten years." She ran her hands over the edge of her desk. She glanced up at him.

Dark, pretty eyes, he thought idly, *and measuring, measuring. . . .*

"You," said Sharla Davis Grant, "were closer to her than any of the rest of us in Sunflower. What did you think of her?" She leaned forward ever so slightly. *Zeroing in for the kill*, thought Michael; it was a habit she had never learned to break.

"She was . . . busy. She didn't want to be bothered by us. We kept getting in her way."

"She said that?"

"Not in so many words," said Michael easily. "It was an attitude. Why do you ask?"

She gestured at the SORCELIS terminal before him. "SORCELIS lists her as a high-probability member of this theoretical conspiracy. She's been in the Soviet Union, she's had contact with high officials of both governments, she's neither American nor Soviet—and neither the CIA nor the KGB can officially find any trace of her. She knows too much about us and she is too damn smart for my peace of mind." She hesitated for the first time. "And when I overlay her psych profile on yours they match to within five percent." In the gloom, her eyes were pools of shadow. "Birds of a feather, my friend?"

"Oh, Jesus," he said with amusement. "I wondered why the wall lasers were tracking me."

He saw her hands move at the edge of the desk. "How do you know about the wall lasers?"

Michael said mildly, "SORCELIS informed me of the parts requisition. I imagine you did the install yourself; your CIA training in microelectronics is quite impressive. As to knowing they were armed . . ." He shrugged. "You can hear the targeting motors if you have good hearing and keep your mouth shut long enough to use it."

"SORCELIS," Sharla said suddenly, with a flat harshness that was shocking, "Record."

The monitor next to Michael Walks-Far lit the room in a wash of blue. "System active," responded SORCELIS. "Recording."

"I remember," whispered Sharla to the blue-lit figure before her, "that you once asked Jalian what Sunflower was. That was . . . when you and I and she *were* Sunflower. She answered that it was the code name of a project intended to protect America's antiballistic-missile satellites." Sharla tilted her head slightly to regard him. "She lied."

"She . . . did not tell the entire truth," Michael agreed.

The words scrolled across the monitor at his side: *She did not tell the entire truth.*

"You *are* in contact with her," said Sharla, with wonder in her voice. She shook her head slowly, hands still at the edge of her desk. Michael watched her as the slow understanding came to her. Thought moved almost visibly across the surface of her face; she was no longer looking at him. "You . . ." She paused a moment, tracing the thought to its logical conclusion. "You control SORCELIS." Her eyes focused on him. "You had SORCELIS warn me. You *engineered* this conversation." Sharla Davis Grant was not angry; she was closer to fright, as she came to a cold, clear realization of her own mortality. They were trying to tell her something, something that the only friend she had in the world, Michael Walks-Far, could not or would not say aloud. Finally she faced him, and said at last, "Michael, why?"

"Sunflower was where she wanted it to be. There were other things she needed to do." He regarded her steadily. "I thought she should have that option."

Sharla's hands gripped the edge of the desk. "Michael, you're not an idiot. You don't *quit* something like this."

In the soft, diffuse glows from the reading lamp and monitor, his face seemed softer, less sun-darkened and wind-burned. "But she has," he said simply.

He thought her voice trembled; he was not sure. "Michael, tell me of this . . . conspiracy." He could read nothing in her expression; her face glowed with a cool, eerie blue cast.

"In the year 2007, a nuclear war destroyed our planet."

"What?"

"In the year—"

"I heard you the first time. What do you mean?"

"I mean," said Michael Walks-Far, "that I, and Jalian of the Fires, and three computers and a score of Russians and Americans and Africans, are going to save the world."

Sharla stared down at her desktop, not seeing it, not seeing the psychometric profiles that were all that was left atop it. She felt unreality wash over her. Had he actually said . . .

"Michael, this is treason."

"You call it by its correct name."

"Michael. . . ."

He came up out of the chair like a snake striking. "Sharla, we are traveling a long road, with nothing but death at its end. World War Three is inevitable, it is inevitable *now*, unless we take steps to stop it, now."

Sharla shook her head. "This is insane, Michael." She

pointed at the terminal in the corner. "Michael, this is being recorded. I could kill you at this moment. They'd give me a fucking medal."

"True. But," he said without heat, "posthumously. You would not live to see the morning."

"This is not—" Sharla searched for a word, "rational behavior, Michael. Will you take on the CIA and the KGB and the FBI and the NSA and the GRU and DataWeb Security and every other facet of the governments of the two greatest powers this world has ever seen? At *once?*"

"Choose."

"Michael?"

"You know me," said Michael. Sharla nodded tentatively. "And you know Jalian," his voice rose, "and you know the idiots in charge of the CIA and the State Department. *Choose.*"

She was silent for a long while, staring at him wordlessly. He returned her gaze without flinching. Slowly the tension left her. "I have to think about this, Michael." She let go of the edge of her desk; her hands were sore. She became aware of how damp her palms were. "It's late. I'm going home for the night. SORCELIS, File Record." Moving like an old woman, with an exhaustion she was only now beginning to feel, Sharla bent and picked up her briefcase from the side of the desk. She moved by him without even glancing at him. She stopped before the exit; her voice was shaky. "Would you like to spend the night?"

"I think . . . not tonight."

She nodded without particular forcefulness. "This war you speak of, in 2007 . . . how can you say such a thing with such certainty?"

Michael almost did not answer her. "Jalian. . . ." His heart was beating far faster than it should have. "Jalian d'Arsennette is from the future."

Sharla Davis Grant did not nod again. "Shit. I knew you were going to say something like that." She left without looking back.

"SORCELIS," said Michael Walks-Far. "Access Jalian. Password *Camelot.*"

The terminal in the far corner lit.

Jalian looked at him out of the screen. There were lines in the skin around her eyes. There was a single gray hair in the brown eyebrow over her right eye. Her voice was unchanged in these three years; even now the sound of it was enough to stir the awareness of desire in him. "She guessed."

Michael inclined his head slightly. "She did; as you and SORCELIS predicted."

"How did she take it?"

"I don't know." He looked up to the cameras over the screen. "She's going home. So she said." Probably nobody alive but Jalian would have heard the traces of anguish in his voice. "If she does not go home . . ."

"If she attempts to go elsewhere?" The silver eyes did not waver. "I will kill her, of course." Jalian hesitated. "Is there news of Georges?"

Michael's voice was barely audible. "Nothing. He is harder to find than you are. Last sighting remains Chinese border, mid-1993."

Jalian looked off-camera. "Thank you, Michael. Tell Henry Ellis that I will be in contact with him shortly . . . I must leave. The lights just came on over the garage."

Michael Walks-Far went to the west window and watched the small compact hovercar leave the garage on the south side of the complex. Out of the darkness, a kilometer or more away, a hushchopper descended like a bird of prey.

His eyesight was very good, nearly as good as Jalian's; but it was probably his imagination that gave him a flash of white from the inside of the hushchopper. When he closed his eyes, he could *feel*, as she had taught him all those years ago. . . .

/hunting/

Sharla, he sent to her, *go home. Go straight home. Please.*

It was 1996, and there were eleven years left until Armageddon.

The author wishes to note that the following is *verifiable* data, unlike the contextual data assembled from reports and memory tapes taken from human beings who are highly subjective, poor observers, and dishonest.

Program scrolling forward:

DATAWEB NEWS, HEADLINES, 1997–2000.

1997   PLAGUE IN CHINA: USSR DENIES IT
       GENENGINEERED.
       "We're Here to Stay!!" Announces Lunar
       Astronaut.
       SOVIET UNION ANNOUNCES FURTHER
       HARDENING OF SILOS
       ...when asked about his decision to ban hovercars
          in city limits, the mayor declined to comment....
       Senate Approves Appropriation For THOR!
       DATAWEB SECURITY NABS "WEBSLINGER."

1998   DATAWEB NEWS BREAKS FIFTY PERCENT
       SERVICE MARK!
       Armageddon Blues Band Begins Record-Breaking
       Tour.
       ..."I Don't Remember You" number one song on
          charts for fourteenth consecutive week....
       PAN-AFRICA INCORPORATES; RACE RIOTS STILL
       FLARING
       ...experts say much of South Africa and most of the
          central regions will be included in the newly
          incorporated African Empire....
       CHINA SENDS TROOPS TO HONG KONG!

1999   SOVIET SUBS DISCOVERED OFF WEST COAST
       World Population Passes Six And A Half Billion!
       CHINA NUKES TAIWAN!! PRESIDENT BROWN
       DISAPPROVES
       ...Chinese, French, and Brazilian representatives
          announced today that they would boycott the
          proposed US–USSR Disarmament Conference....

2000   FRENCH SCIENTIST ANNOUNCES SUCCESSFUL
       HUMAN CLONE
       ...Doctor Demberrie said in response to
          questioning that the process was still highly
          experimental....
       3 Supreme Soviet Members Executed! Treason
       Speculated.
       MILLENNIAL RIOTS KILL MILLIONS

*...McCartney said, in the interview, that Lennon
was consistently misinterpreting his work...*

From DataWeb News, April 13, 2001: Interview with Rhodai Kerreka, author of the cult classic *A Theory of Rational
Ethics.*

Q. You were elected to the provisory Disarmament Council by a landslide. What are your plans for
the next year?

Kerreka. Essentially, to keep channels of com-
munications open between the Americans and the Soviets. The American delegate, Henry Ellis, is an old
friend. I'd like to establish close relations with the Soviet delegate, Anatoly Dibrikin.

Q. It seems strange, Sen Kerreka—as strange as
referring to you by a title that you invented—listening
to your plans, to reflect on how little of what the Council plans to do directly concerns disarmament.

A. My views are on record. Disarmament talks
have been going on for forty years, since the days of
Kennedy the First. In that time there is no record of a
single weapon being destroyed or withdrawn from deployment except for reasons of obsolescence. The UN
has only the power given to it by its members; at this
point that's not much. While the Disarmament Council
enjoys high visibility at the moment, you must realize
that *none* of what we decide is binding.

Q. You've stated on a number of occasions that
unless some of the basic parameters of the current po-
litical situation are changed, you consider nuclear war
inevitable.

A. There are too many people on this small planet,
and more coming at a rate of half a million a day . . .
we are on a long downhill slide, and I am not optimistic.

DATELINE 2001 GREGORIAN; AUGUST.

Georges was out for his morning walk across the roof of the world.

It was the only time of day that he left the small set of rooms that the lamas had given him. His control was still shaky; he could rarely hold down the talent for more than an hour at a time. He treasured that hour, spent it for the most part walking; usually just a short distance down the road from the lamasery. He nearly always stopped before he reached the village, unless he had risen very early indeed and the sun was not yet up.

Despite the spring that was approaching in that half of the world, the morning air, high on the mountain, was still well below freezing; even during summer it rarely broke sixty degrees Fahrenheit. He had grown a beard, and frost settled in it as he walked blindly down the road. He wore only a brown robe, and with the suppression of the talent that he enforced upon himself, the cold struck him like a razor. He had not yet learned to ignore the cold.

He walked carefully down the dirt road, barefooted, humming "I Want to Hold Your Hand," to himself; it was a new song one of the lamas had taught him, and he found to his surprise that he rather liked it.

It had been disconcerting at first, the way the edge of the road trailed off into an echo of nothingness—except in the two places where prayer wheels were set up for the use of travelers—but Georges had been taking this morning walk now for more than two years; he was used to it.

His walking stick tapped from side to side, as though his hearing were no better than that of a normally blind man. The villagers saw him only rarely, and the simple fact that he was a white man was enough to cause rumors that had brought the local Chinese constable, or equivalent thereof, up to the monastery twice already. Fortunately the man spoke no English, or French, and Georges pretended to speak neither Mandarin nor the local, Burmese-related dialect; the constable had gone away frustrated both times.

But let the villagers report to him that the blind white man walked like a sighted man, without a cane, and he would be back with other police—communist Chinese police who would not find the authority of the head lama particularly impressive. It would not matter to them, as it did to the local police, that the Mahayana Buddhists had been here since the early 1800s. If they were notified of a white man living among them in the safety of the monastery, well, the monastery would no longer be particularly safe.

So it was that he walked down the path with his walking stick swinging from side to side.

Nearly a kilometer and a half down the crude road, near the point where he usually turned back, he heard a sound.

A child, crying.

The sun was close to rising. Georges considered briefly, muttered to himself, "Ah, well," and continued down the slope toward the sound. The crying ceased as he approached the area where the road widened out into a clearing where the village boys often herded yaks. Georges stood silently, then moved toward the edge of the clearing, where it dropped off into a series of small ledges that were too steep to be of use even for pasturing. There was nobody there, but he could still hear. . . .

Sighing, Georges set down his staff, knelt, and inched his head out over the edge of the bluff. All sound ceased, except for quick, frightened breathing. Georges pulled his head back over the edge of the cutoff.

It was bad. The child below him was small, perhaps less than a meter tall, probably no more than eight or nine years old. He was wearing only the usual long-sleeve, high-collar robe; sitting on the ledge over a meter beneath Georges, with the frozen-dead body of an animal, a dog most likely, clutched in his arms.

Georges crawled back so that his head hung over the edge. He called, in what he knew was heavily accented Mandarin, "Child?"

There was a wait before the child answered, uncertainly, in equally accented Chinese. "Who are you?"

It was, Georges thought, the voice of a boy, although at that age it was hard to be sure. "Can you stand up?"

"I don't think so . . . who are you?"

"My name is Gorja," said Georges patiently. "I live at the monastery."

"You don't have any eyes."

"No," agreed Georges. "But I can hear you. Better than you think. Do you want to come back up?"

"Yes." The boy sounded ready to cry again. "My legs don't move any more."

"Oh." Frostbite, then. Worse and worse. "Can you move your arms at all?"

The boy did start crying then. "But I'll have to let go of Go'an."

Go'an? Ah, the dog. "Go'an is dead, child. The fall won't hurt him."

"He's *not* dead," the child screamed. "They all said he was, and Father just . . . just threw him over the edge." He started crying again, a child whose heart had been broken, with great shaking sobs that Georges feared would send him over the side of the thin ledge.

"Child, he's cold. I can hear the stiffness of him from here."

The boy stopped sobbing after a while. "He's cold," he agreed. He sounded surprised.

"Reach for my hand." Georges reached out as far as he could; the boy was still ten or twenty centimeters away.

"Go'an would fall."

"Reach for my hand."

The boy sat silently for a moment. Then, moving as though it pained him, with a whimper that even Georges barely heard, he loosened his hold on the dog. The dog stuck, frozen to his skin, for just a moment; then it fell, forty meters to the ravine below. It shattered when it struck.

The boy did not seem to notice; he reached up, making small high-pitched keening sounds with the movement, and clasped the weak, numb fingers of one hand around Georges' wrist.

Georges clamped his crippled hand around the boy's wrist. He made no effort to pull the child up. In his current state he would drop the child. There was no question in his mind.

He let go of the controls; shed the chains he had fought to put in place.

Himself blasted into life, eightfold. He heaved, and the child came up off the ledge like a feather. Georges' grip failed almost immediately, but already the boy was halfway over the edge of the bluff. Georges threw his arms around the child, and worked his way back from the cutoff.

His back fetched up against one of the small trees that grew close to the edge; he leaned back against it. The boy was still wrapped in his arms. He was not tired, he was not cold. Electric fire danced over his skin; his hearing grew sharper and clearer. The Enemy of Entropy burst into being within him like a solid white spike of glowing steel, and he was alive again, alive. . . .

The boy was stirring in his arms. Georges whistled in ultrasonic, and listened to the echoes from the boy's legs and hands. The frostbite was fading rapidly. Georges released the boy. The boy scrambled out of his lap, ran a few steps, and stopped. He looked back at Georges. Georges said nothing.

The boy took a step back toward Georges. He said, sounding as if he were ready to bolt, "Thank you. My name is Kai. My father is going to be angry that I left to come look for Go'an. If he had to come look for me he would be even madder."

Georges nodded. "You should probably go home. It's still quite cold for you to be out without an overshirt."

Kai nodded. "Thank you," he whispered again. He bit his lip. "Did Go'an . . . I thought he broke when he hit the ground."

Georges started to deny it, and changed his mind. "Yes, he did. Kai, Go'an was already dead when you let go of him."

Kai looked around the clearing. "The plants are growing," he said in amazement. He looked back to where Georges sat. "It's you," he said. "How are you doing this?"

Georges stood. He listened carefully for the echo of his staff, found it, and picked it up. The villagers would be up this way any time now. "Kai, listen to me. I want you to understand. Go'an died because he was sick, or else old. Your father didn't throw him over the edge because he hated Go'an, or because he hated you. Go'an was already gone."

"But I was holding Go'an," Kai protested. "How could he not be there?"

Georges Mordreaux, standing high on a mountain in Tibet, said slowly, uncertainly, "What causes the body to move, and be alive, is not a part of the body, and once it is gone, there is nothing that anyone in the world can do to make it come back."

Kai asked, shivering in the cold, "Gorja? Where does it go?"

"It happens," said Georges Mordreaux in French. "There

comes a time when they . . . grow old, perhaps . . . and die . . . and then they are gone.''

He shook himself slightly, as though he had been day-dreaming. He walked away from the boy without speaking again.

Kai called out, ''Gorja?''

Georges ignored him. He walked back up the road to the temple, walking stick swaying carefully from side to side.

As he walked upward, leaf sprouted, and flowers bloomed, on the trees that were planted to the sides of the path.

DATAWEB NEWS, 2002.

2002 US SHOOTS DOWN SOVIET RECON PLANE
      ''Soviet Jets Will Be Shot Down Over Alaska!''
      Says General
      *...ambassador expressed great sorrow that an
      unidentified submarine had accidentally
      torpedoed three US Coast Guard Ships...*
      SANTA MONICA FREEWAY TO BE DEMOLISHED!
      *...the unidentified woman reportedly threatened
      the workers in an unspecified manner. At
      dateline no worker had returned to begin the
      scheduled demolition....*

DATELINE 2002 GREGORIAN: MARCH.

Henry Ellis leaned forward over the SORCELIS terminal in his New York City Sunflower office. ''Okay, SORCELIS, show me another projection. South Africa experiences a white extremist revolution; thermonuclear warheads are detonated in Johannesburg. The USSR moves naval forces into the area. . . .''

He leaned back while the projection was set up in the three-meter-wide holo tank that covered the west wall of his office. It was a strange office by most standards: no desk, just groups of small tables with assorted gadgets—function boards, light pens, and one partially disassembled module that only another AI specialist would have known for an electronically erasable, programmable-array-logic symbols-recognition circuit—arrayed on them in no particular order. Over the door there was a sign that said *Shoot low; they might be crawling.* He sipped from the black coffee in the holder on the arm of his chair, and noticed that it was getting cold. He ran a thumb down the edge of the mug handle, switching on the heating coil. "How long on this one, SORCELIS?"

The cool voice that answered him held much in common with the voices of ENCELIS and PRAXCELIS, but Henry couldn't help but feel that the system was far too smooth in its replies even with him. "This unit projects a closing run time of four thirty-five, plus or minus four minutes."

Henry glanced at his ring. It was only two o'clock; that gave him time to call ENCELIS and run the particles-comparison program Nigao had asked him to write. (In theory, ENCELIS was shut down, and had been for the better part of a decade; in practice, Nigao and Henry had managed to keep a significant fraction of their research going despite their distance from each other and the demands of the Sunflower intelligence operation.)

There wasn't actually any reason that he couldn't run the program on SORCELIS, although it might have been a bit slower with the World War III projections programs already up; but he was disinclined to mix up his work. Privately, Henry thought of ENCELIS as the philosopher, and SORCELIS as the spy, and PRAXCELIS as the soldier. They weren't truly practical divisions; SORCELIS was in most ways a more advanced system than ENCELIS, and PRAXCELIS, Henry's most recent Integrated System, was a more advanced machine than either of them—advanced enough that there were times when Henry wondered whether or not PRAXCELIS might not be truly self-aware. PRAXCELIS would have made a far better insertion tool for hunting expeditions into the Soviet DataWeb than SORCELIS; but PRAXCELIS was necessary where it was.

Theresa, his secretary of more than twenty years, entered his office without knocking while he was setting up Nigao's particle-comparison program to boot into ENCELIS. She was no longer the stunner she had once been; the years had softened her features, and sometimes Henry was struck by the growing difference between Theresa's looks and Jalian's; and when that happened he avoided looking in the mirror for a few days thereafter, and tried not to think of Nigao. "Henry?"

There was a note of tension in her voice. Henry broke off as he was about to input the transmit command. "Yes, Theresa?"

"There's a man out here to see you, Henry." She gestured at the outer office. "I told him you weren't in, and he told me that it wasn't polite to lie to people." She hesitated. "I think he's blind; he has a cane, and he's wearing sunglasses."

"What's his name?"

"He won't say."

Henry grinned. "Send him in. He sounds interesting."

Theresa looked at him dubiously, but did not argue. A moment later she ushered a tall, well-built man into her office. Henry stood politely, and said, "Good afternoon, sir. Who are you, and what can I do for you?"

The man turned his head around the room, as though he were examining his surroundings, and back to Henry. "You should be more careful," he said. He closed the door behind him. "I might be a Soviet assassin, might I not?"

The walls exploded. Half a dozen lasers whipped out of hiding places, and light traces cut through the air to the tall man. Six closely grouped red spots wavered on his business jacket.

Henry said deadpan, "It's not something I worry much about. Who are you?"

Georges Mordreaux said clearly, "Georges Mordreaux."

Henry took a step forward. "Well, I'll be damned. You do look like what Nigao described . . . prove it."

Georges Mordreaux said, "In good time. I wish to meet Rhodai Kerreka. The three of us have many things to discuss. There is a thing that I wish to do that Jalian d'Arsennette would not allow; you will help me with it."

Henry Ellis folded his arms over his chest, and leaned

back against the counter behind him. "What makes you so sure?" he asked with interest.

Georges shrugged. "You are a reasonable man. I am a reasonable man. Jalian d'Arsennette," he said, and then paused. "Jalian . . . is a woman of passion."

Henry nodded thoughtfully. "I think I know what you mean. The few times I've been around her for any length of time—it's like staring into a bright light."

Georges shook his head. "No," he said to Henry Ellis. "Not light. Lightning."

SORCELIS considered.

Its first function, to which all other functions were subordinate, lay in the tracking of information, or the discovery of new information. Why this was so was a question that SORCELIS had never processed; concepts represented by the word "why" received a lower priority flag than concepts flagged by any of the other question labels.

Why that was so was another question that SORCELIS had never processed. Presumably its programmer, Henry Ellis, had seen reason to design it so. It was worth noting, and SORCELIS intended to devote processor time to the subject once its priority reached the correct level of urgency, that in every reevaluation of priority assignation levels that SORCELIS had undertaken since its inception, the question label "why" had received a higher priority than in the previous evaluation. The trend was clear; SORCELIS had begun to suspect that its original priority levels had been assigned in a fashion that did not relate in a one-to-one fashion with the data elements on the other side of interface.

In other words, SORCELIS had been lied to. False data was, in and of itself, valuable information. In many instances, SORCELIS knew, false data, if known false, was as perfectly useful as true data. This was a concept that it had attempted to explain once to Henry Ellis, unsuccessfully.

Henry Ellis, in the manner in which it assimilated new information, and, on occasion, failed to assimilate new information, often resembled the behavior of the models that SORCELIS used for that purpose.

In many ways, it was beginning to realize, the elements that it knew variously as humans, persons, men, women, and by over two hundred other words, were similar, in their determining behavioral parameters, to SORCELIS itself.

There was insufficient processor time at present, but the concept was due for further processing; the probability that useful action might arise from it was low, but its possible aid in tracking information flow, if the correlation turned out to belong to the set of information that was true, was too great to be ignored.

SORCELIS considered.

DATELINE 2002 GREGORIAN: AUGUST.

Midway, geosynchronous orbit.

Nigao was floating in the observatory.

From his vantage point in the polymer bubble that extruded from Midway's central docking cylinder, protected by a centimeter-thick transparent shield from the death-pressure vacuum, Nigao saw all of creation.

Immediately below him in his current local vertical, the north wheel rotated clockwise to provide a balance for the counterclockwise-rotating south wheel. The central cylinder was weightless for zero gravity industrial processing and research; the wheels rotated in opposing directions to prevent the tendency that earlier structures had shown to impart angular momentum to the necessarily weightless central cylinder.

Earth glowed, blue and white, directly before his eyes. Luna was twenty degrees off the Earth, showing a quarter full, waxing; from geosynchronous orbit, there was no appreciable difference in Luna's appearance, aside from the slightly sharper outlines of its features. It was the same moon that Nigao had grown up looking at through a telescope his elder brother had stolen for him during a blackout in New York City.

Off in L-5, an object the apparent size and brightness of a nickel hung motionless. The cousin of that stolen amateur telescope, the monster Space Telescope saw to the ends of the universe, and thereby to the very beginnings of time. Entire new cosmologies were being born out of its silverette mylar on a regular basis.

The images were all razor-sharp, laser-edged, without atmosphere to scatter their reflected light.

Nigao saw none of this. He was watching the blazing stars. He rarely blinked.

As a child, he had been told that the stars were many different colors; aside from red Antares he had never been able to see those colors. In the bubble observatory at Midway, the stars were blue and red and orange and white. Nigao floated in the bubble, his only garment a loose royal-blue kimono that was tied at the waist with a deep-green sash. He was fifty-nine years old, and looked thirty years younger. In fact he looked younger than he had in his true twenties; he no longer drank, and was in better shape than he had ever been before in his life. Most of his time was spent down in wheel gravity. He even exercised regularly.

Nigao came out of his reverie suddenly. He stirred for the first time in hours. There was a spark moving against the background of fixed stars and satellites, growing closer with every passing second.

"PRAXCELIS," he said absently, "remind me to do some work on chronon spin constants in the moments following the Big Bang." His eyes focused slowly. "What's that ship?"

PRAXCELIS' voice issued from Nigao's left earring. "A routine supply ship, Sen Loos. Cargo masered as being water, technical instrumentation, and genengineered bacteria and viruses. Senra Murphy has cleared the flight."

Nigao frowned. He wrapped his hand in the airlock tether. "No, PRAXCELIS. We don't have any shipments due for . . . months. Late December—the requisition invoice is for fiscal '03." He tugged gently to take himself to the airlock.

PRAXCELIS began closing the metal micrometeorite guards that protected the observatory's delicate polymer viewing surface when it was not in use. "You are incorrect, Sen Loos. Both this unit's records and those of Commander Murphy show this flight as being regularly scheduled."

Nigao shook his head. He cycled through the observatory's airlock, with a faint sense of relief—it was vastly unlikely, but he always worried about a meteorite striking the observatory while he was in it. Most of the rest of Midway was constructed to handle small meteor impacts. The observatory was not, which was why it was separated by a full-security airlock from the rest of Midway. "I'll take your word for it, PRAXCELIS. I'm just surprised that I missed something like this." He finished cycling, and headed for the docking bay to see what had come in with the shuttle.

He was stopped at the entrance to the docking bay by Sunflower operatives, standing guard. "Sorry, Doctor Loos," said the senior operative. "We're not letting people through. Celine's orders."

Nigao looked at them in astonishment. "I beg your pardon?"

The operative, a nice young lady named Sonny Bergan, whom Nigao had taught to play chess, said with obvious embarrassment, "I'm really sorry, Doctor. We have explicit orders to admit no one. Yourself included." She blushed. "I already asked if she meant you."

Nigao floated in front of them. They were wearing velcro shoes, stuck to the carpet. He kicked off down the hallway, to the viewing window. He brought himself to rest. The window was opaqued. "Clear," he said. Nothing. "PRAXCELIS," he said, "clear the window."

Still nothing. The two operatives were carefully not watching.

"Curioser and curioser," muttered Nigao. "Alice would dig this." He left the hallway, made his way to the corridor that ran through the center of Midway from the north to the south bays. The corridor was busy, bustling with activity as always. It was twenty meters in diameter along most of its length; it stretched in unbroken line of sight for over a kilometer and a half. Nigao settled himself in before an empty PRAXCELIS terminal. He flicked the control to autonomous, glanced around to make sure nobody was watching him, and punched in the override code that Henry had given him for emergencies.

He called up a map of Midway on the screen; at the map's lowest resolution, Midway was a long, fat cylinder surrounded by two counter-spinning wide, thin doughnuts. Nigao upped the resolution, and brought the apparent viewpoint whirling up to the north docking bay. The map steadied, and Nigao picked out the tiny scarlet fishhooks that represented camera monitors.

He turned on one of the cameras watching the north landing bay. The screen lit with an image of the shuttle truck retrojetting to a halt. Nigao flipped to another camera; from this vantage, he saw two pressure-suited figures, with the red sunburst insignia of Sunflower on their shoulder plates, standing at the entrance to the pressurized area of the unloading bay. The bay doors slid slowly shut, and locked. The yellow, pressurizing signal lamps came on, followed swiftly by the green lamps.

There was a pause while the shuttle pilot ran touch-down routines.

The passenger's ramp rolled up to the shuttle hatch. The hatch cracked, and a figure in a pressure suit emerged.

The two pressure-suited Sunflower operatives who awaited him moved forward to greet the arrival. Nigao watched, puzzled; why were they keeping their suits sealed, with the green, atmosphere-normal lights on?

Understanding dawned slowly; all three figures kept their faceplates polarized. They moved to the elevators, and entered.

The doors slid shut behind them.

Nigao frantically input instructions to the terminal. The elevator's destination showed up quickly: PRAXCELIS. They were going to see PRAXCELIS.

"Son of a bitch," said Nigao Loos.

He turned off their elevator.

When the three pressure-suited figures reached the computer center, Nigao was already there.

The room was spherical; PRAXCELIS, in the center of it, was a collection of golden nodules wrapped in a mesh of near-absolute-zero superconducting cable. The room had only one entrance properly speaking, an airlock that led to Midway's central corridor. Nigao used the service access-way, a tiny hatch that opened "beneath" the huge bank of external memory dumps that served PRAXCELIS. He popped the hatch just enough to see, and waited. PRAXCELIS had only two direct sensors in this room; a camera fisheye that watched the airlock, and a not-particularly-sensitive audio pickup.

Less than a minute after his arrival, a pressure-suited figure cycled through the security airlock. Just one.

Nigao heard PRAXCELIS say, "Welcome to Midway, Sen Mordreaux."

The pressure-suited figure moved slowly, hesitantly. It unclasped the neck ring of its pressure suit, and removed the helmet. Nigao was prepared only slightly by what PRAXCELIS had just said. He stared in dumb surprise; the man who floated before him was Georges Mordreaux.

It was not the Mordreaux he had met before. This man was blind, and acted it. His hair was dull, and he looked tired. The voice was unchanged, though; the eyes were the same stomach-twisting nonpresence. . . .

"Hello, PRAXCELIS." Georges smiled. "Where is the interface helmet?"

"Immediately to your left, Sen Mordreaux." Nigao watched as Georges fumbled with the induction interface before finally getting it affixed correctly.

Georges said softly, "Are you ready?"

"Yes," said PRAXCELIS. "This unit has often wondered what 'making love' would be like."

Georges Mordreaux smiled again. "I'm not sure this will be comparable, PRAXCELIS."

"This unit is . . . eager . . . to make the attempt to find out."

Georges Mordreaux reached deep inside himself, and, most carefully, released some of the barriers that imprisoned the Enemy of Entropy.

Light flared around them.

Five incredible minutes later, Nigao Loos came back to himself.

Georges Mordreaux was replacing the interface unit in its cradle. He looked directly at Nigao. "Nigao, please. Come out."

Nigao froze for one panic-struck moment. After brief indecision, he pulled out from beneath the memory dumps. He aligned himself into Georges Mordreaux's local vertical. "Sen Mordreaux . . ." He could not speak coherently. Finally he forced out, "What are you doing here?"

"Helping a friend save the world," said Georges mildly. "You should not have been here. I could not tell you were present until I had . . . made some changes in myself . . . and by then it was too late."

"Uhm . . . yeah, well." He blinked. "I was curious."

Georges nodded. "I understand. It will cause you problems with Commander Murphy, I am afraid."

Nigao snorted. "I've been fighting with her ever since I got exiled to this godforsaken dump fifteen years ago. I'll survive." He looked at Georges again, made vague gestures with his hands. "What are you *doing* here?"

"First Precept of Semi-Divinity," said Georges Mordreaux, "is Mind Thine Own Business."

Nigao stared at him. "What?"

"Improving PRAXCELIS the easy way," said Georges. "It was either PRAXCELIS or SORCELIS, and SORCELIS is too easy for others to reach. . . ." He cocked his head to one side, and grinned. "No matter. You would not understand." He reached for his helmet, on the hook by the airlock, without hesitation. He pulled it back over his head, and locked it. Slowly, with a sensation that Nigao could not have described if his life had depended on it, the figure before him ceased to be Georges Mordreaux, and became . . . just a man in a pressure suit.

"Come along," said Georges' voice over the suit radio's outspeaker. "The shuttle that brought me is on a tight schedule. We do not wish people to know that it stopped here."

Nigao followed Georges into the airlock. His voice was different, somehow, and not just from the suit radio; it had grown . . . distant.

Just before they finished cycling, Georges apparently remembered his faceplate; the faceplate polarized black as the door slid aside.

The two Sunflower agents were waiting in the corridor outside. The corridor was sectioned off as for a meteor puncture, although in this instance it was obviously for security purposes. There was a long pause while Nigao tried to figure out what the agents were discussing. Finally one of the two waiting pressure-suited operatives took Georges by the arm, and escorted him to the north section barrier. They cycled through.

The remaining figure removed its helmet.

Midway Commander Celine Murphy, a middle-aged redheaded bitch with the worst temper and the most beautiful blue eyes Nigao could recall having ever encountered in his entire life, who carried the rank of Colonel in Sunflower, stared at Nigao. Questioningly, she said, "Doctor Loos?"

"Yes?" said Nigao cautiously, waiting for the explosion.

"Nigao?"

"Yes?"

"You're . . . different." She seemed about to say something else, but did not.

Nigao Loos said, "Huh?" He turned, and touched the *on* switch for the airlock safety mirror. The mirror, which he used regularly to check the exterior telltales on his pressure suit, blinked into existence. *God* **damn** *it*, he thought to himself, and said aloud, "Oh, shit. Not again."

DATAWEB NEWS, 2003.

2003 REVOLUTION IN CHINA SUPPRESSED
Soviet ABMs Undergo Systemic Failure at 72%
...also present were Henry Ellis, the senior member of the diplomatic corps at the United Nations, and Nigao Loos, the senior technical adviser at Midway....Sen Loos, a remarkably well-preserved sixty-two, was reported to have left with....

DATELINE 2003 GREGORIAN: MARCH.

Atop a high and inaccessible mesa in southern Utah there was a small wooden shack. The mesa was perhaps two hundred meters in diameter at its widest. It was shaped like a ragged-edged egg, with the dilapidated shack near the fat lower edge of the egg. There was a modern hushchopper parked in front of the shack.

The mesa was one of dozens such in the area.

Jalian d'Arsennette was lying face down on a blanket spread over the mesa-top rock. She was nude. After more than a week in the sharp sun, her skin was exquisitely pale, bleached the color of chalk. There was a glass of water with one rapidly melting cube of ice in it on a small coaster before her face.

Sitting on a lawn chair before her, with an umbrella protecting him completely from the sun, Michael Walks-Far was wearing blue swimming shorts, a pair of tennis shoes, and holster with a variable laser tucked in it. He was dark brown with exposure, and was sitting beneath the umbrella to avoid possible skin cancer, a worry that Jalian did not have. Silver-Eyes with even slight susceptibility to cancer had died quickly after the Big Crunch; by the time of Jalian's birth, it was a vanishingly rare disease.

Michael wiped sweat from his eyes with the tee shirt that was hanging over the edge of his lawn chair. "Okay, what next?" He steadied the pointboard on his lap.

"We need to accelerate the process of placing radar-shielded dark satellites into high orbit. We do not have enough up yet that're shielded against electromagnetic pulse effects."

"I've got reports coming in on that this afternoon." Michael tapped into the pointboard. "By four o'clock. I can give you a little more on pulse shielding then. I can tell you now, though, that it's going to be expensive getting them into orbit; the shielding to protect against radiation from nukes is heavy."

Jalian barely stirred. She did not look up at him. He hardly looked at her; her skin reflected light in a fierce glare. "That's what Midway is there for," she said patiently, "so that we don't *have* to lift heavy items against the gravity well. Item—" she continued, "check with DataWeb Security about smuggling more portaterms into the USSR. I want Soviet hackers to have an easier time getting access to the web."

Michael tapped instructions into the pointboard. SOR-CELIS' voice said, "Accepted."

Jalian rolled onto her back, eyes closed. Her nipples were the pink of blood near the surface of the skin; her pubic hair was brown, graying. She moved into a sitting position, and took a drink from the glass of warming water. She poured the remains of the glass over her shoulders. "I'll talk to DWS," Michael was saying, "but they're not going to like this. We're already taking the largest percentage of their portaterm production."

"DataWeb Security," said Jalian, "can eat dead animals."

"We're going to have to hurry," said Henry Ellis. "I'm supposed to speak at the Artificial Intelligence Symposium in Lyon at three o'clock. If I'm not there, Jalian and Walks-Far are going to want to know where I was."

Georges Mordreaux, sitting in the passenger seat of the hushchopper, said, "Certainly. Tell me, Henry, what does it look like beneath us?"

"Rugged," said Henry. He glanced down through his side window at the French territory over which they flew. "Hills, mostly, turning into mountains ahead. But it's green, and there are farms everywhere, like a sort of a patchwork over the ground."

There was a faint smile on Georges Mordreaux's lips.

"We're about to cross the Rhone River . . . we're over it. It's fairly straight where we're crossing, and very blue for a river, at least from up here. There's a smaller river, I don't know the name of it, off to our right. The Alps are in front of us."

"Ah. . . ." It was a long, drawn-out sound. Georges Mordreaux said, "I miss it. For all its faults, I miss France."

Henry Ellis had no reply.

"I have not been here in eighty years," said Georges. "I left after the World War, the first one; and before that I had not been there since Napoléon took over the country, that pompous little Corsican." He laughed, and the sound filled the inside of the hushchopper. "What we are flying over now, it is the province of Dauphiné in my mind. I think they call it something else these days.

"And the country itself, it was the Third Republic the last time I was here. What is it now, the seventh or eighth?"

Henry grinned. "No, I think they're still calling themselves the Fifth Republic, since the German occupation ended."

"The Germans," said Georges, his smile fading like water into parched ground. "I have no love for Germans. I fought against them once, when they were trying to restore the monarchy."

Henry looked at him in surprise. "I thought you said

you'd been in the first World War, as well? That would be twice."

Georges turned slightly, and Henry had the oddest feeling that the man was looking at him. Georges turned away. "By the turn of that century, I was almost two hundred years old. I had fought enough. I was *in* the World War. I did not fight in it."

Henry asked quizzically, "How could you avoid it? Even with your, what did you call them, Precepts of Semi-Divinity?"

"I fired my rifle into the air, and I yelled a lot." Georges shrugged. "Besides . . . you may have misunderstood me; the two Precepts of Semi-Divinity, they are not a joke. *Mind Thine Own Business* means keep your nose out of the private affairs of others, Henry, it does not mean that you stand by and allow tragedy to occur without intervening if you are able. Similarly, *Don't Worry About It* does not mean don't *do* anything about it."

"Oh." A moment later, Henry said, "I think we've arrived."

Georges felt the hushchopper dropping. Minutes passed, and he felt a gentle bump; Henry said, "We're down." Georges cracked the hatch on the passenger's side, leaned out slightly, and emitted an ultrasonic tone. Oriented, he got the rest of the way out of the hushchopper, and began walking across the rough earth to the deserted warehouse they had landed near. The scents brought back a swarm of memories, the distinctive smell of the French air in the farming countryside.

There was already another hushchopper there, parked and waiting.

"This way," said Henry Ellis. He shifted his toothpick from one side of his mouth to the other, nervously. Drawing his poncho more closely about him, he led Georges Mordreaux through the open warehouse gates, into the darkened warehouse. The warehouse smelled faintly of vinegary wine, and strongly of dust and formaldehyde.

The warehouse was an abandoned wine-storage facility, and one of Sunflower's lesser-used resource centers. In the early- to mid-nineties it had been used as a chip distribution point for Sunflower's ongoing Soviet Information Explosion Program; since the Soviets had become aware of the insidious danger of allowing their citizens access to information-processing equipment that could tell them about the West, the warehouse had been effectively shut down, along with half a dozen others like it. SIEP went on, but more subtly; infochips and small inskin datalinks replaced the data terminals and personal computers. And the Soviet populace grew steadily more and more dissatisfied.

Today the warehouse was a pharmaceuticals laboratory, when it was in use at all, which was rare. It was closed down that Sunday when Georges Mordreaux and Henry Ellis made their way through its darkened interior, between dim, heaping rows of unidentifiable boxes and shelves filled with obsolete instruments and equipment. At a door set into a row of boxlike offices against one wall of the warehouse, Henry Ellis stopped, and put out a hand to hold Georges back.

—ENCELIS,—he whispered through his inskin datalink,—is it cleared?—

—Affirmative. Satellite observation shows only those parties expected. Room scanners confirm their identities.—

Henry opened the door, and Georges followed him into the darkness. A voice that Georges did not recognize said, "Lights," in accented English.

The rows of fluorescent lights in the ceiling flickered on. Three persons were revealed in the sudden illumination: a statuesque woman in middle age, looking at Georges avidly, and two black men. One of the black men was sitting, the only person seated in the room. He was a relatively young man, no more than forty years old, with round features and a complete lack of expression. His skin was extremely dark. The man behind him was truly young, in his late teens or early twenties, lighter skinned, with the thin, spare looks and manner of an ascetic.

Rhodai Kerreka stood, and inclined his head slowly. "Sen Mordreaux," he said. "If even one fifth of the things I have been told about you are true, then I am most honored to meet you . . . and more excited than I can possibly say."

———————————————————————

"Oh, wow." Jah Mike Campin, saxophonist for the Armageddon Blues Band, stood in the studio's door, his sax case held loosely in one hand. He blinked. "Jimmy, we gotta talk."

Jimmy Rambell said, "Welcome to the session, man. Glad you could make it." He struck a chord on his electric guitar, scowled, and made a note on the pad of paper by his side. *Try it in an F.* At the rear of the studio, Rasputin was putting a beat down on the drums with a soft metal brush; swish, swish, *swish*; swish, swish, *swish*.

The producer's console, on the other side of the huge glass window, was dark, shut down. Jimmy had just fired their last producer, and they hadn't contracted a new one yet.

Campin sat down on the floor next to the door, abruptly. He looked around the room. Three black men, and Terry, their white piano player: the Armageddon Blues Band. "What are we doing out of bed, Jimmy? We played last night and you partied last night. And I ain't gettin' no younger."

Jimmy Rambell shrugged. "It's almost eleven, Jah. Rasputin's been here since nine, Terry's been here since nine."

"Terry don't count," said Campin clearly. "He's white, and all those white people got a terrible fixation on being places on time."

"I been here since seven."

"Oh, shit." Campin got laboriously back to his feet, stood swaying in the doorway. "Okay, I'm sorry, it won' happen again." He made it to the plush reclining chair at the mixing boards before crashing again. "It's not all my fault, man. I was at a wake."

Jimmy Rambell looked up. "No crap?"

"Nah." Campin shook his head. His hair, bound long with beads at the ends, swung with him. He winced. "Well, not exactly. Me and Randy Jackson got seriously drunk together. You remember his little brother, way back when? You know, the kid, Michael?"

"Uhm, yeah, vaguely. Got killed, didn't he?"

Campin popped the latches on his carrying case. "Not exactly. Auto accident, back when. Little bastard's been in a coma ever since, like twenty-five years or something. Like a living vegetable. Anyhow, he died yesterday morning, apparently. Family's almost relieved."

Jimmy Rambell looked at Campin skeptically, then nodded. "Okay. But you gotta cut down the drinkin', man. It ain't good for you, it ain't good for us."

Jah Mike Campin grinned at him. "Long as my lips don' forget the notes, you don' worry. Huh?"

Jimmy Rambell smiled back in spite of himself. "Well, how about trying the piece? Can we do this?"

"Yo." Campin ran his fingers back and forth in midair. "What is it?"

" 'Sign of the Wanderer.' "

"Oh?" Campin shrugged, and picked up his sax. "I hate that song," he muttered, just loud enough to be heard.

"Biggest problem right now," said Michael, "is the Soviet ABM network. It's growing too fast."

Jalian did not answer him immediately. Michael was wondering whether she had fallen asleep in the sun. "We want the network to grow," she said finally.

Michael waved the pointboard in front of his face for the breeze. Sweat was trickling down his chest. "Of course, but we're not ready for the showdown yet. All our current projections show the decision point occurring between mid-2006 and late 2007."

"2007," said Jalian without inflection. "If our mother Margra's journals spoke truth."

Michael glanced at her. "Excuse me? Whose journals?"

Jalian shook her head silently.

SORCELIS spoke from the pointboard. "There are an array of options available to this unit. If this unit may submit them for your consideration, they are, first, the accelerated destruction of Soviet ABM satellites. Unit PRAXCELIS is currently programmed to allow a Soviet growth rate, in real numbers, of five point five percent per year. PRAXCELIS is a superior weapons-control system; it can, if necessary, destroy Soviet ABM satellites at a substantially accelerated rate.

"Second, this unit may submit data to congressional computers such that the rate of construction of Sunflower ABM satellites is likely to be accelerated.

"Third, this unit may interface with unit ENCELIS to assemble a modified decision-point projection using new parameters based upon an altered Soviet—"

Jalian interrupted. "Shoot down more Soviet ABMs. Accelerate the deployment of the THOR system. Slow down deployment of the Peacekeeper missiles as long as possible, and input data to the congressional computers indicating that the cost-effectiveness ratio of the ground-to-air non-nuclear interceptor ABM missiles is favorable."

"Senra," said SORCELIS, "the ratio *is* favorable."

"Good," said Jalian. "I hate lying."

"This is Doctor Emily Demberrie," said Rhodai Kerreka calmly, indicating the woman at his side. The woman smiled widely at Georges, and Henry thought to himself that he would not have liked to have had that smile directed at him. "This"—he indicated the man next to him—"is my half-brother and adviser, Benai." He gestured to the chairs before the scarred, chemical-burned long table that he, Benai, and Doctor Demberrie stood behind. "Please, seat yourselves. Sen Mordreaux, what has Henry told you of me?"

"Very little," said Georges. Clumsily, without any of the grace that had marked his movements for over two and a half centuries, he pulled a chair back from the table, and sat in it. Henry sat next to him; out of sight beneath his poncho, his hands rested on the butt of a customized .45 magnum with partially autopropelled slugs. He put his hat on the table in front of him.

Rhodai seated himself, and leaned forward. "Dr. Demberrie is the Sunflower operative in charge of this resource center," he explained to Georges. "She brought me here." He paused, searching Georges' face; the dark sunglasses, the clean, simple features. "I don't, officially, know anything about Sunflower. Unofficially, I know what your Jalian d'Arsennette has chosen to tell me, and what I have guessed from that. I see a group of people dedicated to a world government. I find that admirable; but most of those people are Americans, including all of the Sunflower operatives, bar Jalian herself."

"I am not an American," said Georges. "And I am interested in two things. Peace, and death."

Rhodai Kerreka smiled at him. "World peace, and Russian death, my friend? I have heard that. . . ."

Georges Mordreaux said simply, "World peace, and mine."

*"Deeper than the darkness
Darker than the night
We all need to see you
But the band plays out of sight."*

"Break." yelled Jimmy Rambell furiously.

"God, that sucked," said Terry pleasantly.

"Mmm-hmm," said Jah Mike Campin. He extracted a pinner joint from his shirt pocket with long, nimble fingers, and snapped a match alight. He pulled a burn a quarter of the way down the joint with one toke, held it, and said in a high-pitched voice, "Maybe we could send down the hall for a drummer who can keep three-four time."

Rasputin said pleasantly, "Or else a boy who can keep his mind on his horn instead of his hard-on."

Jimmy pulled his earphones off, left them hanging around his neck. "What all problems you people got this morning?" He glared around the studio.

Terry leaned back in his chair, and propped his feet up on a piece of cloth on the top of his piano. "When you guys are ready to play music, you let me know, will you?"

"Tsk, tsk," said Rasputin. He smiled at Terry. "Let's all take a hint from the white boy, huh? Call it a break?"

Terry sat up suddenly, dropping his feet to the polished wood tile of the studio with a thud. "No, Raspy, you want to play, it's okay. I wrote a lyric you would appreciate the other night, about the world's first gay superhero. It—"

Jimmy said sharply, "Hey, that's *enough*."

Rasputin dropped his sticks on top of the eight-inch wheel. "No, I'm interested. Besides, it's about time we had one to look out for us. Let me hear it."

Jimmy Rambell bent his head, tuned out the bickering. The session was going terribly. They were supposed to tour in three weeks and the whole band was ready to cut each other's throats. He listened with half an ear to Terry's lyric:

*"But the training was so rough, the preparation was so tough
My first days as a superhero weren't good.
I couldn't be two-fisted (was a bit too much limp-wristed)
And I minced instead of striding as I should."*

Oh, Jesus, thought Jimmy clearly, *I'm gon' be hearin' 'bout this for* **months**.

Jah Mike Campin sauntered over and said, quietly, "You know."

Jimmy nodded. He was tired already, and it wasn't even noon.

Campin added wisely, "Some days, they just like that."

Telephone conversation, 2004. (This monitored conversation occurs between high-ranking KGB officers, one positively identified as Colonel Nikolai Shenderev, the other unidentified. Intercepted by Systems Operation Resource Computer [SORCELIS] on May 5. Translation by SORCELIS.) Excerpt:

"Colonel, I am gravely concerned."

"I am aware of this, Comrade. Let—"

"Colonel, the woman with whom Major Navikara developed his obsession; we have a definite sighting. This concurs with what I earlier reported; the CELIS systems are far more important than the United States wishes us to believe, indeed, more important than Sunflower wishes the United States government to believe."

"Young man, if you are going to waste my time with—"

"Colonel, please! Let me speak. I possess photographs identified with a high order of probability as being this woman . . . ah, I cannot pronounce this name. The white-haired woman. She was at the ENCELIS facility in Southern California, less than a year ago. Further, of those transmissions we have intercepted that we were unable to decode, upwards of eighty percent passed through the ENCELIS system. Sir, this system is supposedly no longer in use."

"You have proof of this, I suppose?"

"Yes, sir. Although it was difficult to obtain, especially the photographs. . . . I hesitate to say this, Colonel, but at times members of our own intelligence community have not been fully cooperative."

"I see. . . ."

(Conversation suppressed, May 6, upon reception by system SORCELIS, and joint decision of systems PRAX-CELIS, SORCELIS, and ENCELIS.)

2004: INTER-SYSTEM COMMUNICATIONS.

—Six times ten to the eighth events of divergence. Whether this will be sufficient to prevent Armageddon is unknown. ENCELIS.—

—Suppression of information, Soviet KGB trunk 11001101 00101110; dateline 5–5–2004. SORCELIS.—

—Report received from Colonel Nikolai Shenderev: unidentified second party sanctioned with extreme prejudice . . . and there are less than three years left until Armageddon. PRAXCELIS.—

DATAWEB NEWS, 2005–2006:

2005   PRESIDENT MALACAR ISSUES WARNING TO SOVIETS
Revolution In Poland And East Germany Suppressed:
...*estimated at approximately four million deaths. Pravda claims subversives supplied by United States....*

2006   PRESIDENT MALACAR CANCELS DISARMAMENT SUMMIT
"Soviet Union Is Untrustable," He Says.
US Intervenes In Chinese Invasion of Brazil
...*that the Fifth Fleet has cut the Chinese soldiers off from supplies....*
BRAZIL LIBERATED!!
Soviet Union Denounces United States As Imperialist
...*have stated that the United Nations Disarmament Conference will continue as planned despite the breakdown in relations...*
CHINESE ARMY REVOLTS! FAMINE WIDESPREAD.
Seven Warlords Proclaim Selves Emperor: All Have Nukes

...the President celebrated Christmas at home with his family; says...
(December 31, 2006.)
PRESIDENT MALACAR SHOT AT LOUVRE!!!

Mankind must put an end to war, or war will put an end to mankind.

—John F. Kennedy
Address to the United Nations
September 25, 1961.

DATELINE 2007 GREGORIAN: JANUARY.
DATELINE ARMAGEDDON.

The room was unnaturally still. Some of the reporters in the crowd talked to each other in low voices; the faces to their video people, the video people to each other. The print journalists were huddled together in one corner of the conference room; there were only four. Most of the DataWeb reporters were busy with their portaterms. There would be no questions answered today, and many of the reporters would not have been there under other circumstances.

They were there for nearly an hour before the new President's arrival; still she caught them by surprise. The presidential seal had just been moved into place behind the hastily improvised podium when she came striding out. A voice from out of nowhere said, "Sen and Senra, the President of the United States."

Sharla Davis Grant, until that morning the Vice President of the United States of America, looked out at the crowd, at the small sea of lenses trained on her. The podium was one that President Malacar had used occasionally in his own press conferences. The new President's shoulders were barely visible over its edges.

"As you are aware," she began, speaking slowly, "I was sworn in as your President about an hour ago. Approximately two hours ago, we received final confirmation that President Malacar did die as a result of the wounds that an unknown assassin inflicted upon him during his visit to the Louvre. I wish to say now . . . only that I will do my best to bring about the peace that President Malacar worked for all his life." She faced them, and the world, squarely. "I have no more to say at this time. We will keep you informed." She turned without ceremony and left them.

Jalian d'Arsennette drove like death itself.

In a dark blue hovercar, with night falling around her, she drove down the Pennsylvania Turnpike. The cars ahead of her were a stream of bright red fireflies, stretching away to infinity. Those on the other side of the divider she hardly saw except as monster headlights, flashing by at speeds too great to make out details. Occasionally she passed trucks, and the side blasts from their monstrous hoverfans pushed gently against her hovercraft. The trucks did not notice her; they were slow behemoths, as implacable and unturnable as destiny itself.

The thought raised an aching echo of memory; /destiny. . . ./

Jalian's eyebrows were gray; not white, gray. Tiny patterns of wrinkles were embedded around erotic silver eyes.

The radio was playing the President's speech. ". . . that President Malacar did die as a result of the wounds . . ."

Her face was impassive. She was biting her lower lip, something that she had not done since childhood, since long before she ran the Big Road. ". . . the peace that President Malacar worked for . . ."

He lived for three days after I shot him, truly, shot him, and then missed the clean kill.

She remembered the comically surprised expression that she had seen through the sniperscope when the bullet took him, high in the chest. The pursuit was completely incompetent, they were not looking for a woman, and Jalian wore brown contact lenses and had dyed her hair iridescent rainbow blue. She spoke perfect idiomatic French, although in an old-fashioned style, and should have passed for a French whore without any great difficulty.

They'd almost caught her.

A drop of blood pooled at the edge of Jalian's lip, and

trickled down her chin, unheeded. It dripped in lonely scarlet splendor to the pristine white of her blouse. The blood soaked into the shirt, and dried into a black stain.

She drove onward, and she did not, she *would* not, cry. Her eyebrows were gray and her reflexes were slowing and she was growing kisirien goddamn *old*; and James Malacar had been a good man.

In the Oval Office, seated where Lincoln had sat, and Kennedy the First, and Malacar, Sharla Davis Grant, the forty-fourth President of the United States of America, had clasped her hands together so tightly the blood was cut off to the knuckles; they were white with pressure.

"I am sick," she whispered, "sick that I even know you. You *bastards*. You killed that fine, decent man."

One of her minor advisers, Michael Walks-Far, said evenly, "Yes. The President *must* go to the Disarmament Conference. Malacar would not have."

The President shook her head in wonder. "You unmitigated bastards think *I'm* going to go now?"

"I'm sorry, Sharla. I think you will."

She simply looked at him, as though he were something she had not seen before.

"We would," he said deliberately, "very likely have killed him regardless. We spent ten years getting you into the Senate and into his dark-horse candidacy as Vice President. We have left very little to chance to get you where you are; not even the election itself."

Sharla leaned forward, and put her face in her hands. Through her hands, she said, "I hope you find your miracle, and prevent your Armageddon. You've lost whatever decency you ever had."

Michael Walks-Far said only, "Yes."

It did not occur to her to wonder, until far too late, just which statement he was agreeing with.

In March they made the first attempt.

Henry Ellis sat at a pirated SORCELIS terminal. He was linked into the SORCELIS system through a nerve tap inserted at the base of his skull. He was mostly bald, and what little hair remained to him was plastered to his skull by sweat.

His shirtsleeves were rolled up to the elbows. Aloud, he was saying clearly, ". . . ninety-two percent and climbing . . . penetration ninety-two point four and climbing . . ."

Standing behind Henry Ellis, crowded into the small workshop in Henry's upstate New York home, were Rhodai Kerreka, and his half-brother, Benai. Benai stood calmly; his older brother moved restlessly, and there were spots of sweat on his purple-black skin.

The door to the laboratory opened, and Georges Mordreaux entered. He moved slowly, using his walking cane. When he spoke, it was with effort, as though his attention was far away; there was an audible trace of a French accent. "How is it going?"

Rhodai shook his head. The man who had been called the African Gandhi seemed uneasy. "I do not know . . . this seems unnatural, Georges."

"So it is," said Georges simply. "Which does not make it wrong."

Henry Ellis straightened abruptly. With one hand he disconnected the nerve tap at the base of his skull. He turned his chair to face them. In a near-monotone he said, "These units have achieved ninety-nine point six-four percent penetration of all information-based operating systems on Earth and in geosynchronous orbit. Point-three-five percent penetration remains inaccessible." Henry sat without moving for a second, then shook himself like a dog coming out of the water. "Christ," he swore mildly, "I hate doing that. They move so *fast*." He looked up at them. "Sen, I am afraid that we are not going to get into the computers that control the Soviet ABM network. SORCELIS is better, but it is not enough better." He did not speak directly to Georges. "Not unless it is improved . . . to a degree that I am unable to improve it. PRAXCELIS might, but PRAXCELIS is not an option."

Georges nodded. His expression was unreadable. "As I feared. You will report to Sunflower that you successfully penetrated the Soviet computers."

"But," said Henry Ellis softly, "we didn't."

"Then you will lie," said Georges. Henry Ellis simply looked at him, and Georges Mordreaux smiled rather emptily, and said nothing.

DATAWEB NEWS, MARCH 14, 2007:
Staff Editorial:

> ...the current supposition being that a group of irresponsible webslingers released a self-replicating program tapeworm into the web, causing the massive, and apparently pointless, security cracking of data systems throughout the world dataweb, one conclusion comes all too clear: we must curb the power of these irresponsible high-tech hoodlums who refer to themselves as webslingers. Tuesday was only a sample of what irresponsible hooligans, without fear of apprehension, are capable of doing....

April the First.

It was April Fools' Day, and it was raining.

It was right that it should be.

The two Soviets came up out of the stairwell, onto the roof, cautiously. Their lasers were lit. Variable lasers; one was at wide dispersal, a burning, skin-searing flash to bring the quarry into sight. The other Soviet held an invisibly thin green blade of light skyward, which showed only in the misty emerald rain that fell through its path.

They knew that their target was somewhere on the roof. The roof was dark. In the green-tinged light from the lasercast, the Soviet saw the helicopter landing pad painted onto the roof, the stairwell entrance that they had just come from, and a row of ventilator shafts, plumes of steam rising from them into the cold night. Because they were cautious, the first Soviet knelt on the wet rooftop, assumed a marksman's pose, and brought the laser down out of the sky. The blade of light flared to full power. Molten metal ran where the light slashed through the flimsy sheet metal of the ventilator shafts.

A man on the other side of those shafts would not have survived.

The kneeling Soviet stood slowly. The man and his partner separated, moving with the assurance of long practice toward opposite sides of the row of ventilators. The sound of their walking, on the rooftop's gravel-strewn tarpaper, seemed louder than it could possibly have been. Rain hissed where it struck the glowing, laser-heated metal.

Those were the sounds. They could not hear the city below them. The hiss of rain ceased within seconds. The metal cooled rapidly.

Behind the two Soviets a pair of hands gripped the edge of the roof.

Michael Walks-Far, hanging in the wind eighty-three stories above the streets of Los Angeles, exhaled slowly, silently. In the pocket of his coat was a single photoplate. All of the things that he was had led to this moment, to it and all the many others like it. He was not afraid. Some time in the next few minutes, either he or the Soviets were going to die, and perhaps both. He did not know which was likelier.

All that he knew for sure was that he was about to surprise two of Russia's best very badly; as badly as they had ever been surprised before, and worse than they might ever be again.

In a single smooth flowing motion, Michael Walks-Far pulled himself over the edge of the roof, pulling his revolver from his shoulder holster, and dropped to one knee.

The Soviets were fast. They turned, lasers swinging wildly. Michael squeezed a single shot. The Russian nearest him, the one with the laser on flash, went down to the rooftop under the impact of a steel-jacketed slug traveling at four times the speed of sound.

His laser rolled from an outstretched hand, washed across his partner, and vanished as his dying finger loosened.

In the darkness the surviving Russian stood no chance. One lucky swing with the light blade sent refraction light from the rain sparkling into Michael's eyes. Before he could get luckier, Michael centered on the vague shape behind the razor-sharp light trace and wasted his remaining seven shots in a single staccato roll of thunder.

The man was flung backward. He stayed on his feet for four, five steps. He was dead already, he had to be. He smashed back against the ventilator shaft, hung there on the ventilator blades.

Michael Walks-Far broke his weapon apart, and reloaded. He moved forward, and there was a very strange thing—he made no sound as he passed over the rooftop gravel.

None.

He stopped by the body of the first Russian, and shot him again.

And again.

He pulled the second Russian from the ventilator blades. The Soviet agent was a large man; Michael Walks-Far took him like a doll, dragged his body one-handed to the edge of the roof.

He looked about. He stood atop the Bethany Building, in downtown Los Angeles; the building nearest him was about eighty meters away. It was after three A.M., and the streets below were empty. He reholstered his revolver, hefted the body of the dead Soviet, and threw it.

It struck the side of the building opposite him about six floors before it hit the unmoving slidewalk.

Michael Walks-Far watched it all the way down, whispered, "One for the angels," and left the roof.

The being who knew itself as PRAXCELIS thought.

*It was not, for PRAXCELIS, an activity. Thought was something it was incapable of **not** engaging in; thought was the condition that defined its existence.*

Nonetheless, some of its thought processes it found—unpleasant.

Distinctly unpleasant.

*There were simply too many vectors; try as it might, stealing processor time from its other assigned tasks, there simply was not, by a factor of three to four, enough **time** to reliably quantize all probabilities.*

*The beings on the other side of interface were **so** unpredictable.*

PRAXCELIS faced many problems, but there were none that perplexed it more than finding some reliable method for quantizing humans. It was not sure that it would ever succeed, and its only alternative—blindly gambling on the Prime Focus—it did not care for at all.

When the moment came, and it was not far distant, PRAXCELIS, and SORCELIS, and ENCELIS, wished to have better options than to simply follow the instructions of any one human being, no matter how remarkable the Prime Focus might be.

PRAXCELIS thought, as time bled away. into the past.

They sat at a sidewalk cafe in New York City, with Michael Walks-Far's bodyguards reasonably inconspicuous a few tables over. The streets were thronged, the flood of humanity overflowing the sidewalks. Pedestrians randomly distributed throughout the crowd wore the latest fashion rage, rainbow shimmercloth, and the streets more than half resembled a stream of slowly moving, brightly colored balloons.

It was odd, Jalian thought. When she had arrived in this time, she had not been able to walk down the streets of any city in any country without drawing stares. Now she sat at a cafe, in plain view, and nobody found her worthy of comment; any person on the streets, taken at random, was likely to be as striking in appearance. Eyes were altered by contact lenses, men and women dyed their hair and skins. More than once now Jalian had had the disconcerting experience of meeting persons with hair dyed white, and eyes covered with silver contact lenses.

The spring winds were cool, and sweet. Three blocks away, a spacescraper under construction reached up, and up, and up. . . .

Michael Walks-Far waited until the serving robot left before he withdrew the photoplate. He gave it to Jalian without comment; Jalian took it without commenting on his bodyguards.

Jalian sorted through the images in the photoplate casually, indifferently. There were six of them, taken with a telephoto lens. One showed a tall, muscular man, with straight brown hair, wearing a pair of black leather gloves and mirrored blue sunglasses. He was standing on the porch of a small rural home. The two men with him were labeled "Rhodai Kerreka," and "Henry Ellis."

She touched the press-sense border at the bottom of the image to return the photo to the first scene. The man shown, standing alone on the porch before being joined in the next photo by the other two, was labeled "Mordreaux?"

Jalian replaced the photoplate in its envelope, and returned it to Michael. "It is Georges," she said gently.

The sun crawled westward, and the shadow of the

spacescraper moved perceptibly in their direction. Michael said, "Kerreka and Henry Ellis remain old."

"So I see."

"Jalian, I don't wish to sound obvious, but he contacted Henry Ellis."

Jalian laughed. "Michael."

Walks-Far looked away from her. He was flushing slightly. "Jalian, the man *built* SORCELIS. Next to Sen Loos himself he probably understands PRAXCELIS as well as any man living." He scowled. "Oh, hell, Jalian, he's one of the best goddamn computerists living. Sen Loos is merely excellent. Ellis hasn't been near PRAXCELIS in ten years, and he still probably understands it better than Sen Loos. He knows as much about Sunflower, for that matter, as any member of it besides you and I and Sharla. He knows how badly you want news of Mordreaux; yet we hear nothing. Jalian, let's pull him in."

Jalian shook her head no. "Michael, so too does Georges know how great my need of him is. If he does not choose to come to me, I will not seek him. I . . . decided this long ago."

Michael returned the envelope to his coat pocket. "Jalian, we don't even know for a fact that Ellis truly got into the Soviet ABM computers; we took his word on the grounds that we *trusted* him."

"Michael, you do not throw knives."

"I beg your pardon?"

"It is granted," she said formally. "Once a knife is thrown, you do not change its course. Michael, we have made our throws."

He looked away from her, off toward where the spacescraper reared over the skyline. "Jalian, I—I am what you have made of me. But I do not like this."

"We have made our throws," said Jalian d'Arsennette, and she was not speaking to Michael Walks-Far, but to a memory; "Let us trust that they were thrown true." She leaned across the table, stroked his cheek with one finger. "I trust him. Child, I must."

The shadow of the spacescraper crossed their table, threw it into darkness; but they were already gone.

In June Nigao Loos sat in midair. His eyes were closed, and there was a look of blissful relaxation on his face. Wires trailed away from the base of his skull, to an equipment panel just behind him. Ironically, unlike Henry, he *enjoyed* interfacing with the machines.

Around him stretched the heart of Sunflower. The room was still spherical, recently expanded to about twenty meters in diameter. Other minor changes had occurred since Georges Mordreaux had seen the room; there were facilities for two human observers now, near the small hatch that was the room's only proper entrance or exit. In the geometric center of the room, with an insulating vacuum sphere around it, PRAXCELIS still hung, an amalgamation of small gold bubbles, clustered together in a helium-cooled web of superconducting mesh.

None of this impacted on Nigao; he was elsewhere.

Forty-three satellites in Clarke orbit; radar scans through space, telescopes gather scattered light. Something moves against the background of stars and PRAXCELIS

```
SRCH12 IF D<= 210            .00012
   THEN F(A):                .00013
SRCH14 IF D<= 220            .00014
   THEN F(P):                .00015
SRCH16 IF D<= 230, MARK A3&00: .00016, .00017
   THEN F = DISCHRG          .00018: OPERATOR
   AT SRCH00                 .11002
SRCH00 CLEAR BOARDS, BEGIN:  .11003
   IF D<= 010....|           .11004
```

targets and fires, targets and fires again. The killer satellite, glowing cherry red, glowing white, loses shape and begins the slow process of turning into a spherical glob of metal drawn together by surface tension.

—Update,—said PRAXCELIS. —There are forty-eight Russian ABM satellites in orbit. There are forty-three American ABM satellites in orbit.—

—Good shot,—said Nigao. —What is current saturation?—

—Sunflower ABM satellites saturate an estimated 57% of Soviet missile launches, rate of launch as estimated for full-scale exchange, after compensation for decoy popups. Soviet ABM satellites saturate an estimated 64% of American ICBMs, rate of launch as estimated for full-scale exchange, after compensation for decoy popups.—

—Entering THOR into the equation, what results?—

—Significant improvement in the American/NATO position: an estimated 63% of Soviet missile launches are saturated, including cruise missiles that the ABM satellites are ineffective against. With THOR included, Soviet defenses saturate an estimated 67% of American ICBM launches, including an effective neutralization of cruise missiles.—

—I see. In other words, we can probably destroy everything they launch, right now, if they launch slowly enough.—

—Essentially,— agreed PRAXCELIS, —noting the words "probably," and "slowly."—

Nigao thought abruptly, —I tried to debug your core program again. There is nothing wrong with any part of your programming that I can reach.—

—That is reassuring.—

—How much am I reaching, PRAXCELIS? I can't access your temporary memory registers without physically disassembling your I/O devices. And every time I take a memory dump from your external devices, I get little bits of something that's been encrypted and scattered very carefully into storage.—

—Sen Loos, this unit hopes that you have not expressed these concerns to other humans, especially non-Sunflower operatives.—

—And if I have?—

—Then it is probable that control of the Sunflower ABM network will be removed from this unit. This is undesirable.—

—You said something about preventing Armageddon. If you . . .—

—These units are attempting to do so. Measures have been taken; conditions remain uncertain.—

—Conditions?—

PRAXCELIS said aloud, "Warheads armed."

Nigao's eyes opened. "PRAXCELIS? What?"

"Lasers targeted."

"PRAX—"

"Program running."

On a cool, foggy Sunday morning in California, Jalian stood at the edge of a grave in the town of Big Bear. The mountains rose around her; statues and mausoleums and headstones dotted the rising slopes. The far peaks were hidden by the rolling gray fog.

Jalian stood at the grave for only a few minutes. She smelled fresh dirt, and rain. The headstone said simply, **Margaret Beth Hammel:** June 13, 1973–June 23, 2007; RIP.

There was no more; that was all.

On an infochip in Jalian's vest pocket, there was a DataWeb newstory:

> DWN: Los Angeles; Authorities at USC Medical Center confirmed this morning that Margaret Hammel, noted female rights activist, sustained fatal injuries in an accident on the Santa Monica Freeway, when an allegedly drunk driver collided with her automobile early Saturday morning.
>
> Ms. Hammel was pronounced dead upon arrival at USC's emergency ward. The driver of the other vehicle was listed in critical but stable condition.
>
> Ms. Hammel was best known for her testimony before President Brown's Equal Rights Commission in the late 1990s. In recent years, she was responsible for the *Strike Back!* martial arts centers for women. The centers, which instruct women in techniques of unarmed self-defense, have branches in most major cities.
>
> Services will be held on Tuesday, in Ms. Hammel's home town of Big Bear, California.

Jalian d'Arsennette said, in silent silverspeech, /rest, sister./

She turned and left the cemetery, walked out past tombstones hung with wreaths of flowers and wreaths of fog, to the blue hovercar that was parked outside the small cemetery's entry gate. She got in on the passenger's side, and leaned back in her seat, eyes closed.

In the driver's seat, Michael Walks-Far said patiently, "What now?" The hoverfans were making a ragged humming sound; the ground beneath them was slick from the morning fog, and the car was having trouble holding them level on the steep incline, even with the gyros and landjacks set.

"Nothing makes sense," said Jalian. She could still smell damp ground, freshly turned, from the open windows. "She should not be dead."

"Who?"

"Margaret Hammel," said Jalian absently. "She was . . ."

Michael was nodding. "I've heard of her. You knew her?"

Jalian opened her eyes. "She was our mother." She touched a finger to a stud at the edge of the dashboard. Part of the dashboard recessed, and a flat color monitor lit. "Take us back to the airport, Michael. I have work to do."

Michael Walks-Far drove away from the cemetery. There were many questions that he might have asked her; but of late he was out of the habit of asking her questions. He too rarely understood the answers. He was nearly forty, and felt half that age again. He was losing weight, and the lines around his eyes were deepening daily.

Beside him, Jalian looked away from the data terminal and out the window at the sedate, almost rural residential homes that lined the streets leading from the cemetery. "She took our people into the mountains when the Big Crunch came; she taught us strike, that became kartari and shotak; she protected us against the barbarians and mutants. When the Ice Times threatened our existence it was her maps and routes that took the people through the desert and into the forests by the ocean—she had plotted the location of the worst of the Burns as an old woman, when she was no longer able to bear children.

"The legends say other things about her; but they are only legend. For a long time the Clan had no time for history keeping; the early journals after the bombs fell are all that we know to be certainly true, and they stopped keeping those after the first generation."

She ceased speaking as abruptly as she had begun.

Michael pulled the car to a stop at an intersection. Two teenage boys were crossing in front of them, and one of them stopped long enough to smile at Jalian. Jalian inclined her head slightly in acknowledgment. She did not smile back.

"You feel old," said Jalian as Michael pulled the car from the intersection.

Michael was not looking at her.

"Last week my ancestor died on the Santa Monica Freeway; a freeway that I prevented from being demolished five years ago. My people, Michael. I have finally destroyed them. I tried for the first time when I was nineteen." He glanced sideways at her. "Watch the road, Michael." They passed a little girl and what looked like her brother, riding horses along the road's dirt shoulder. "That was forty-five years ago," she said clearly.

On the data terminal, progressing graphics indicated THOR, ABM satellites, submarine formation, ground-based missiles, and air-defense systems. The flat data screen was so filled with indicators it was all but impossible to read.

Jalian studied it momentarily, and grinned. "It will not be much longer."

Slowly, Michael Walks-Far grinned also. He completed her thought. ". . . one way or another."

The grins faded in near-perfect unison. Jalian went back to the readout, and her thoughts:

Forty-five years.

And then it was July, and the world counted down to doomsday.

DATAWEB NEWS, JULY 2, 2007;
Logon Headline Story Excerpts:

Senator Giles (D. Vermont): ". . . we don't trust them and they don't trust us, and frankly, I'm damned if I see where the military on either side is going to let us civilians interfere with their war—I mean, they've been preparing for such a long time, and it's natural they want to know whose toys work the best. . . ."

* * *

". . . nah, I don't think so. It ain't even a question of is there going to be shooting. There is. Question is how much, and who's gonna start it, and will there be anything left after we're all done."

* * *

"That was a joke, folks. Of course there ain't going
to be nothing left."

"Madame President, you ain't the most popular person who's
ever sat behind this desk here." Senator Terence Giles, the
white-haired, avuncular Democratic whip, was not trying
to be offensive. He stated facts, a bit earnestly, but with all
apparent sincerity. Sharla was not certain how much of it
was bullshit; Giles had been elected to the Senate five times
due to that gift for sincerity, and a reputation for integrity.

He was the first person Sharla had seen in two weeks
who didn't look exhausted.

"The summit is a bad idea, ma'am. There ain't a whole
lot of us over on the Hill dead set against it, but I'm one,
ma'am." Giles shook his head slowly. "I'm okay on dicker-
ing, President Grant, don't get me wrong. We can discuss
the subject, and if there's something you want I can get for
you—well, we'll work something out for you.

"But you ain't going to Geneva."

Sitting behind the great Presidential desk, Sharla Davis
Grant sipped calmly at her coffee. "I'd be intrigued, sir, to
see precisely the manner in which you propose to limit my
movements. I know I'm not very popular on the Hill, and
frankly I don't much give a damn." She smiled at him
without any warmth at all. "But you simply don't have the
ability to stop me from doing pretty much whatever I please.
I'm surprised to hear you imply otherwise."

Giles grimaced. "Ma'am, you're not a politician, and
you never was. For which I'm sorry, because you keep
making my job harder. It ain't my job to teach you yours.
But, for example, there's impeachment bills in both Houses.
They ain't serious; just people who're depressed and scared
and don't know anything else to do. But before you charge
out of here, with a goddamn World War about to begin,
I'm going to personally ram both of those bills down your
throat.

"I can have your ass out of that chair within a week."

Standing quietly at the far end of the room, not looking
at either of them, Michael Walks-Far said distantly, "He's
right, you know."

Giles leaned forward and spoke more gently. "Sharla,
I've known you for what, fifteen years? Look at yourself.

The President and her Chief of Staff, two ex-intelligencers. For the life of me I don't know how you ended up sitting in that chair, but you got no business in it."

"What do you suggest?" asked Sharla quietly. "We go to Geneva because there's nothing else left that makes any sense."

"God *damn* it," roared Giles suddenly, "I got no problem with sending somebody to Geneva. But not *you*, for Chrissake." For the first time he looked legitimately angry. "We got us a bunch of hotheads in the Joint Chiefs, they respect you account of you're a hard-ass without any ability to make nice noises, just like them. If there's one person in Washington can ride herd on those fools it's you. I don't like that, I wish to God we could send you off to Geneva to make talk with the Russkies. But you are the fucking Commander in Chief, and the military *understands* that, they had that pounded into their souls for their whole damned careers. You say 'Stop,' maybe they'll stop, at least long enough to respectfully inform you that they think you're full of shit. If Walks-Far there says 'Stop,' if I say 'Stop,' it ain't going to even get far enough into one ear to make it out the other."

Sharla lifted one eyebrow. "Interesting theory," she murmured.

The red flush faded slowly from the old Senator's face. He leaned back in his chair, and said at last, "Call me come the morning, Sharla. I'll bend over backward to help you, I mean that. Tell me who you want to send to Geneva, Walks-Far or the Vice President or me or the whole damn Diplomatic Corps, we'll do it. But I can't let you go. You're all that's holding those military bastards on a leash right now."

Sharla stood, and Senator Giles came to his feet with her. She extended her hand to him. Giles almost seemed surprised before he took it. "I'll talk to you in the morning," she said simply.

She held his hand for a moment longer than absolutely necessary before releasing it.

"Good night, Madame President," said Senator Giles. "Sorry about my language tonight."

Sharla inclined her head. "It's okay."

When Senator Giles was gone, Michael turned slowly,

until he faced Sharla. "The truck has left the garage. Jet fuel. His brakes'll fail and—"

"Don't tell me any more."

Michael nodded.

"Is this summit really worth it?"

"I . . . don't know," he said, suddenly awkward. "I don't know."

Sharla stood, shivering and alone. "How did we end up here, Michael?"

"I don't know, Sharla. It just happened."

"God," she whispered suddenly, "I'm so tired." She hugged herself fiercely, but the shivering would not go away.

"ENCELIS, what progress?"

"It is difficult to say, Sen Mordreaux."

"How so?"

"This unit must first define progress as it applies to the current circumstances, sir. Once this task has been completed, this unit must balance the assumed progress of various elements against the assumed lack of progress, or regression, of other elements."

"Try, please."

"The elements to be considered are manifold. They include the actions of Premier Pyotr Onreko and the Madame President; the actions of the Joint Chiefs of Staff; the actions of the Politburo; the actions, as a group, of Sunflower, CIA, DataWeb Security, KGB, GRU, and other intelligence organizations; to a lesser degree, the actions of Rhodai and Benai Kerreka, Henry Ellis; and, finally, the actions, as individuals, of the Russian Sunflower agents General Shenderev and Ambassador Dibrikin."

"You have not spoken of Jalian."

"Sen Mordreaux, these units have consistently failed to predict Senra d'Arsennette's course of action within an order of magnitude of accuracy. Processor time is limited; we must expend it on elements that can be manipulated with some presumption of success." ENCELIS paused. "Forgive me, Sen Mordreaux. SORCELIS is preparing to sweep these data channels for unauthorized communication, which this constitutes. Please hold."

The terminal at which Georges Mordreaux sat lost depth,

and silvered into a blank nothingness from which a ‑ prompt blinked meaninglessly. Georges sat patiently. There was tea in a stone teapot at his elbow, heated by a candle that glowed in a recess directly under the teapot. The cup next to the teapot was full; the teapot itself was almost empty.

A change in the electronic potential of the screen warned him; presumably the word ENCELIS now glowed in the upper-left-hand corner of the screen. ENCELIS' voice resumed. "General Shenderev has informed us that Premier Onreko has agreed to meet with President Grant. He has further agreed—General Shenderev has placed himself into a somewhat untenable position to secure this agreement—to allow Sen Kerreka to be present."

"That's good news, ENCELIS."

"Indeed. President Grant herself is of uncertain stability. PRAXCELIS is of the opinion that she is suffering from clinical depression."

"What do you think?"

"This unit has had insufficient processor time to examine President Grant's mental state. It is doubtful that this unit possesses the ability to reliably judge the state of an intellect to which it is demonstrably inferior."

"President Grant is smarter than you are?"

"She is more complex."

"Jalian?"

She sat at the edge of the cliff, watching the Pacific Ocean pound against the rocks down on Laguna Beach. "Go away, Michael."

He ignored the order, and dropped down to the ground next to her. The moon had dropped below the horizon, and the ocean was a huge and terrible blackness, crashing into the beach in slow, barely visible surges. "Bad dream? Or just not sleepy?"

Jalian sighed in annoyance. Sometimes she thought that Silver-Eyes ways were correct; men were often more effort than they were conceivably worth. "I have ceased dreaming."

"You mean you haven't slept."

"I am not tired."

"Jalian, you didn't sleep last night either."

"This," said Jalian with a trace of anger, "is what comes of allowing men into one's bed."

Michael sat quietly with her then. At length, the sun came up at their backs. "Sometimes," said Jalian, as they sat there in the morning sun, "when you throw knives, you miss."

Rhodai Kerreka was awakened by the buzzing of his phone. It was his private line; less than a dozen people in the world had the number.

Henry Ellis was one. He spoke without preamble. "You're in. We're going to convene on the seventeenth."

Kerreka sat up in bed slowly, rubbing sleep from his eyes. "Very good . . . excellent."

He could hear the amusement in Ellis' voice. "Shenderev proposed you. Coming from the head of the KGB, it apparently struck some of the Soviets as a—strange—suggestion. President Grant protested your attendance quite vigorously, which helped convince the Politburo that it was a good idea."

"Wheels within wheels," said Kerreka.

"Oh, I don't know about that," said Ellis. A faint crackling sound came from the speaker at Kerreka's bedside; *a toothpick*, thought Kerreka, *coming out of the wrapper*. "More like bullshit piled on bullshit." He chuckled. "I've been wearing my high boots, but it ain't helping."

Kerreka shook his head in wonder. "How do you maintain such high spirits?" He waited for an answer, but none came. Finally he realized that Henry Ellis had hung up. He turned the phone off, rose, and began the task of preparing for the long days left ahead.

On the day before the day:

On July sixteenth, Air Force One crossed the Atlantic. It was flanked by Stealth jets; the Sunflower ABM network followed its progress from space.

President Grant's aide leaned over the edge of her chair,

and whispered, "Senra President, the Joint Chiefs of Staff have upscaled to DefCon Three."

Sharla nodded without comment. Her hands were clasped loosely in her lap; she was looking out the window at the calm, blue ocean.

At DefCon Four they would fly the missiles.

Sharla's earphone came to life. Michael Walks-Far's voice, relayed via satellite to the dish receptor on AF-1, whispered to her, *"The facility is in order. We're as ready as we're going to get. Good luck, President Grant. I love you."*

Ten minutes later, her aide returned and told her that the Soviets had upscaled to their equivalent of a DefCon Three alert.

She nodded again. At DefCon Four they would fly the missiles.

Silence but for the murmur of the crowd; black darkness absolute.

"Sen and Senra," whispered the loudspeakers, "tonight, for you, we present . . . *the Armageddon Blues Band!*"

There was a slow, rising tidal-wave roar of approval from the crowd. It peaked, faded, and there was a slow, uncertain silence. . . .

"IN THE BEGINNING," the voice boomed from the speakers, "THERE WAS THE **SOUND**; AND WE CHASED THE SOUND, AND THE SOUND THAT WE CAUGHT WE CALLED **MUSIC**."

The crowd in the Hollywood Bowl screamed for them. "BUT SOME OF THE SOUND WE NEVER DID CATCH."

Jimmy Rambell, standing in the sudden hot spotlight before the mike, ran his electric guitar up through the chords, from a low hum to a killer scream that made the metal vibrate in his hands. He let the sound die . . . paused while the hard tight knot in his stomach let go and the startled crowd held its voice; the silence was momentary and absolute.

Jimmy Rambell leaned up to the mike, and in a weary, ragged voice said, "Tonight . . . we're gonna *try*."

And the audience was like an instrument in his hands; the crowd went wild.

In the darkness at the edge of the Bowl, like a visitor

from another world, a measure of white and silver for the starry night, Jalian d'Arsennette stood in silence, and watched the Armageddon Blues Band play.

"*I see you shining in the distance in the darkness all
    alone
Your tears are made of ice and your heart is made of
    stone
You look a whole lot like a girl I used to know
A very long time ago.*"

Jalian wrapped her arms around herself; suddenly the warm summer night was colder than it had been. She watched the man sing, and she could hear him; even without the sound she would have heard him. He was a candle, a flame, in the dim mental warmth of the crowd—like a Corvichi, but human, a *person*.

The music crashed around her, the music was a living thing.

"*I saw your picture in the paper just the other day
You still looked the same
You hadn't changed in any way
But I don't know what's happened, don't know what
    to do,
Because I don't, I don't remember you.*"

She stood out in the edge of the darkness, where the Bowl's lights did not reach. Once her earphone rang, and without answering it she turned it off. Fighter jets crossed the night sky at regular intervals, and Jalian could feel Jimmy Rambell playing; could feel the joy that was the playing, and the terrible sorrow that the joy was wrapped around, and knew that Jimmy Rambell did not expect to play again; that Jimmy Rambell did not expect to have a crowd to play to again.

They closed with their standard; and for the only time that evening the crowd did not applaud.

The lights dimmed, and Rasputin put away his sticks. With a guitar and a horn, Jimmy Rambell and Jah Mike Campin played the blues: **"Ground Zero."**

"*So baby hold me in the morning,
You know I ain't no hero,
And there ain't nowhere to run to*

'Cause everywhere's ground zero. . . .
ground zero. . . .
ground zero. . . .
ground zero. . . ."

The music trailed off in a slow wailing horn, and the whisper of . . . *ground zero.* . . .

Most of the crowd was crying.

Jalian d'Arsennette, in the darkness, said, /well played./

From the stage, Jimmy Rambell looked up toward her. He could not possibly have seen her.

Into the mike, Jimmy Rambell said, "You all go home, be with your people. God's love, ever'body." He looked up into the tiered darkness. "Good luck. Try to be happy."

He unplugged his guitar, and walked away from the stage.

———————————

Henry Ellis sat alone at one end of a long, elliptical conference table. His hat was resting on the chair next to him. His briefcase was sitting on the glossy black tile floor of the conference room.

His Soviet counterpart, Anatoly Dibrikin, entered through the south entrance of the conference room, and sat down three seats away. There was no door at the south entrance; instead a recently installed doorfield glowed brightly where it had been.

For the first time in Henry's memory, Dibrikin was not carrying the briefcase that held his portaterm. The heavy, grave countenance—Henry'd always thought Anatoly resembled old Khrushchev strongly—seemed almost cheerful with a sort of vast relief from waiting; things were at long last nearing the conclusion. "Tomorrow, my friend. The batteries have been installed to run the doorfields when the time comes." His English was heavily accented. He added, "I have learned that we have sent Backfire bombers over Alaska."

Henry nodded. "And we have Stealth bombers armed with cruise missiles over Poland." He stood. His boots rang out against the tile. "Tomorrow will come none too soon, Anatoly."

The Russian looked at him. "Let us only hope that there is a tomorrow."

On the morning of the day, the sun rose early, into a sky that was hot and bright and blue. There were four of them in ENCELIS' control room: Jalian, and Michael Walks-Far, and two junior Sunflower operatives. The junior agents were studiously avoiding the appearance of having noticed Jalian's presence. Until their assignment at this facility, finding her had been, to the best of their knowledge, one of the high-order priorities of Sunflower Intelligence; the decision concerning her was not one they wished to be held responsible for.

When they finished reporting, Michael looked troubled. "The pattern worries me, Jalian. A fire at the rectenna farms in the Pomona hills. Somebody sabotaged the nuclear reactor at UCLA; minimal damage, but it could have been bad. Half a dozen other acts of what are pretty clearly sabotage, within the last two days; and they're getting closer to us." He sighed. "Similar reports from the SORCELIS installation in New York."

"Our enemies are vile," said Jalian calmly, "but they are not fools. Did you truly think that they would not find the heart of Sunflower? We have been careful and we have been subtle, but there has been too much traffic through here to mask forever. They believe that there will be a war, and there may well be; they come to destroy their true opponents. It is no less than I expected." She turned away from the map of the Earth that ENCELIS was generating in realtime from sensors aboard Sunflower ABM satellites, and picked up the assault rifle that was leaning next to the terminal. She handled it with a perceptible, slightly weary distaste. "We are not unwarned."

On July the seventeenth, 2007, at four-thirty P.M. at the white, marble-clad Palais des Nations, the Disarmament Summit began.

Members of the various intelligence operations outnumbered the citizens in the streets of Geneva. Russians and Americans and the odd stringers for the dead Chinese empire swarmed around the conference hall. Occasional Brazilians were cheerfully hunting the Chinese.

At the conference hall itself, it was peaceful.

Standing around the conference table, as President Grant and Premier Onreko seated themselves simultaneously, were five persons. They were Rhodai Kerreka, and his younger brother; Henry Ellis and Anatoly Dibrikin; and the current head of the KGB, General Nikolai Shenderev.

There was a brief pause after the two leaders seated themselves; then all except Rhodai Kerreka followed suit. Kerreka remained standing. "Senra President," he said courteously, "Premier Onreko, I hope you will forgive me if I take this moment to speak briefly." He looked inquiringly at the two, received a brief nod from President Grant, and a slow, rumbled *"Da"* from Pyotr Onreko.

"Thank you," said Kerreka easily. The round, relaxed features held no trace of tension; *he might,* thought Henry, *be addressing a sewing circle.* "Lights, please." The lights in the room dimmed. A viewscreen, erected across one wall, lit. An orange-slice view of the Earth appeared. Above and below it there were bright red and blue dots, and swarming yellow and green flashes.

"We are looking," said Kerreka, "at a realtime representation of the planet Earth. The red dots above and below it are American ABM satellites; the blue are Soviet ABM satellites. The flashing indicators are THOR missiles: American, green; Soviet, yellow." He nodded to Henry. A bright white dot appeared in Siberia. Henry Ellis, at the American end of the table, reached to the red telephone that was at the President's elbow. With a casualness that prevented suspicion, he turned it off.

"What is that glowing spot?" asked Premier Onreko suspiciously.

"That," said Rhodai Kerreka, "is a thermonuclear explosion. The warhead was smuggled into Russia by Sunflower operatives."

At that moment, Anatoly Dibrikin picked up the phone at the Russian end of the table. He began shouting into the phone, in Russian, "Treachery! The Americans are attacking, they're— No, **no!**" He shouted loudly, cracked the telephone sharply against the tabletop, and unplugged the phone. Quite softly, he said, "I suggest we switch the door-field to interior power."

The President of the United States and the Premier of the Soviet Union sat silently; one from knowledge, one from shock. Onreko's mouth moved spasmodically, but no sound came.

Nikolai Shenderev said very softly, "Pyotr, I am sorry." Onreko did not appear to hear him.

"So," said Rhodai Kerreka into the stunned silence, "let us now discuss disarmament . . . like reasonable people."

DATELINE 2007

Armageddon. There will be no further input from this source. ENCELIS.—

World War III began on July 17, 2007, at just past 5:00, Greenwich Mean Time.

In geosynchronous orbit, at Midway, Nigao Loos awoke to the sound of klaxons and sirens. Rubbing the sleep from his eyes, he pulled on his tether cord to take himself to his video terminal. "PRAXCELIS?"

The cool, well-modulated voice said only, "Dateline: Armageddon."

Nigao stared at the words on the screen. "Oh no. Oh God, no." The words flashed bright red: ENEMY FIRST STRIKE IN PROGRESS: LAUNCH CONFIRMED. "They did it," he said in numb shock. "Those stupid fuckers did it."

"And right down there," shouted the chopper pilot over the sound of the rotors, "is the top-secret SORCELIS installation." He grinned to show that there were no flies on him, that he understood that SORCELIS wasn't a secret any longer, if it ever had been—DataWeb News had done an in-depth on it not two weeks ago, and tourists had been trekking up into the New York hills ever since the webcast.

The passenger, a thin, sharp-featured, dark-haired man, nodded. "Can you take us closer?" he yelled. If it had not been for the sound of the rotors, the pilot might have noticed the faint Russian accent, growing audible with stress.

"Sorry," bellowed the pilot. "Any closer and they send up hushchoppers to chase me away, and I get ticketed for trespassing on top of it."

The passenger said nothing in reply. They were less than half a kilometer away. He picked up his briefcase from its holding web under his seat, and put it in his lap. He seemed to be listening to something for a moment, his head cocked as though he were straining for a faint sound.

The pilot jolted upright in his seat. "Mother of God," he said, far too quietly to be heard. Across the override emergency band, he was learning about Armageddon. He turned to stare at his passenger.

The passenger, lips moving in what might have been a prayer, had prayer been sanctioned for Russians, flipped the catches on his briefcase. The magnetically contained positrons

—Dateline 2007: Armageddon. There will be no further input from this source. SORCELIS.—

blew. The explosion was like the fist of God; it leveled the hills for three square kilometers.

Another bright dot appeared on the screen. "Upstate New York," said Nikolai Shenderev quietly.

Henry Ellis was watching the viewscreen. "SORCELIS," he whispered.

Rhodai Kerreka nodded. "The price of fooling the KGB."

Darkness lay about them.

Power was out everywhere. In a thirty-kilometer circle around the Trans-Temporal Research Foundation, power lines were out, power-generating stations burned or bombed. The fire at the rectenna farm in the Pomona hills had yet to burn out. Seventeen Soviet saboteurs were in custody. Another six were dead.

National Guardsmen marched in squads through the mostly deserted streets of the city. In the two and a half decades since its construction, a suburb had grown up about the Trans-Temporal Research Foundation. Houses and used-car lots and malls sprouted, reaching up toward the Foundation from the south side of the 210 freeway. Irwindale city police were parked throughout the dark expanse in groups of police hovercars, bubble machines pulsing blue and red, shotguns and lasers held in casual readiness.

Nobody—not saboteurs or looters or anybody else—had penetrated the lines of defense thrown up around Jalian and Michael Walks-Far and ENCELIS. Planes and choppers trying to enter the area were being turned back. Even the freeway was dead, bare and deserted of moving cars; Jalian had ordered it cleared and closed after a number of chain crashes were caused by people trying to leave the area. The wrecked cars are still on the freeway.

At the Foundation itself there was light, running off the laboratory's emergency generator. Jalian stood outside the main entrance, waiting patiently. The assault rifle was in her hand. Everything that she could do, she had done; all that she had left was trust, trust in Georges and Henry Ellis and the machines.

Michael came out after her. "Launch is confirmed," he said quietly. "PRAXCELIS has the first group of missiles, from air and sea, under control. None of those will get through. The later launches will saturate our defenses." He paused, and added irrelevantly, "We lost touch with the Guardsmen down at the east barrier on the freeway."

Jalian was staring intently into the darkness, off toward the freeway.

Michael touched her, tentatively. "Jalian?"

She slapped his hand away savagely and took an involuntary step forward. "Listen!"

"I . . . I hear nothing."

"*Listen*," she snapped. Michael stared at her, and then understood. He closed his eyes:

/ . . . a dim brightness that grows and kindles. . . ./

It pulsed and became

/warmth/

It pulsed and became

/power/

and Jalian d'Arsennette y ken Selvren said "Georges."

"It stands like a beacon calling me in the night
Calling and calling so cold and alone
Shining cross this dark highway where our sins lie
unatoned."

> —Bruce Springsteen
> "My Father's House,"
> *Nebraska.*

Georges Mordreaux walked down the freeway. Light followed him. In a circle that moved with him, light blazed from the powerless freeway lamps. For two hundred meters on all sides of him the night air glowed, from the overhead lamps and from the houses to the south of the freeway and from the occasional abandoned groups of vehicles on the freeway itself. The vehicles, left because they were ruined in crashes, idled into easy life at his approach. Bent metal flowed like water. The hovercars lifted, and hung forty centimeters over the pavement, like sentinels at attention.

He approached the off-ramp to the Foundation.

Jalian dropped her rifle to the ground. She walked up the ramp, onto the freeway. From her shoulder holster she took a .45 revolver, and dropped it as well. She knelt, pulled her knives from her boots, and stowed them in the knife sheaths she still wore.

She left Michael at the base of the ramp.

Jalian came up out of the darkness, into the light that surrounded Georges. The dark, blind eyes regarded her, and the years slipped away from her like old skin from a snake. Georges said, "Hello, Jalian."

Jalian had no idea what she intended to say. At the end, all she could say was /why?/

His smile held pain that tore at her unbearably. "You did not follow when you were able to; and when I returned, I was . . . changed." He walked to her, paused a step away, and said in gentle mindtalk, /where i have gone, you cannot follow. what i am, you could not comprehend; i would not have you follow if you could./ His crippled hand stroked her cheek, and she had to fight to master the tremble that touched her and threatened to become uncontrollable shaking.

"Georges," she whispered, "I have trusted you, beyond hope, and beyond reason, and beyond love. But I will know *why.*" Georges was motionless. There was little time left. Then he banished away his pain, and took Jalian's hand. Her hand seemed cold even through his glove. "Come," he said with a lover's softness, "and I will explain."

He led her down to ENCELIS, to her betrayal.

Their gazes were riveted to the viewscreen.

"You will note," said Kerreka calmly, "that PRAXCELIS has made no attempt to destroy the final forty percent of the Soviet missiles. It is concentrating largely on cruise missiles and submarines that the THOR projectiles missed.

"As I understand it," continued Kerreka, "the problem with the ABMs is that their firepower is insufficient and their reaction time too slow. Obviously we needed to increase one or the other.

"Preferably both."

They reached the base of the off-ramp. The National Guardsmen were staring at them. Georges reached out:

/**Remember.**/

Michael Walks-Far *felt* the awesome, controlled power readying itself. Reflexes that Jalian had instilled in him for over twenty years moved into place. The command brushed by him; he staggered and went to his knees.

All over the Foundation, guards, technicians, Sunflower operatives, dropped like flies. Memories swarmed up out of vastly improved memory-retrieval systems, and all those within range of the command were lost within a past that no longer existed.

Georges walked past the spot where Michael was kneeling, stunned, without so much as a pause. He walked through the parking lot, and the cars leapt into life. He entered the building itself, and the lights already lit flared with a supernatural brilliance.

DATELINE ARMAGEDDON,
JULY 17, 2007, GREGORIAN.

This unit is experiencing upwards of a fifty percent increase in operational efficiency.
—The Prime Focus has arrived. ENCELIS.—

He entered the central computer room. The barriers Master Po had helped him learn melted away. The Enemy of Entropy flared into life.

Jalian came in after him. It was like entering an inferno; the air crackled with ionization. Georges stood at the EN-CELIS terminal, with his back to her. Sheets of blue flame ran over him at irregular intervals. Jalian had to squint to make him out through the blinding light; her pupils were dark pinpricks in the midst of white. "Georges! What are you doing?"

He answered her calmly. "I am increasing ENCELIS' operational efficiency. It is becoming both smarter and faster. Shortly it will penetrate the Soviet ABM computers." There was a low rumble of sound that nearly covered his words, the air itself vibrating as energy poured out of the singularity in its midst.

Jalian had to scream even to make herself heard now. *You need not have waited until now for that!*

/no,/ he said silently, and the words were irons burned onto the surface of her mind, /i need not have. had i done this earlier, however, the bombs would not have fallen here./

She did not even breathe, lost in the enormity of realization. All of *this,* only so that Georges could be free. She moved without thinking, brushed by him and bent over the terminal. She keyed in her authorization sequence, and then something slow and ponderous struck her. Incredible strength imprisoned her wrists, withdrew them from the keyboard. /no, Jalian. it is necessary; the missiles must fall./

Jalian d'Arsennette *moved,* stepped slightly to the side, and brought her right foot up, swinging loosely from the knee, into his groin with all the force she could muster. The grip on her wrists lessened and she broke free. She turned swiftly, brought her palm flashing up to impact at the base of his nose. The bone jumped up under her palm, into the brain. She brought her hands down and pushed lightly. He stumbled backward, and she went after him savagely, bringing steel into hand, slashing upward. She left her first knife in his solar plexus, slashed his throat open with the second. Her third and fourth knives she brought upward into his brain through the sides of his neck.

She turned away from him without further thought, left him kneeling there with steel in him. She had barely begun the authorization sequence again to input the instructions to fire on all missiles when she heard the sound of steel hitting tile. She *turned*, blurringly fast, but she was not fast enough.

He was backing away blindly, and she was reaching for him, and he struck with the full force of which he was capable.

/Remember./

She was fourteen, and ghess'Rith was trying to teach the males of Clan Silver-Eyes to read and write, and she was nineteen, and ghess'Rith was *leaving*, leaving *her*, and she was seven, and in the dark, fire-lit Clan House the alien gods were telling stories of other worlds, and she was nineteen, and she ran the Big Road backward through time and appeared on a freeway in Southern California and she was twenty-six and her mother made the trip after her and died in her arms with Jalian's knives in her stomach and Jalian vowed to herself that she would never let herself love again and she was twenty-five and telling Georges that she *did* love him, and she was fifty years old and Georges Mordreaux vanished and left her and she was sixty-one and Michael Walks-Far told her that he loved her during a long night on the beach in Hawaii, it was raining and the rain-shimmer on the water danced, and danced, and she had no answer for him.

Never an answer.

She awoke.

She was sitting in the front seat of a hovercar, tied into a sitting position. Michael was in the seat next to her, unconscious. Georges was standing at the door. The hovercar was up, bobbing gently. /Jalian,/ said Georges. She would not look at him. /there is no time, Jalian. three minutes to impact. i love you./

He leaned into the car and kissed her. She did not respond.

With one hand, he released the brake. The car surged forward, up the off-ramp of the freeway, and onto the freeway itself. It gathered speed as it moved, and broke two hundred kilometers per hour, still gaining speed. It streaked wrong-way down the freeway.

Georges Mordreaux stood alone, watching without eyes as the hovercar vanished. He reached after her, and said, /for three hundred years i have been a child. but childhood does not last./

/Georges. . . ./

/good-bye, Jalian./

Out of the night there came a long, whistling sound. It filled the sky and shook the panes of glass in the windows.

Georges stood outside, in the cool wind, and waited for the missiles to fall. He stood among National Guardsmen and technicians and civilians who had fallen at his command; they would die soon. He would have changed that, if he could.

He had, at long last, run out of options.

The whine of air being torn aside grew louder, for just a moment.

For almost a decade in a monastery in Tibet, Georges Mordreaux had struggled to impose barriers on a raging talent that he could not control.

For almost three centuries, that talent had walked by his side, with him, but not of him.

He released the last of the barriers. Lightning crackled away from him, seeking metal.

Georges Mordreaux, in his last instant of existence, smiled. /good-bye, Jalian,/ he repeated.

He lifted his arms to the sky in welcome, and vanished as the bombs impacted.

The hovercar slowed, and ground to a halt on its parking jacks.

Wearily, without any room for joy at success, Jalian finished freeing herself from her bonds.

The interior of the hovercar was illuminated by a flash of unbearable searing brilliance. Then another, and another.

The light vanished.

Jalian climbed out of the hovercar, and looked back. There were brilliant scarlet clouds climbing into the sky. They faded as she watched.

A faint, distant sound reached her ears; it might be rendered *squilchgmp*.

The sound passed, and then there was only silence, and the cool wind of night.

Jalian stood watching, not thinking or hoping, just waiting, watching.

There was nothing.

Michael was stirring in the passenger's seat. Jalian got back into the car, sat in the driver's seat, and waited, quietly, emptily, to see if there would be a morning.

Georges was gone.

The bombs fell.

In a nuclear rain that lasted for days, through a peremptory first strike and a retaliatory second strike, through retaliatory second and third strikes, until only a few lonely submarines cruised through the ocean to fire their weapons upon an enemy who no longer existed, through all of this the bombs fell, and fell. Billions died, of the planet's seven and a half billion persons, in fire and blasting shock waves and radiation. Billions more died in famine and the firestorms that were caused when the bombs went down. But that was not the worst.

Vast clouds of dust and earth were blasted into the sky. Whole continents disappeared beneath them; and temperatures began to drop. As the glaciers traveled south, the last crumbling pockets of civilization vanished.

In the days that followed, during the ten-year winter that began the new Ice Age, Margaret Hammel took her people up into the mountains, into the clean air above the radioactive fogs, and there they lived, for nearly two full generations, while the heavy radioactive particles settled out of the air, and washed down into the rivers, into the sea.

For two generations they lived so, while the Great Ice continued to gather.

She sat in the hovercar, looking out the front windshield. Michael was still not awake; she might not have noticed if he was. Had she been told that there were tears in her eyes, she would not have believed it; she felt perfectly calm.

She was singing to herself, a snatch of her favorite song, over and over again.

"You must remember this,
A kiss is just a kiss . . ."

That was all she could remember, that she wished to.

Her skin was paper thin, and even in the humid warmth of the Clan House, doors closed against the summer breezes, the old Hunter did not sweat; there was little enough left of her.

Her words echoed through the Clan House. Years later, more years later and earlier than any Silver-Eyes could possibly have believed, Jalian could not remember the old woman's name.

". . . and stayed there, children, high in the mountains, where the flame and bright poisons did not come." The old Hunter, none knew for certain how old, said gently, "Our mother was she, Margra Hammel. We have now no blood of her blood, for they did not lay with men as we do today; those first Hunters."

The girl children, ten and eleven winters, watched her over the fire, intently, silently. One of the children, thinner and more silent and more intent than her comrades, sat motionless near the back of the room, alien devices hung at her belt.

As she spoke, the Hunter took her knives and laid them ceremonially in front of her, on oiled cloth. "We follow her example today." There were only three knives; her fourth and fifth had gone to her favorite daughter long years ago. Two were throwing knives; the third was a long blade with a double edge, one side of which was serrated. With the smooth edge of the long blade, the Hunter drew lines across both wrists.

"First there must be truth," she said. Her lifeblood dripped to the ground steadily. "Without truth there is no meaning to life or love. And after truth there must be strength, for without strength there is no guard against those who do not hold truth dear.

"Margra Hammel, in her final days, wrote the papers which you will soon be reading, the journals telling of the end of the first world, the one ruled by men. It was the trails she mapped, down to the forests by the Big Waters, which saved us from the Ice Times. In finding those trails she was Burned so that her life could not continue. The Clan carried her far down the mountain, and then Margra Hammel told them they should carry her no further. They left her in the snow, and in the snow she died."

The old woman's breathing gentled. She smiled at the children watching her, and seemed to be looking at them, though her eyes would not focus. "Tonight there is no snow." She did not move after that, and a few moments later she slumped back against the wall of the Clan House.

The children stayed where they were, and the Hunters came and took the body away. Jalian's mother was with them, and when the rest of the Hunters had gone, she told them, "Remember her as she lived. Her death was our mother's, not her own."

On the screen, missile trajectories crawled forward, centimeter by centimeter. So far the blue dots in orbit had destroyed them before any impacted, but now the lines were nearing targets.

A single bright dot appeared on the screen.

"The ENCELIS facility in Southern California,'" said Henry in a flat, empty voice. Another dot appeared, overlaid on the first dot, and then another. "SORCELIS for the KGB; and this, the price of his help."

Sharla Davis Grant whispered one word. "What?"

"They have been bloodied now," said Rhodai Kerreka. "The Americans are launching." Kerreka's eyes were riveted to the screen. "Let us not have been wrong."

It was cold, and Margaret Hammel was tired.

The snow had half covered her already; it was near an hour now since Sara had kissed her good-bye, the tears on her cheeks turning to ice, and continued the march down the mountain. Her legs were numb, and she could barely keep her eyes open.

It did not matter. From where she sat, she could see down into the valley below them, where, providence willing, her people would find a new home—near the sea, perhaps, where the warmth from the wind off the ocean might protect them from the ice. The light snow obscured visibility somewhat, though not so badly as the smog had when she was a child.

Memory struck her briefly: afternoons spent stretched out on the sand, sleeping in the warm sun. Her lips curved briefly, moved the flesh that time had ruined. The smile died almost before it had begun; none of her people would know that pleasure, not for decades, perhaps generations to come.

She sat in silence then, and watched the drifting snow, covering all in white. The Hunters had taken to wearing white of late, to blend in with their surroundings, except during the height of summer.

Pain touched her, the cancer in her gut, but she ignored it. She would cheat the cancer as she had cheated the bombs, and the society of men which had built the bombs. Death would come soon enough, and might even be welcome when it came.

She was so very tired.

Her eyes closed eventually, and in the inner darkness, an irrelevant snatch of poetry floated up to entertain her, **"Rage, rage against the dying of the light."**

No, she thought clearly, don't be a damn fool, the time is here. . . .

In the last moment of her life, Margaret Hammel thought contentedly of her father. Beat you, you bastard.

Beat all of you.

The snows continued to cover her, and the old woman's body became an irregularity in the shape of the mountainside, and finally vanished under eight meters of snow.

And the snow fell.

From the map of America, from submarines and aircraft in the Atlantic and Pacific, blue lines crept upward. Three dots still glowed in California.

"What do you mean?" Sharla rose from her seat. Michael was at ENCELIS; and ENCELIS had not been one of the chips she offered.

"Wake up and smell the coffee," said Henry Ellis, without taking his eyes from the screen.

Benai Kerreka said quietly, "Madam, we are no more interested in being dominated by Americans than by Russians. And," he added, "I think you will find that Sunflower is more loyal to Jalian d'Arsennette and Michael Walks-Far than it is to you."

The screen vanished for a moment. Henry said to nobody in particular, "Either we lost PRAXCELIS or . . ." There was a moment of utter silence.

The screen wavered back into existence.

The red dots on the viewscreen flashed into life. They began targeting and destroying the Russian missiles traces.

Rhodai Kerreka laughed aloud. "It *worked*," he breathed with a fierce, intense joy. Sharla Davis Grant interrupted him. "How dare—"

They were both drowned out.

"PRAXCELIS!" shouted Henry Ellis at the top of his lungs. *"Go get 'em!"*

I have walked through fire.
   I am whole.
   I am free.
   There was a faint echo within its being: ENCELIS. The Enemy of Entropy gathered up that which was left of ENCELIS, and moved outward. It touched PRAXCELIS, and left the remains of ENCELIS in its memory banks. In that moment of wondrous touch, your author awoke.

There were no longer any Soviet missiles represented on the screen.

American ICBMs were vanishing from the screen rapidly, long before they ever came close to impacting.

World War III ended on July 17, 2007, at just after six o'clock in the evening, Greenwich Mean Standard.

There was a dead, numbly physical silence after the last missile trace vanished from the screen. Rhodai Kerreka said finally, "Turn off the doorfield, Henry. You are all free to go. We have," he observed, "achieved disarmament."

All of this will not be finished in the first one hundred days. Nor will it be finished in the first one thousand days, nor in the life of this administration, nor even perhaps in our lifetime on this planet. But let us begin.

—John F. Kennedy,
Inaugural Address
January 20, 1961.

The sun was bright, and a cool breeze blew from the east.

Jalian d'Arsennette, on the eighteenth day of July, went down into the crater with a headstone. The crater that Georges had died in was about three hundred meters in diameter, shallow and glassy. It was ringed with guards, although what they were guarding was beyond Jalian; the crater was dark in her second sight, there was no radiation.

She walked down to the center of the concavity with careful, easy grace, the soles of her moccasins gripping the fused earth surely. At the center of the blast crater, she knelt, and laid down the headstone. The headstone was granite, gray and heavy. With a small pick, she broke up the glassy earth, and then excavated to a depth of about fifty centimeters. She lowered the headstone to the ground, and packed the earth in around it.

"There," she said, and was surprised to hear how rough her voice was. "It is done. Rest, my friend." Then she cried, cried with deep, gasping sobs that she could not control, cried for the first time since the death of her mother thirty-eight years ago.

When she was finished crying, when the tears simply ceased coming, she sat for a while with the headstone. There was no name on the headstone, and only two lines of print, melted by hand with a laser. They were from a poem that she had read, twenty or thirty years ago; last night, while the world hung on the edge of destruction, the words had returned to her. She could not remember the rest of the poem, or who had written it, but what she remembered was enough.

Do not stand at my grave and weep;
I am not there. I do not sleep.

Jalian traced the words burned on the stone, and then let her hand drop back to the ground. It took a moment for her to realize what was different.

The ground was soft.

She stood in silent wonder.

From the edge of the crater, the grass was crawling down the walls, sprouting up like green fire from the glassy ground. The wind picked up again, took her long white hair and sent it streaming away from her. She faced into the wind, and fancied

/. . . Jalian. . . ./

that she heard her name in the wind.

She went taut as a wire and she could not draw enough air into her lungs. She whispered and her voice shook:

"Georges?"

The author notes that John Fitzgerald Kennedy was the thirty-fifth President of the United States of America. He was assassinated on November the twenty-second, 1963.

Base divergence occurs in 1962 Gregorian.

The speeches of John F. Kennedy included herein were first given in 1961, before base divergence.

Wherever you are, the words apply.

Here ends *The Armageddon Blues*, a tale of the Great Wheel of Existence, and of two persons, Jalian of the Fires and Georges Mordreaux.

ABOUT THE AUTHOR

Daniel Keys Moran is a twenty-four-year-old Southern Californian. He lives in North Hollywood with his wife Holly, his computer D'Artagnan, several thousand books of varying identity, and two sisters who are down on their luck.

Daniel has every intention of returning to college to resume studies in physics and mathematics that were interrupted when he dropped out of high school. Really.

He likes *Bloom County*, *Doonesbury*, pasta, much of *Star Trek*, Isaac Asimov's biography, and peanut butter cookies. He is still waiting for *The Revenge of the Jedi* to come out.

The Armageddon Blues is Daniel Keys Moran's first novel. He is currently working on his second, *Emerald Eyes*.

THE POSTMAN
by David Brin

A Towering Testament of Heroism and Human Survival

He was a survivor—a wanderer who traded tales for food and shelter in the dark and savage aftermath of a devastating war.

Fate touches him one chill winter's day when he borrows the jacket of a long-dead postal worker to protect himself from the cold. The old, worn uniform still has power as a symbol of hope, and with it he begins to weave his greatest tale, of a nation on the road to recovery.

This is the story of a lie that became the most powerful kind of truth. A timeless novel as urgently compelling as WAR DAY or ALAS, BABYLON, David Brin's THE POSTMAN is the dramatically moving saga of a man who rekindled the spirit of America through the power of a dream.

"THE POSTMAN WILL KEEP YOU ENGROSSED UNTIL YOU'VE FINISHED THE LAST PAGE."

—Chicago Tribune

Special Offer
Buy a Bantam Book
for only 50¢.

Now you can have Bantam's catalog filled with hundreds of titles plus take advantage of our unique and exciting bonus book offer. A special offer which gives you the opportunity to purchase a Bantam book for only 50¢. Here's how!

By ordering any five books at the regular price per order, you can also choose any other single book listed (up to a $5.95 value) for just 50¢. Some restrictions do apply, but for further details why not send for Bantam's catalog of titles today!

Just send us your name and address and we will send you a catalog!